ABA BAYEFSKY
in
Kensington Market

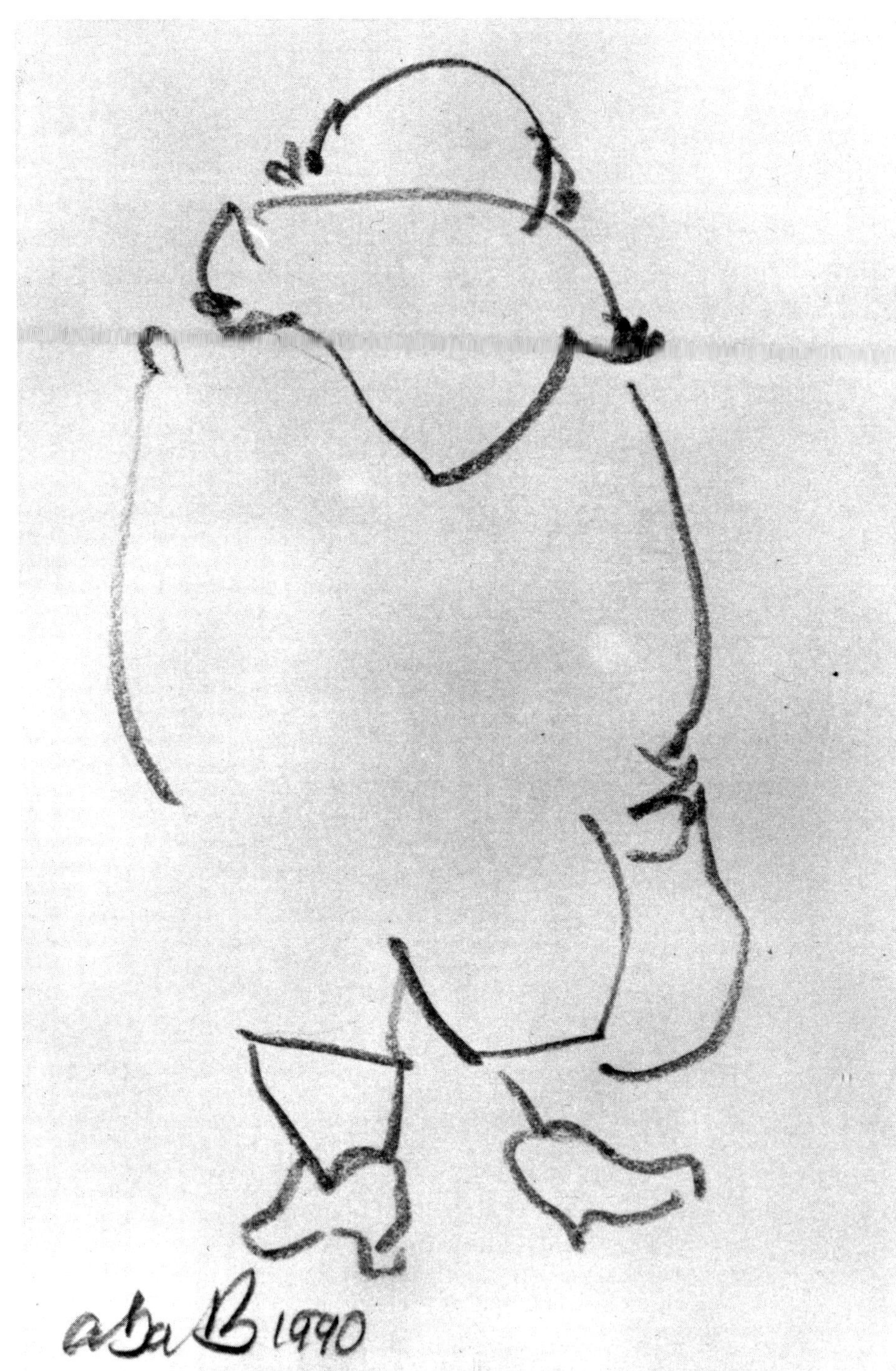

aba B 1990

ABA BAYEFSKY
in
Kensington Market

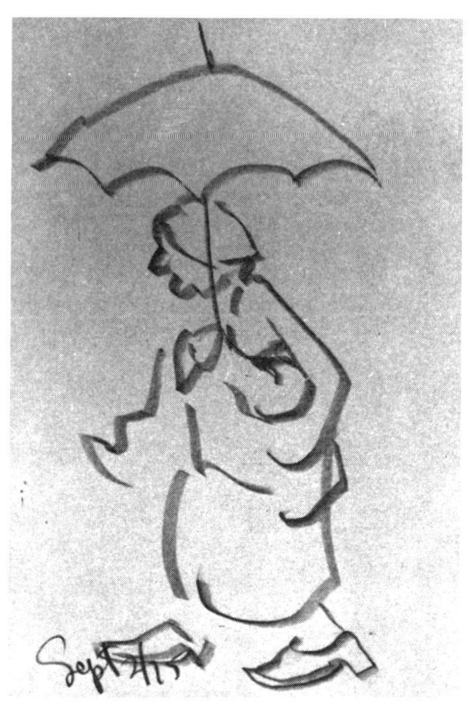

Introduction by Paul Duval
A Memoir by Ben Lappin

MOSAIC PRESS
Oakville-New York-London

Canadian Cataloguing in Publication Data

Bayefsky, Aba, 1923-
   Aba Bayefsky in Kensington Market

ISBN 0-88962-496-8 HC   ISBN 0-88962-506-9 P B

1. Kensington Market (Toronto, Ont.) - Description Views. I. Duval, Paul, 1922- .II. Lappin, Ben, 1916- .III. Title.

FC3097.52.B38 1991   971.3'541   C91-095546-8 F1059.5.T686K42 1991

No part of this book may be reproduced or transmitted in any form, by any means, electronic or mechanical, including photocopying and recording information storage and retrieval systems, without permission in writing from the publisher, except by a reviewer who may quote brief passages in a review.

Published by MOSAIC PRESS, P.O. Box 1032, Oakville, Ontario, L6J 5E9, Canada. Offices and warehouse at 1252 Speers Road, Units # 1&2, Oakville, Ontario L6L 5N9, Canada.

Mosaic Press acknowledges the assistance of the Canada Council and the Ontario Arts Council in support of its publishing programme.

Photograghs by Harry Lieberman and See Spot Run Inc.

Acknowledgement From the Collections of:
McMichael Gallery
Dr. & Mrs. Collin Wolfe
Mr. & Mrs. Wolfe D. Goodman
Market Gallery
Mr. & Mrs. Milton Harris

Design by Ruth Scheffler
Cover Design by Ruth Scheffler
Typeset by Hedda Bowler

Printed and bound in Canada.

MOSAIC PRESS
In Canada:
          MOSAIC PRESS, 1252 Speers Road, Units 1 & 2, Oakville, Ontario L6L 5N9, Canada,
P.O. Box 1032, Oakville, Ontario L6J 5E9

In the United States:
          Distributed to the trade in the United States by: National Book Network, Inc., 4720-A Boston Way, Lanham, M.D.,20706 USA

In the U.K.:

          John Calder (Publishers).,Ltd.,9-15 Neal Street, London, WCZH 9TU, England.

CONTENTS

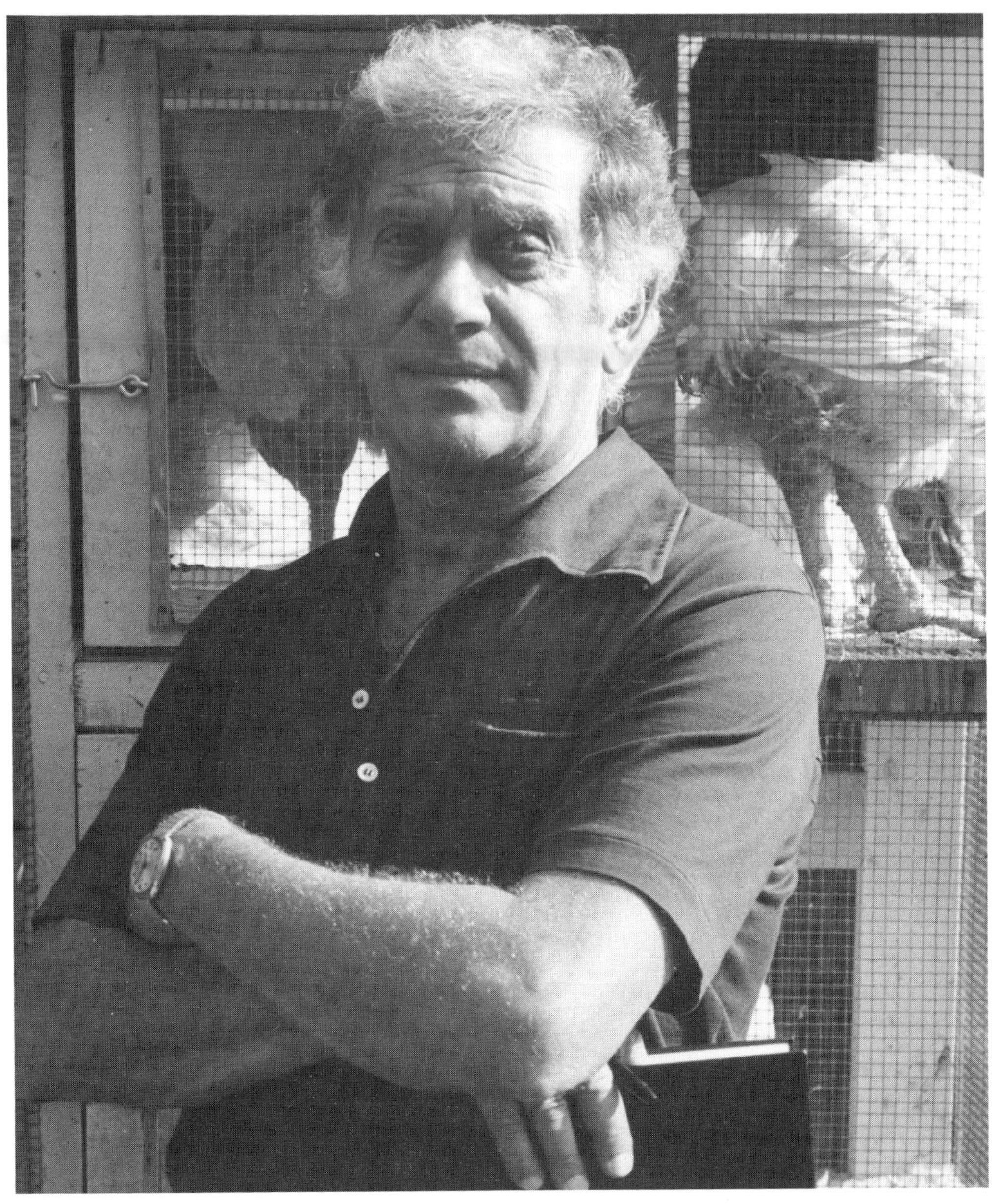

INTRODUCTION
by Paul Duval

From Catalogue 1978

These drawings represent an artist's affectionate return to the sketching grounds of his youth. Aba Bayefsky first portrayed the Kensington Market of Toronto in his middle teens, while he was a student at the Grange Art Centre under Arthur Lismer from 1937 to 1942.

Bayefsky's first drawings of the market were executed at a time when the idea of people as an artist's major concern was just emerging in Canada - a people then clinging perilously to the edge of a great depression. Life was simpler, and the market was a popular forum, almost exclusively Jewish - as well as a vehicle for buying and selling. Political views were exchanged with each sale, for it was a desperate era, and everyone seemed to have his own firm notion of what desperate measures might cure it. Since then, Bayefsky has watched the market through its up times and down times. He also has seen many art fashions come and go in the ensuing four decades, without straying from his early dedication to humanity as his theme or from his personal style, which was substantially formed by the time he was in his early twenties though he has since rung many subtle changes and refinements on that basic style.

The fifty drawings reproduced here were executed from 1976 to 1978. They consist of selected pages from his sketchbooks, and all are drawn in lead pencil. They represent the current denizens of the market caught on the fly, often in the freezing weather of winter, when the artist had his hands in and out of his coat pockets to keep warm. These drawings are not illustrations or mere factual reportage. Nothing is described for its own sake. It is a totality of form and mood that Bayefsky captures in these rapidly inscribed images.

Each element takes its place within the weaving calligraphy of his pencil and is converted into a rhythmic pattern without destroying its reality.

They are, above all, optimistic drawings. The people in them are not mendicants, or dispossessed or tentative; they belong solidly where they are portrayed, at home in the market with their familiar wares. The forms of these citizens of Kensington have been searched out with a fond awareness. Bayefsky cares, and the concern shows in the very character of his graphic strokes. There is no analytical finality in these drawings, no searching out of telling detail, but a summary sort of caress with the pencil which capture the entirety of form in motion. This is the knowing shorthand of an artist who can create the subtle nuances of his subject from a few inscribed gestures.

During its evolution, Aba Bayefsky's art has presented many aspects of the human condition. It has known terror, in his series of canvases of the abysmal pits of Belsen completed during the war when he was an R.C.A.F. Official War Artist. It has known religious celebration in his synagogue murals. It has contained fantasy, in his Paul Bunyan series. But if I were to pinpoint Bayefsky's creative home, I would place it in those few downtown Toronto blocks which are called Kensington Market.

These drawings represent both a celebration and a requiem. Kensington, as Bayefsky has known it, is inexorably changing, even disappearing. Together, his market drawings compose both a vivid portrait of a vanishing place and a memorable creative statement. Other Canadian artists have chosen to celebrate a given neighborhood or city, but I know of none who has been more constant in his attentions, or evocative in his interpretations.

1991

Aba Bayefsky's life-long affection for Kensington Market has emerged in three distinct creative periods - the 1940's, when he painted his dramatic and forceful watercolours of a Jewish merchant community that then dominated the area; the late 1970's when he drew his first pencil impressions of a gradually changing ethnic scene; and this latest group of drawings created between the early spring of 1990 and the summer of 1991.

These 1990-91 works reproduced in this volume exist partly because of the thrice-weekly dialysis treatments that the artist was then undergoing at Toronto's Western Hospital, situated on the edge of Kensington Market. Each Monday, Wednesday and Friday early afternoon before his medical appointments, Aba, sketchbook in hand, would stroll among the stalls of Kensington, stopping to record the diverse people, still-lifes and architecture that compose its byways.

Though the resulting drawings, executed in 4b and 6b pencils, relate closely to the earlier market studies of 1976-78, they offer a dramatic contrast in theme. During the intervening thirteen years, Kensington had changed from a primarily Jewish sector to a truly multi-cultured one. The few Jewish shops that remained were surrounded by an exotic mix of merchants from around the world. The kosher chickens that once hung in shop windows were replaced by Chinese, West Indian, Asiatic, Middle Eastern and European fare. Bayefsky's eyes were delighted in these changes, and he recorded them with a skill and sensibility that encapsulates the spirit of the place.

Kensington Market, like London's Covent Garden, may soon be threatened with dissolution. If, like Covent Garden, it does disappear, its people and places will persist in these small vivid drawings, born of a half-century of familiarity and love.

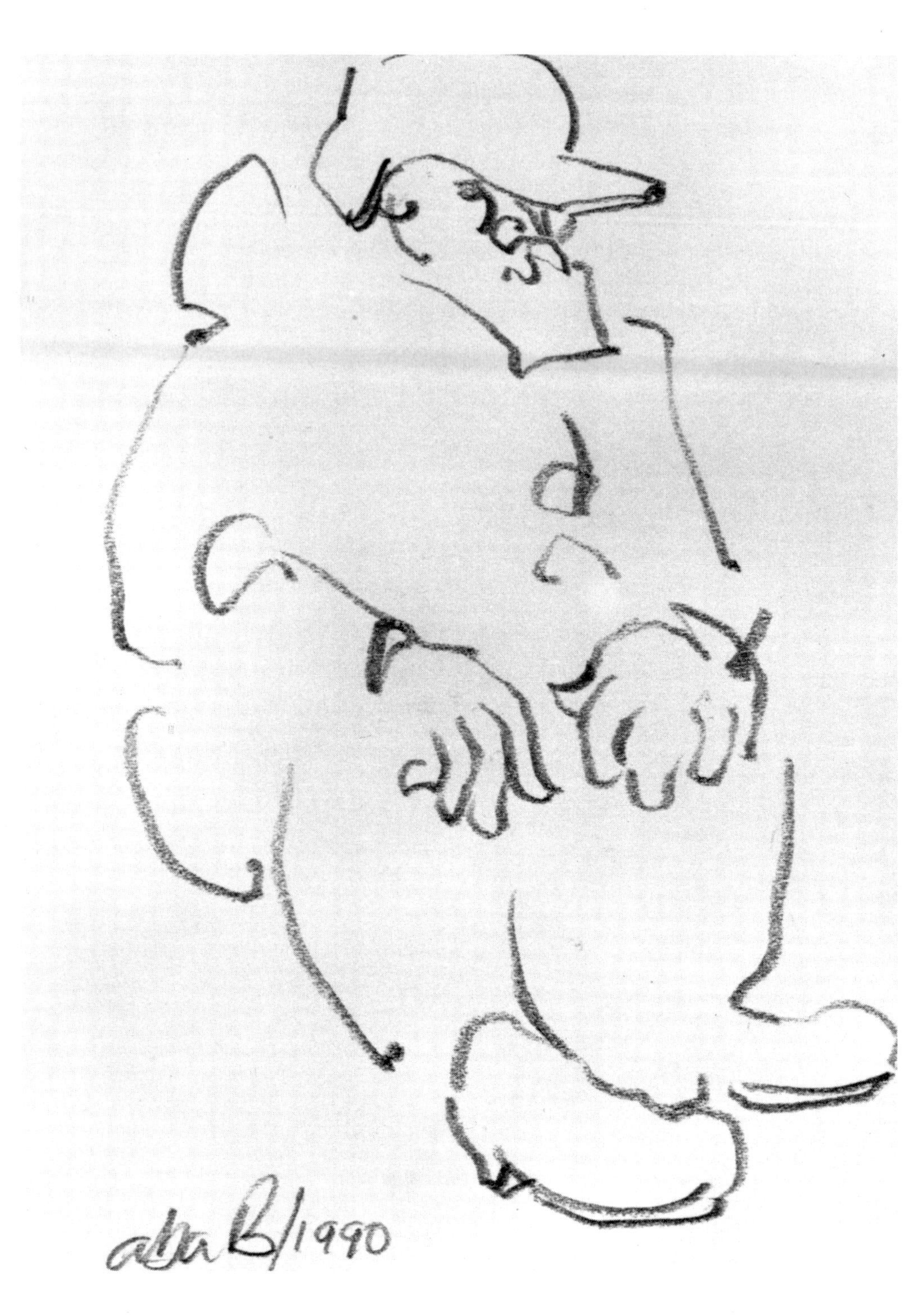

alan B/1990

FROM THE ARTIST'S NOTEBOOK....

Many immigrants have begun their Canadian experience in Kensington.

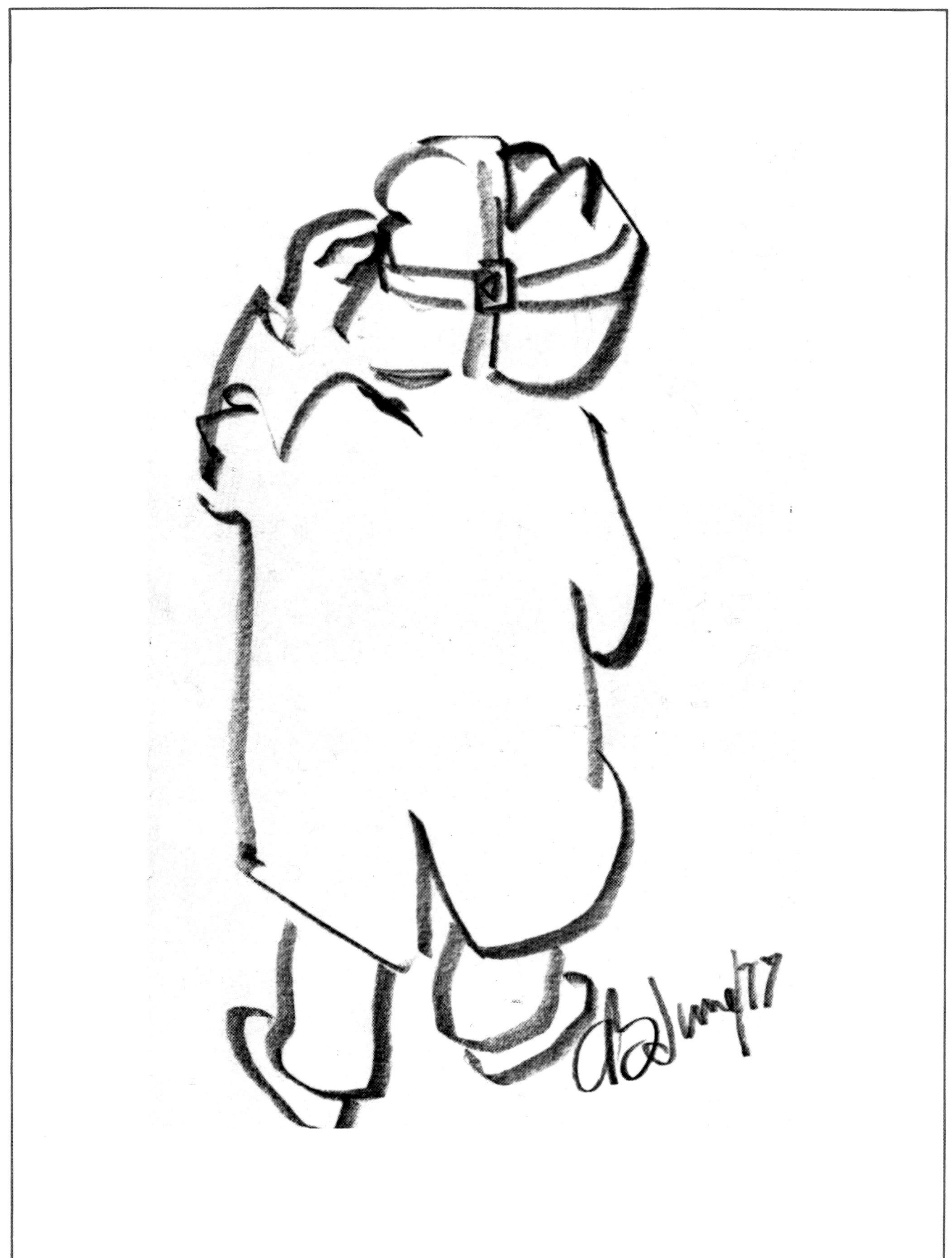

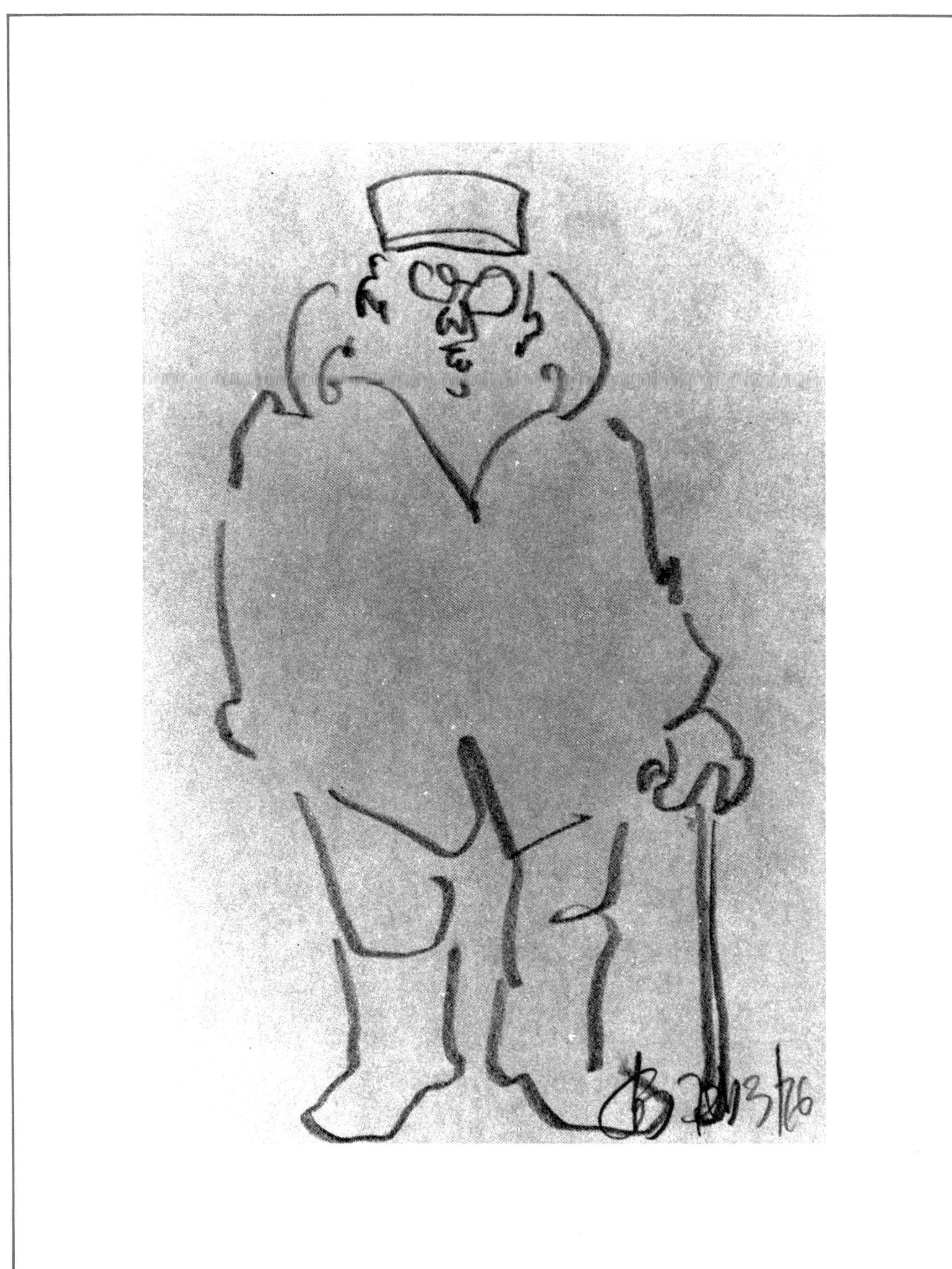

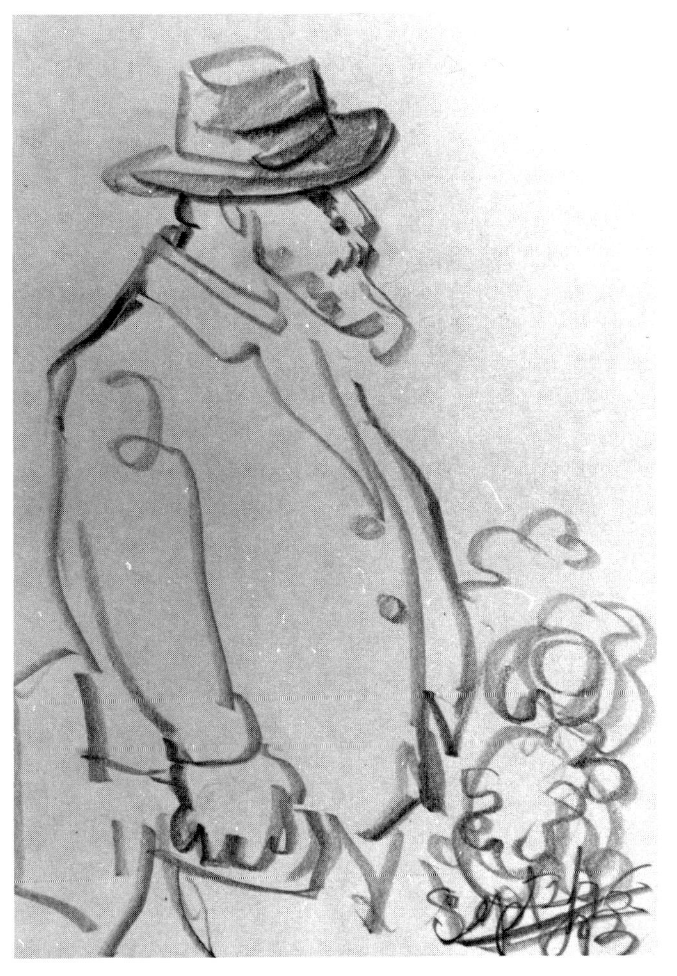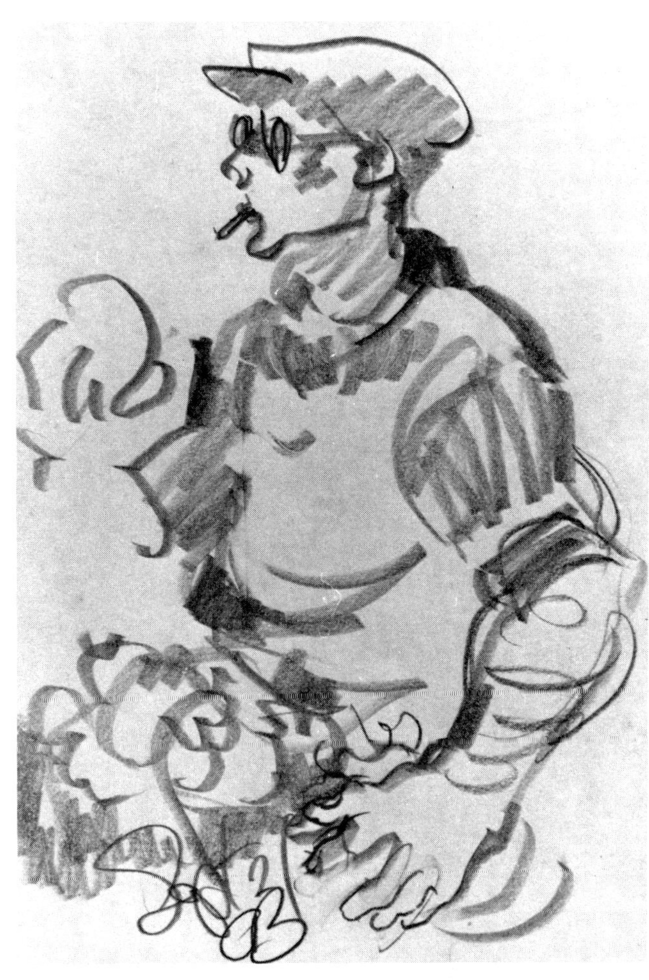

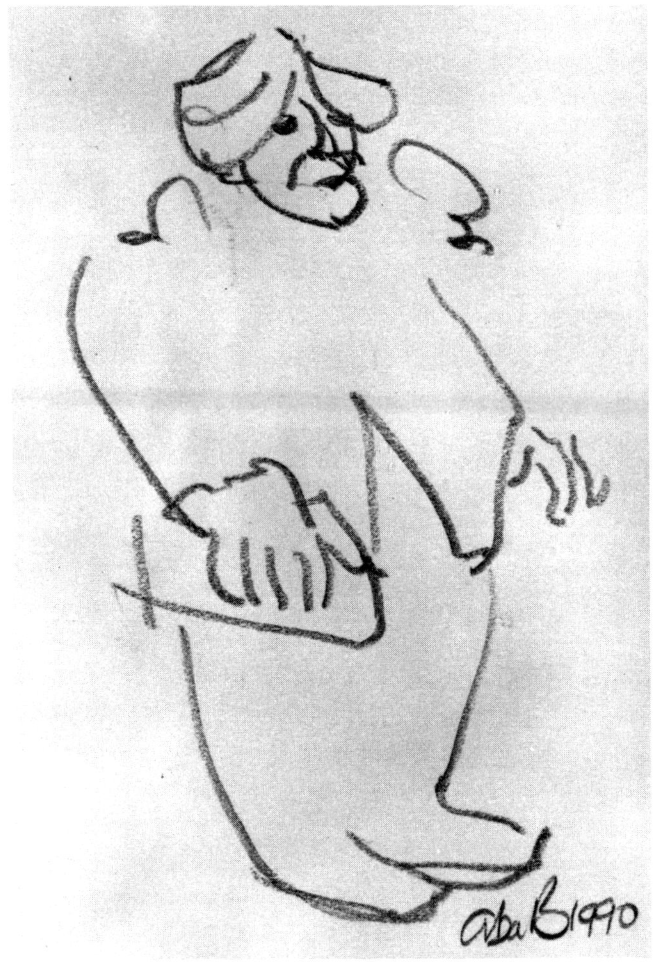
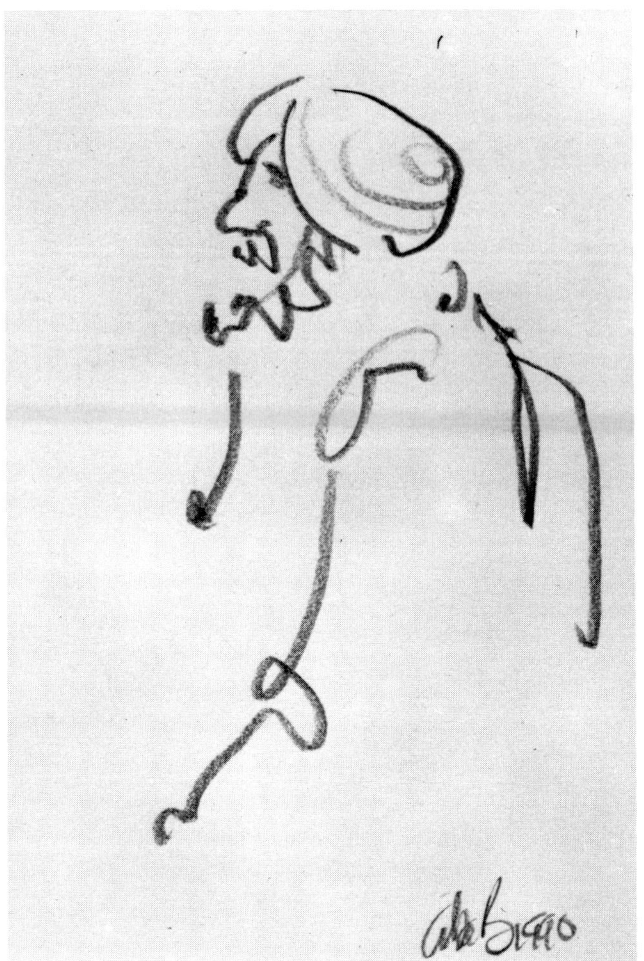

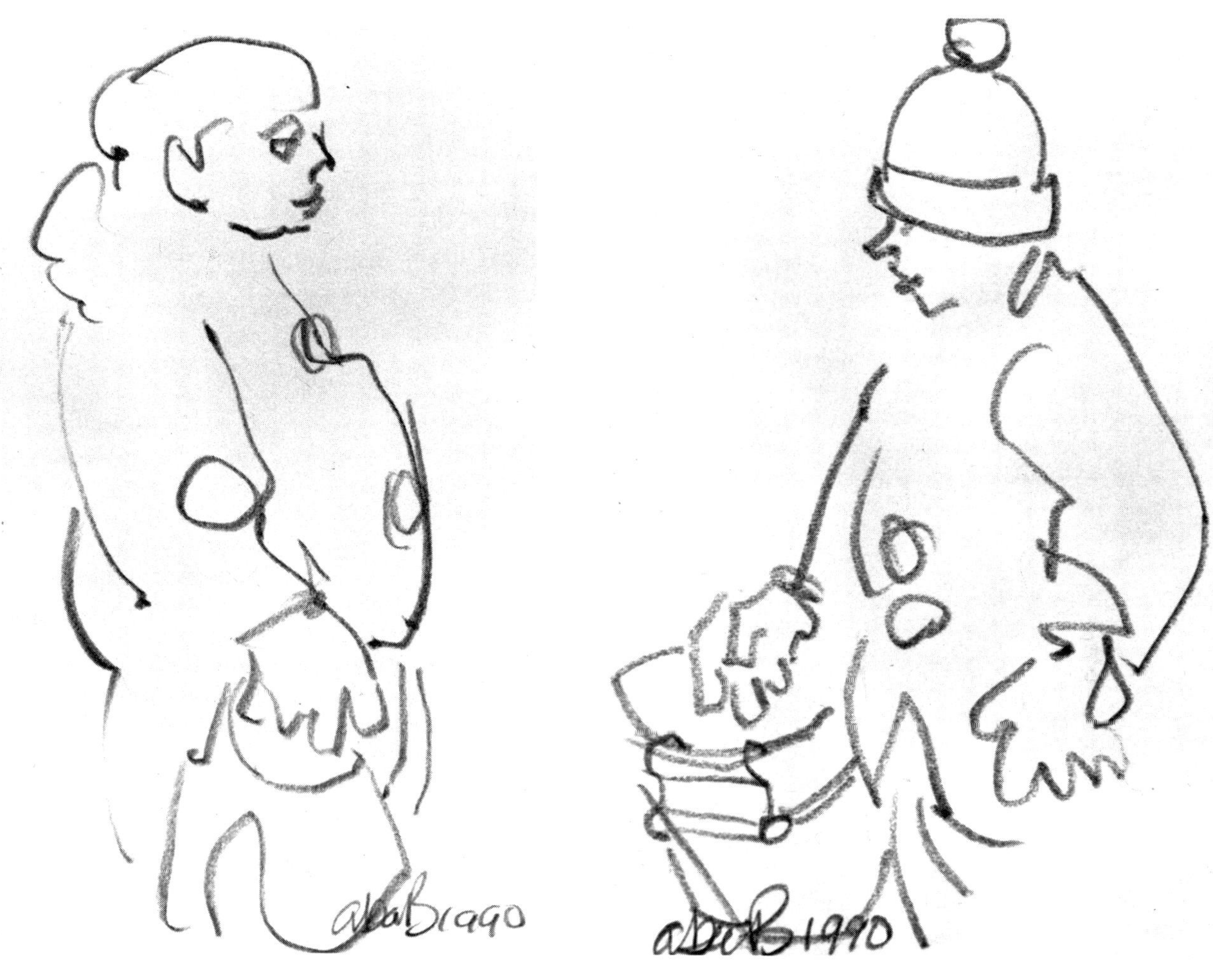

aDaB1990
aDaB1990

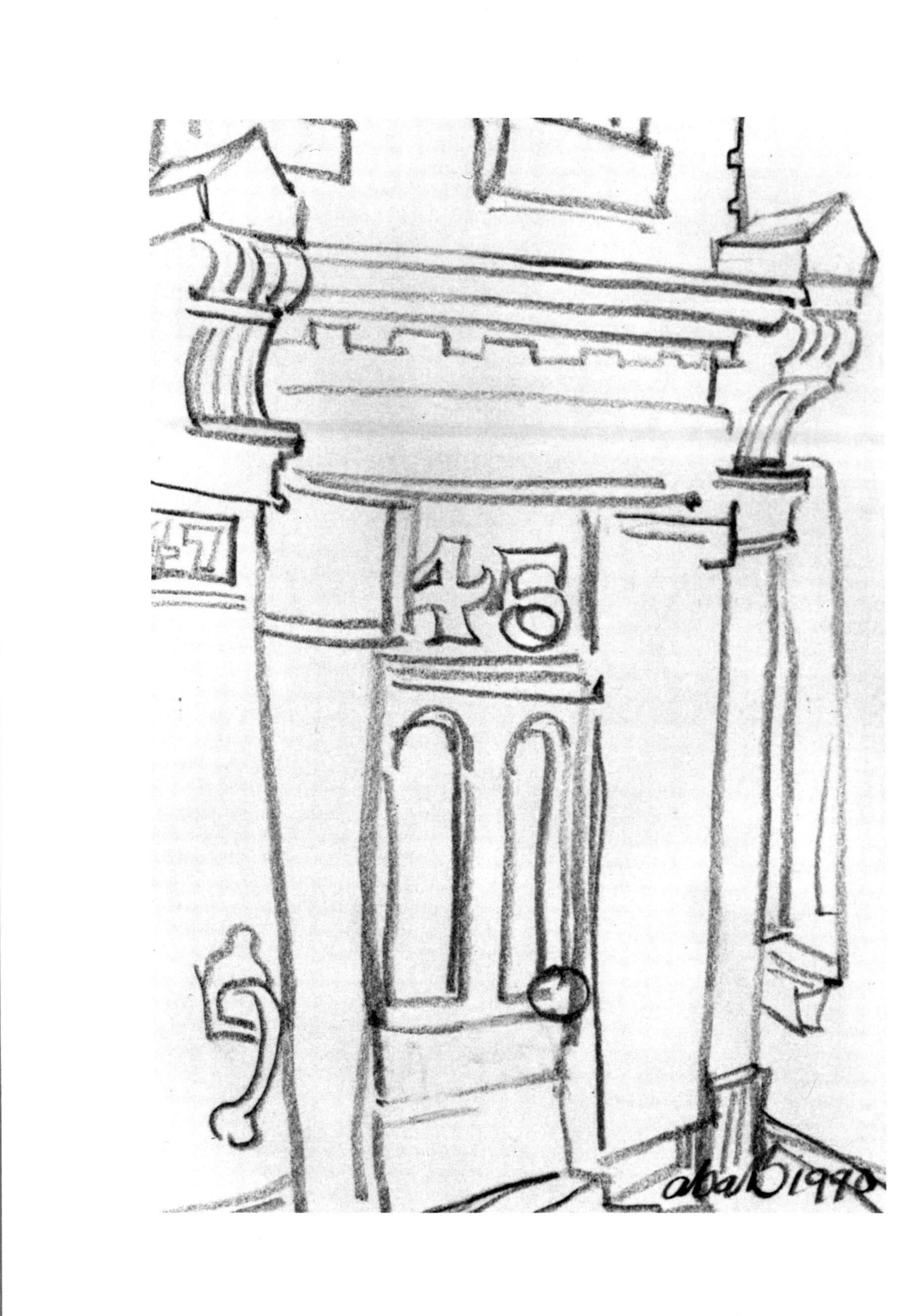

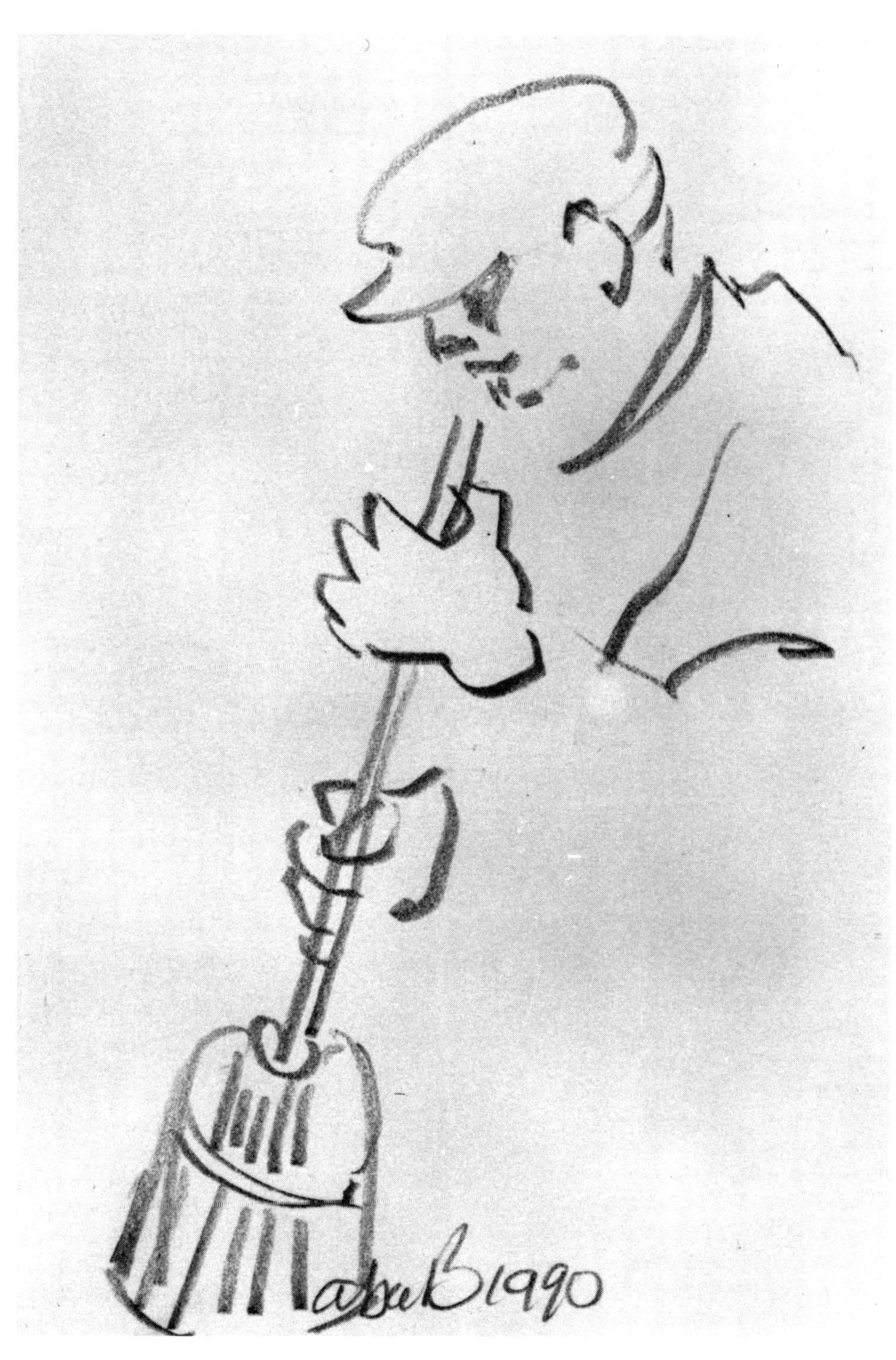

abul 1990

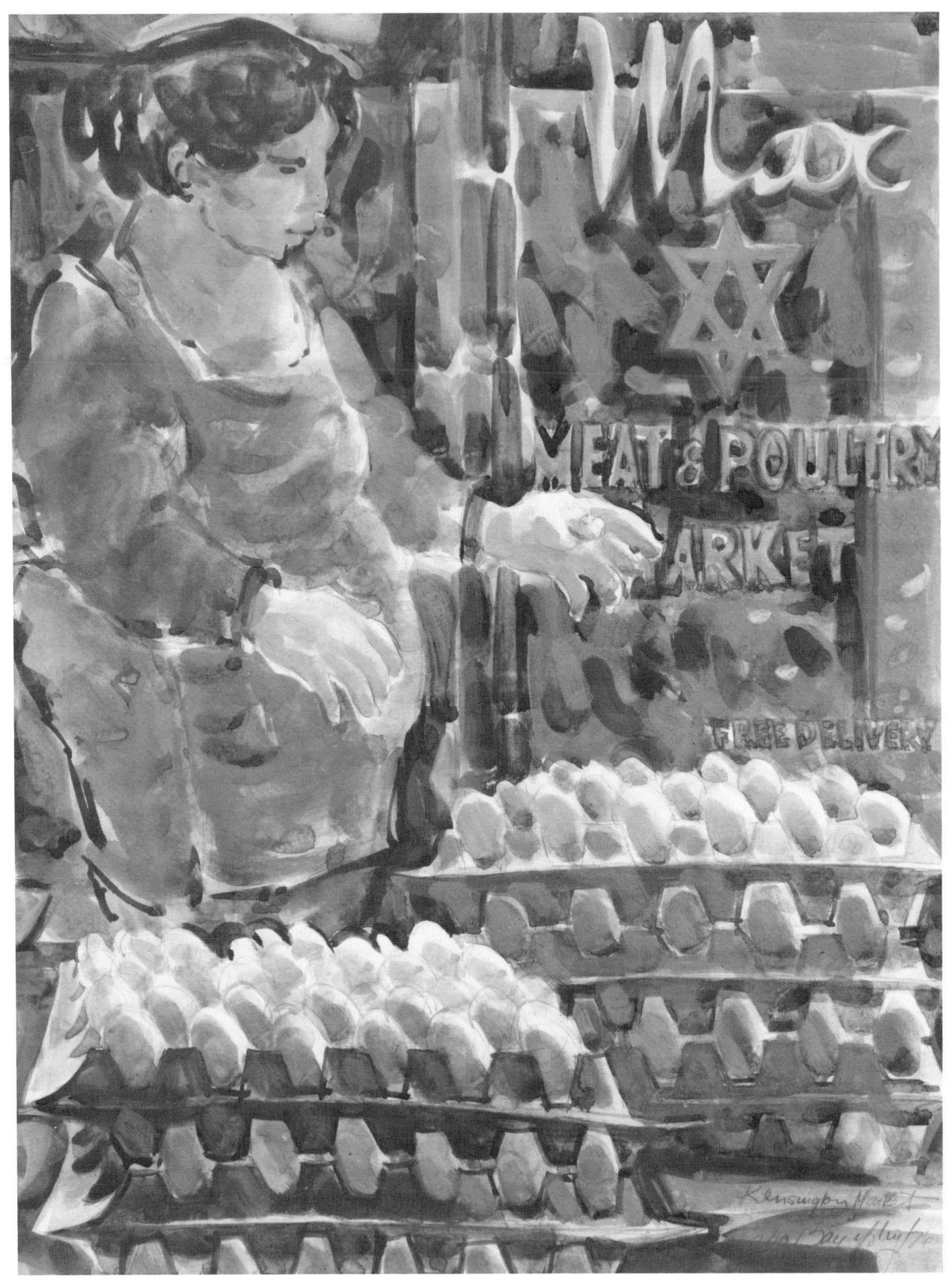
Max
MEAT & POULTRY
ARKET
FREE DELIVERY

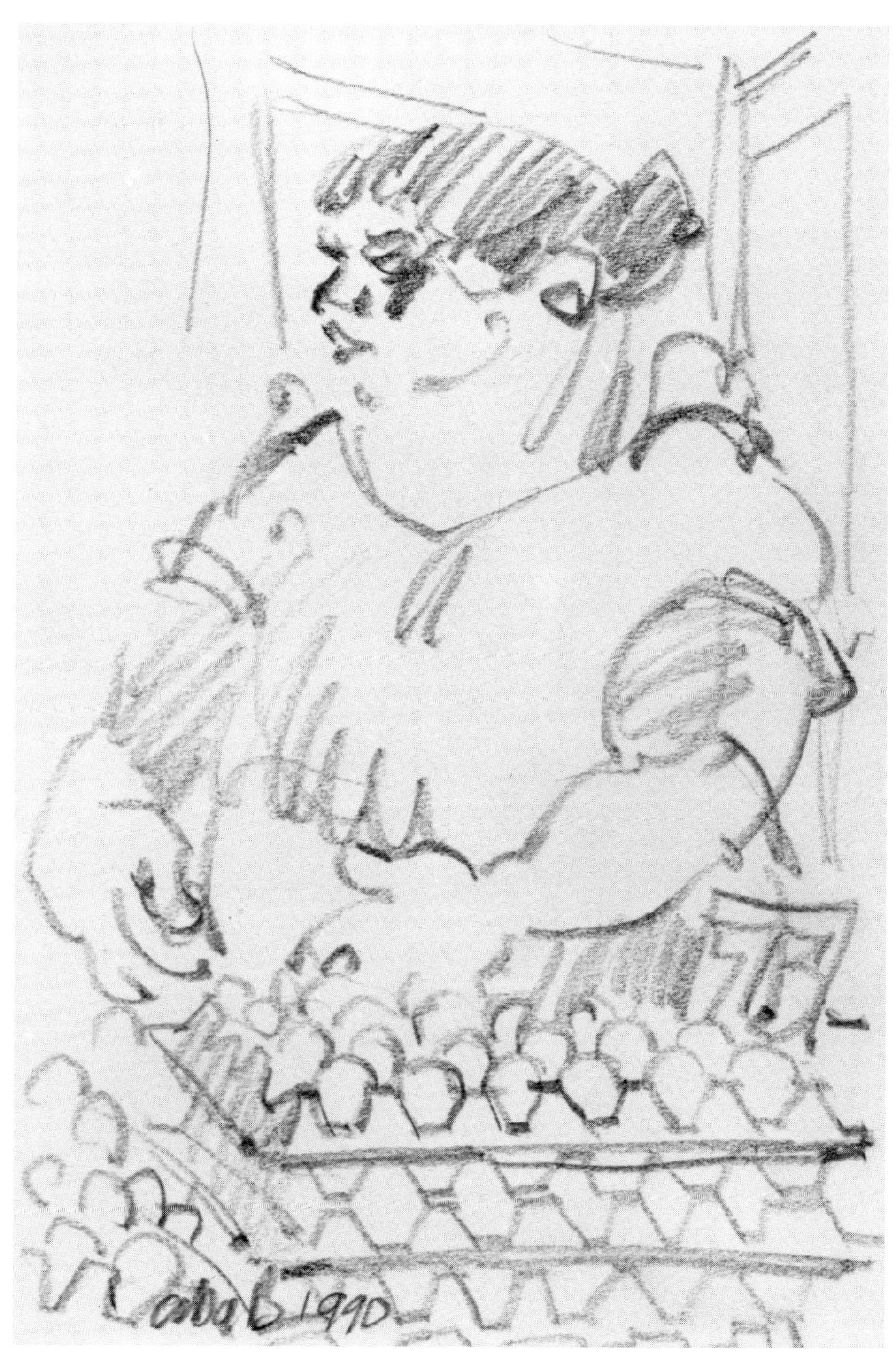

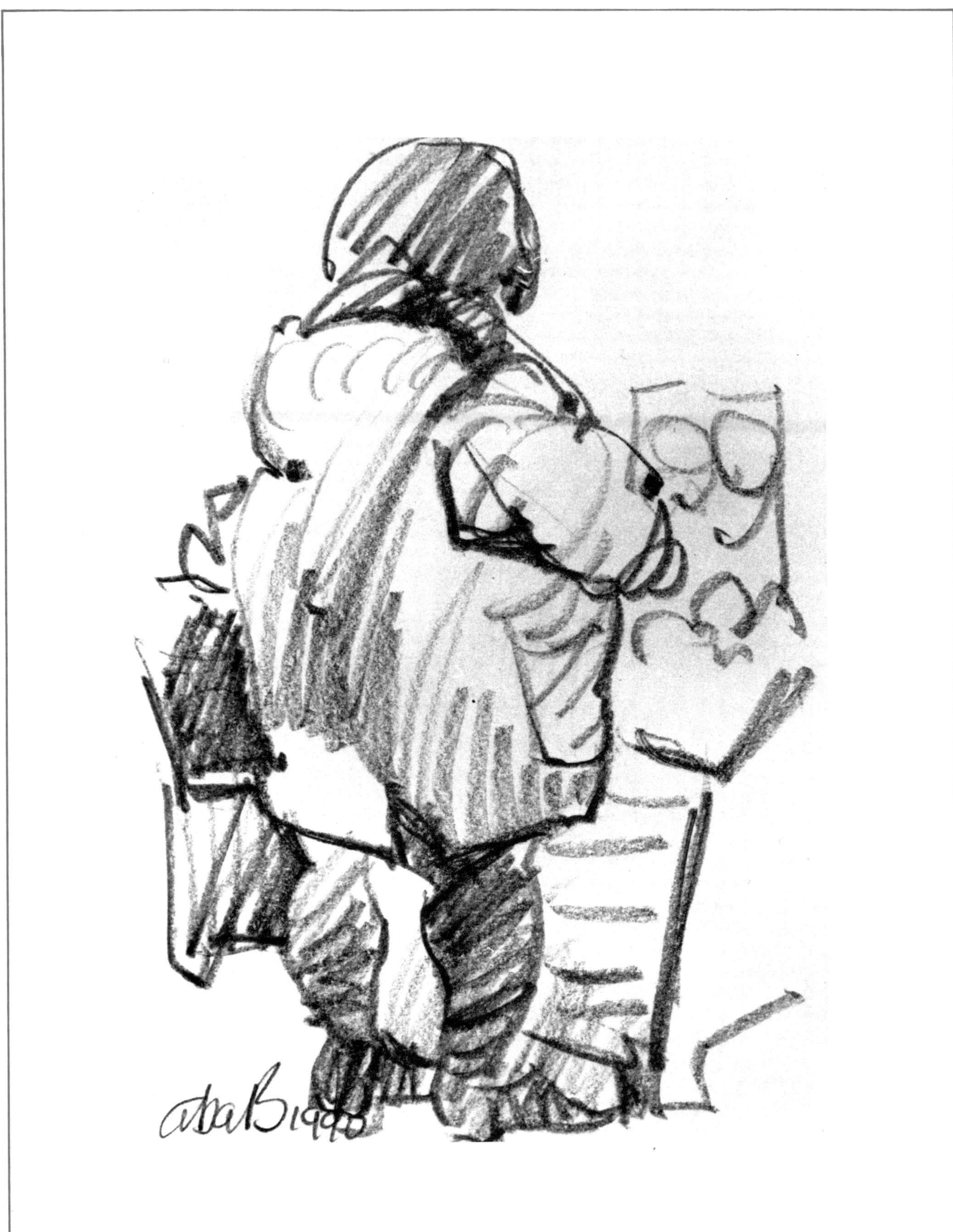

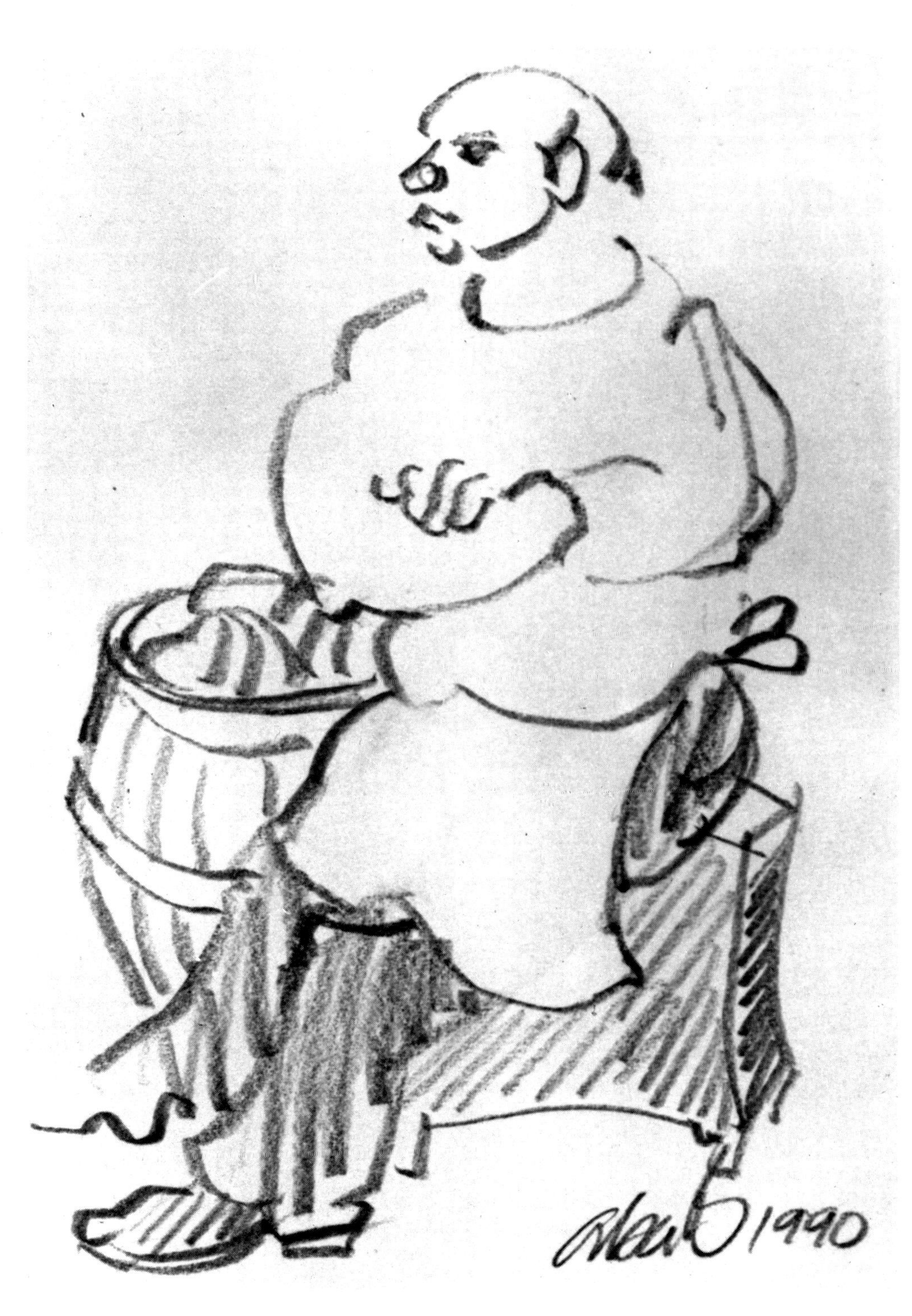

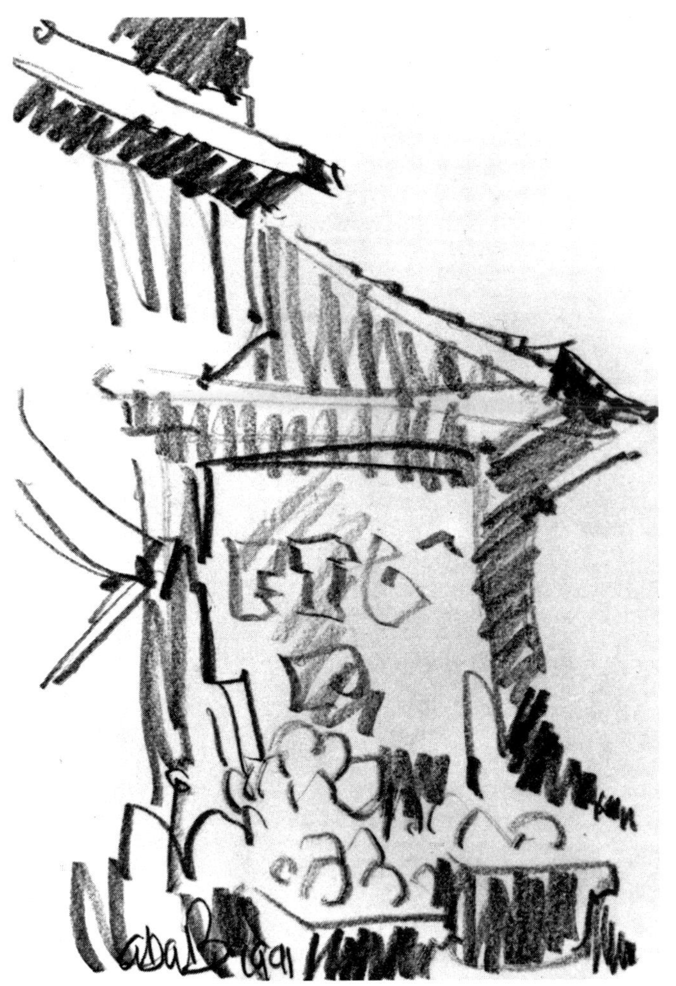

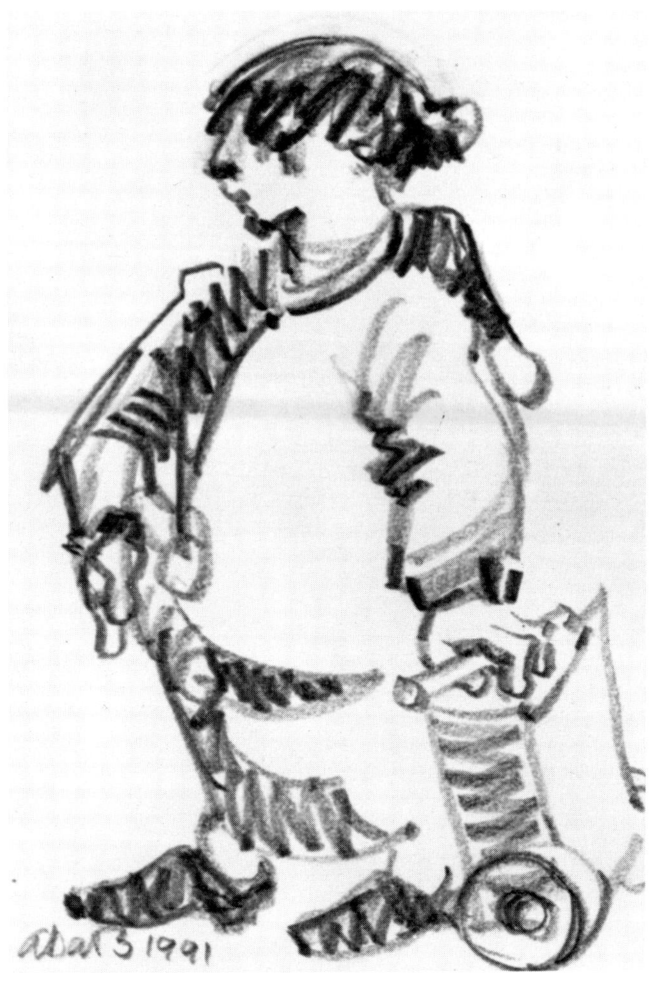

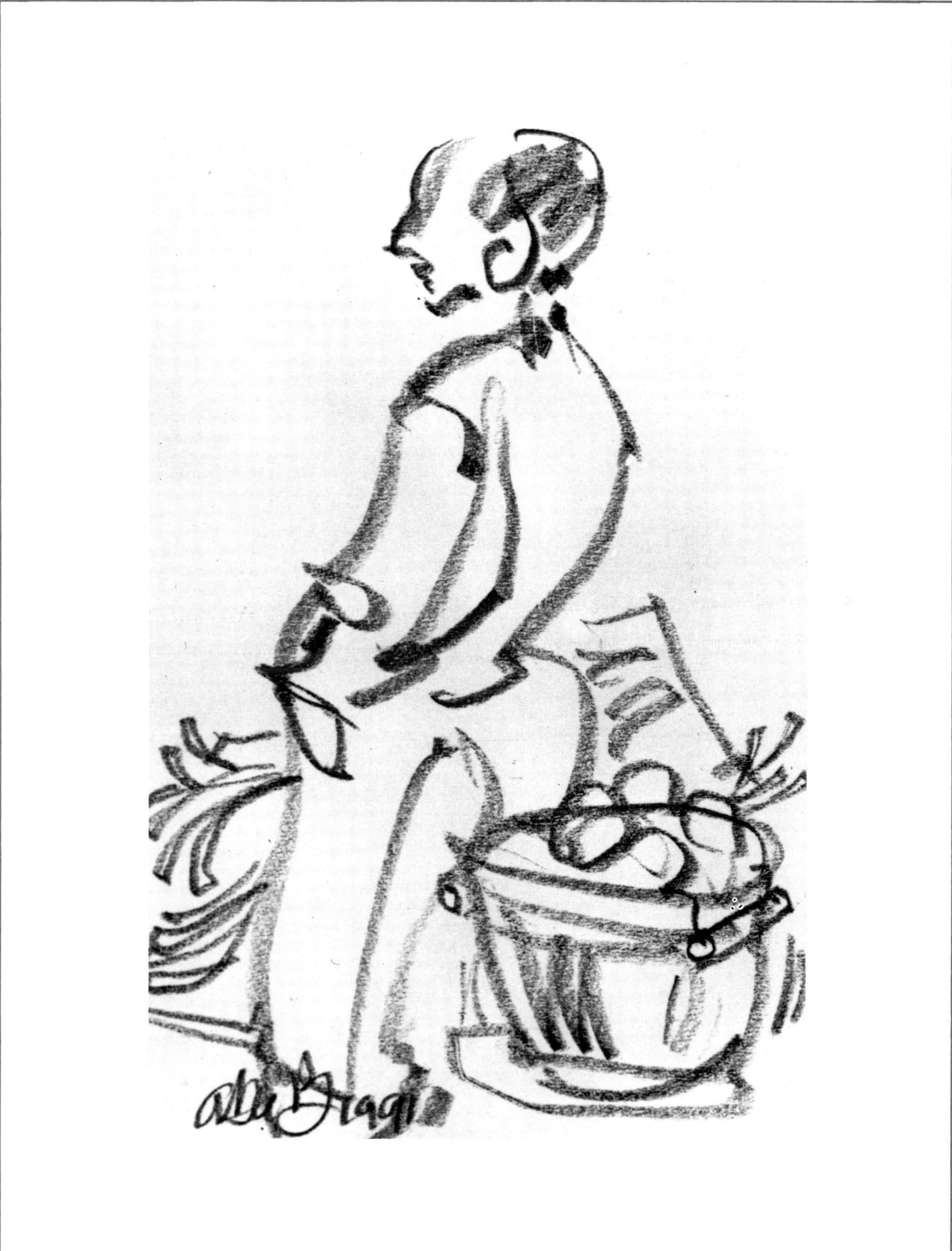

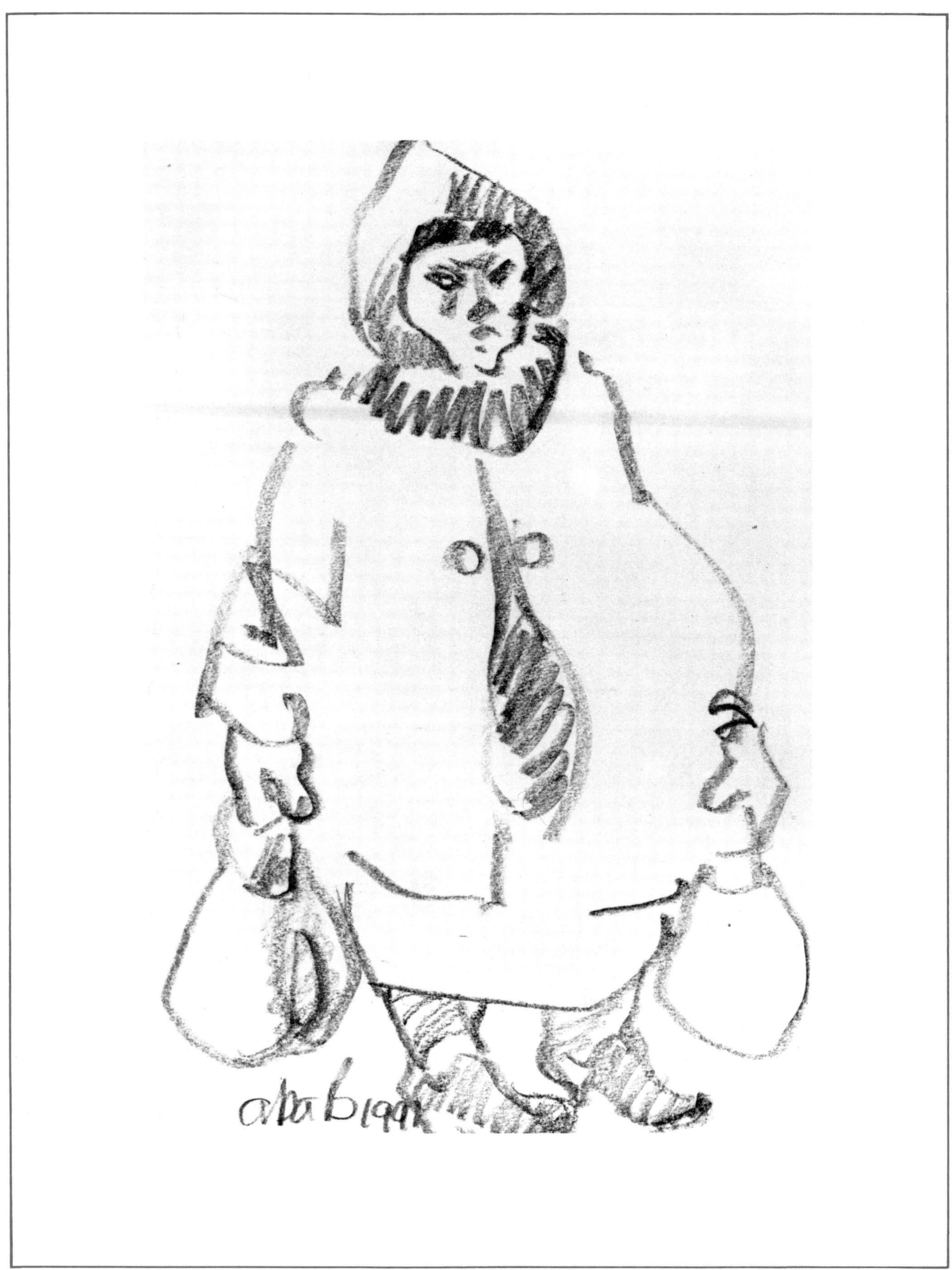

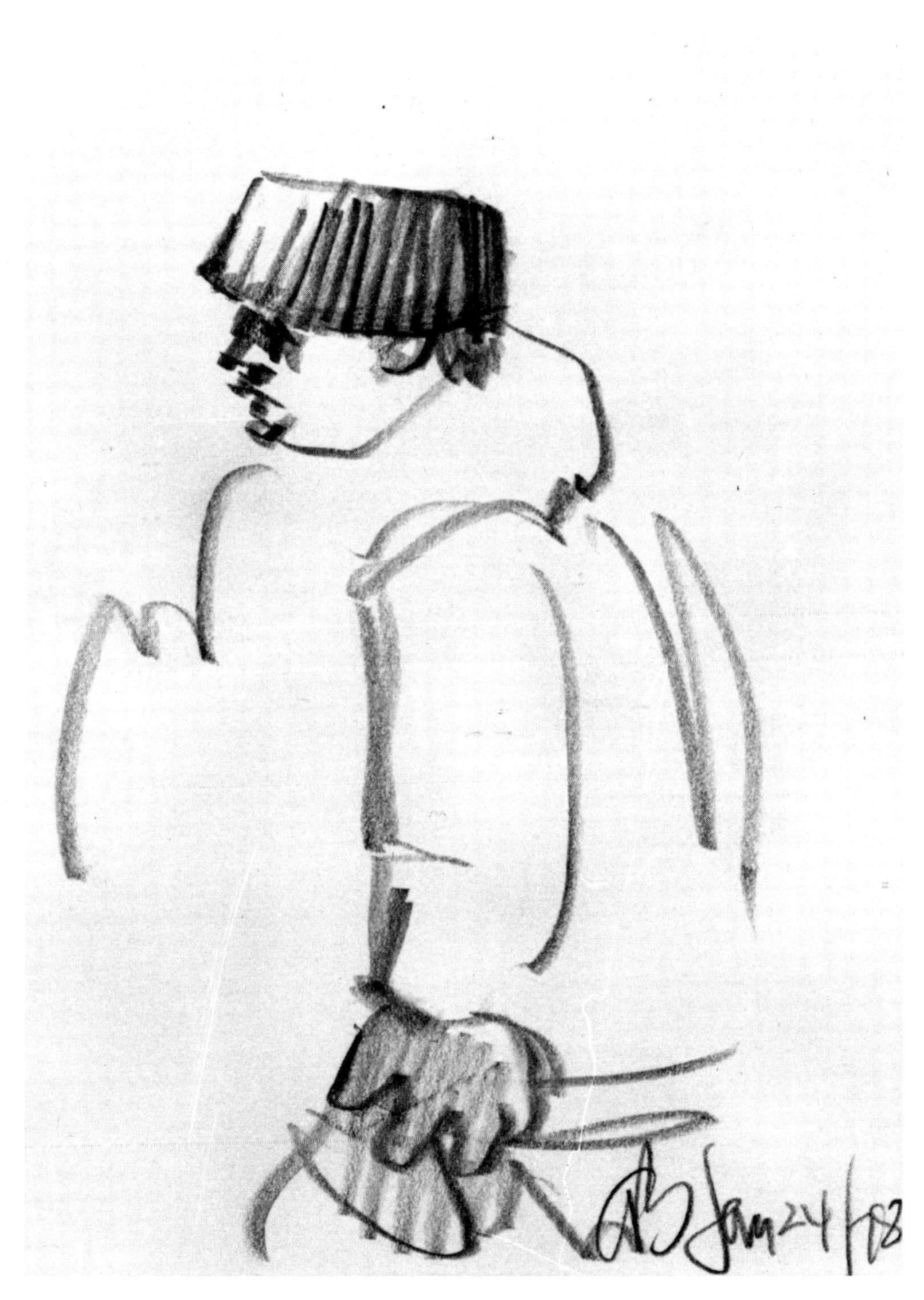

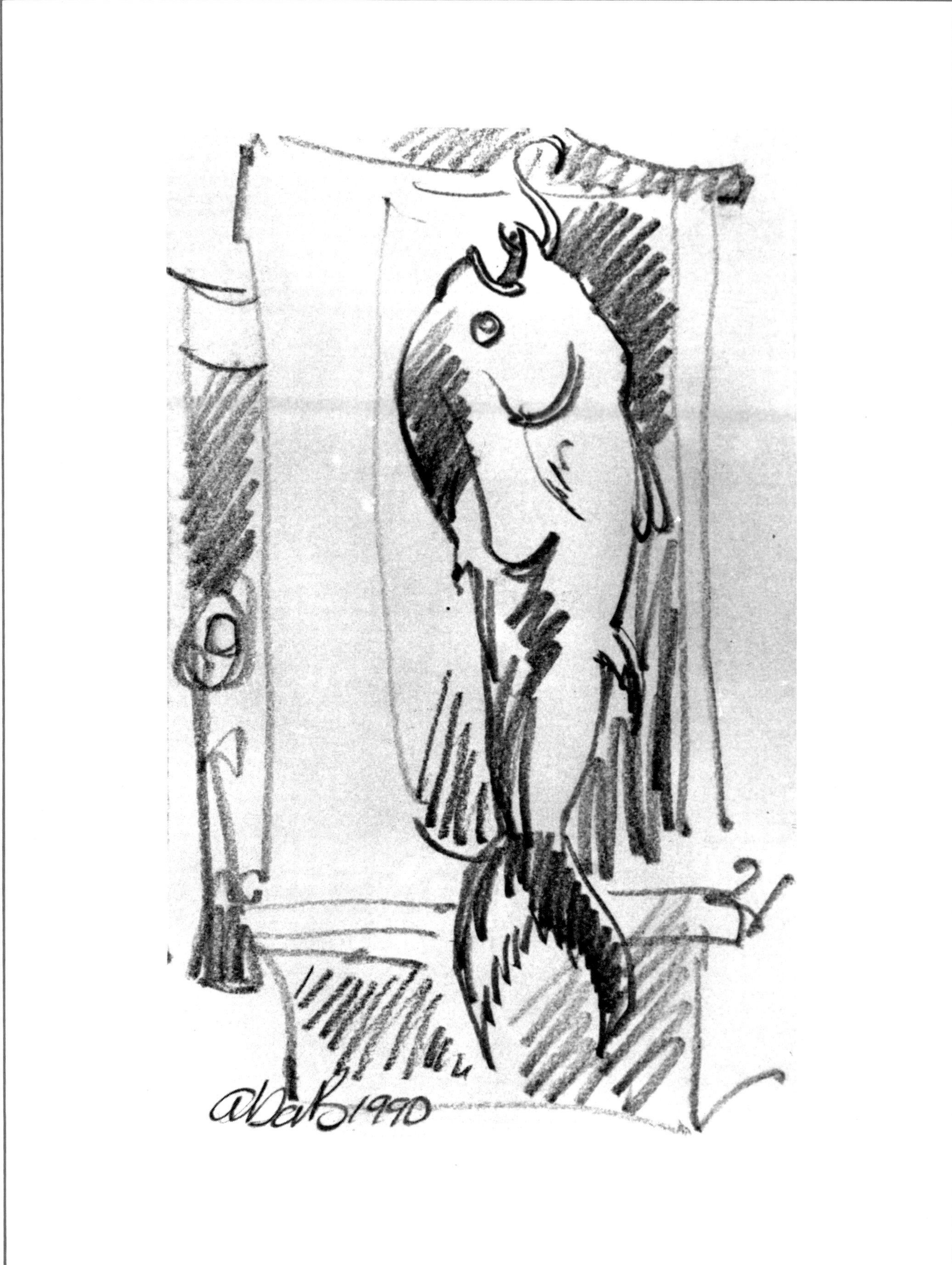

ADale 1990

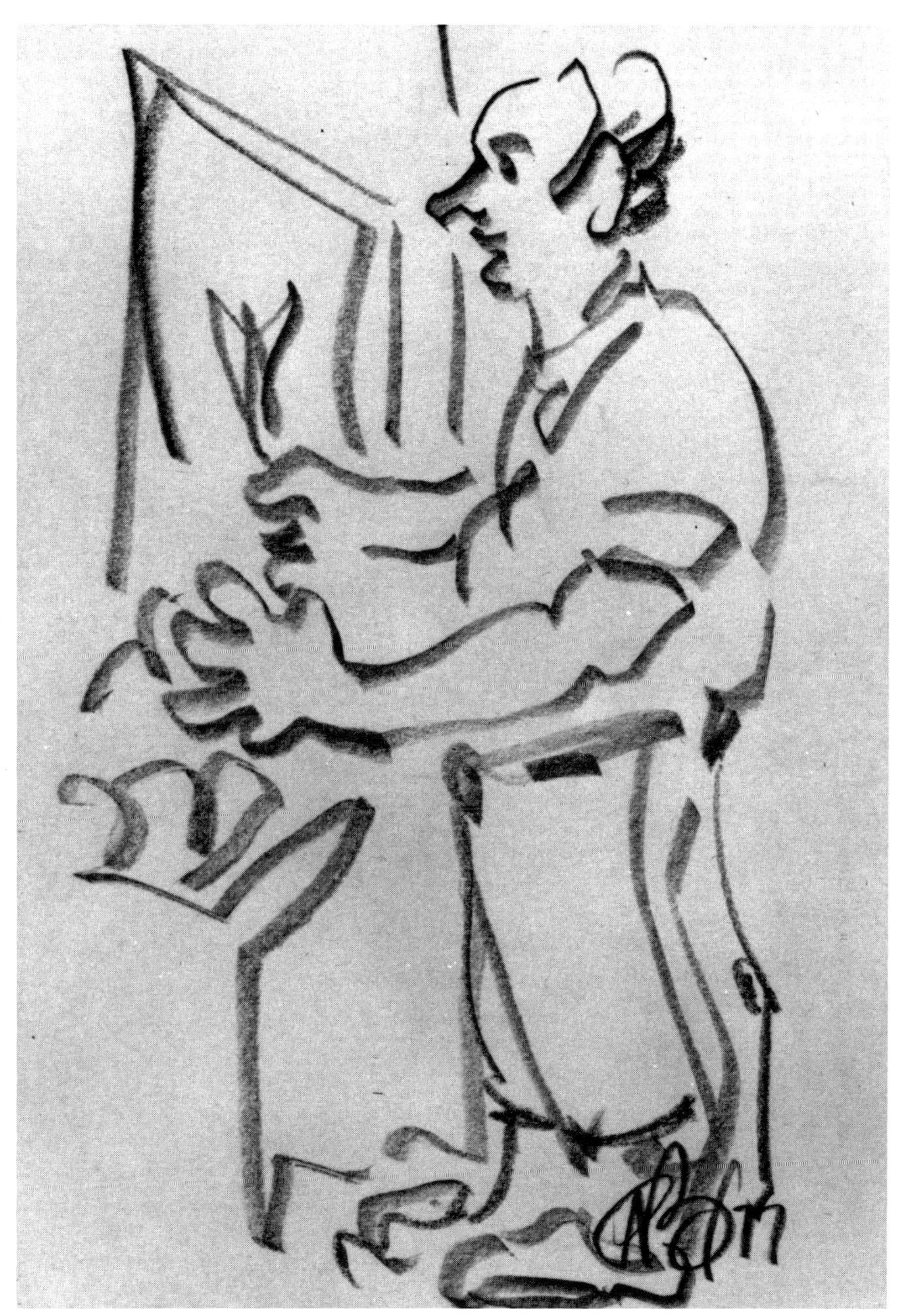

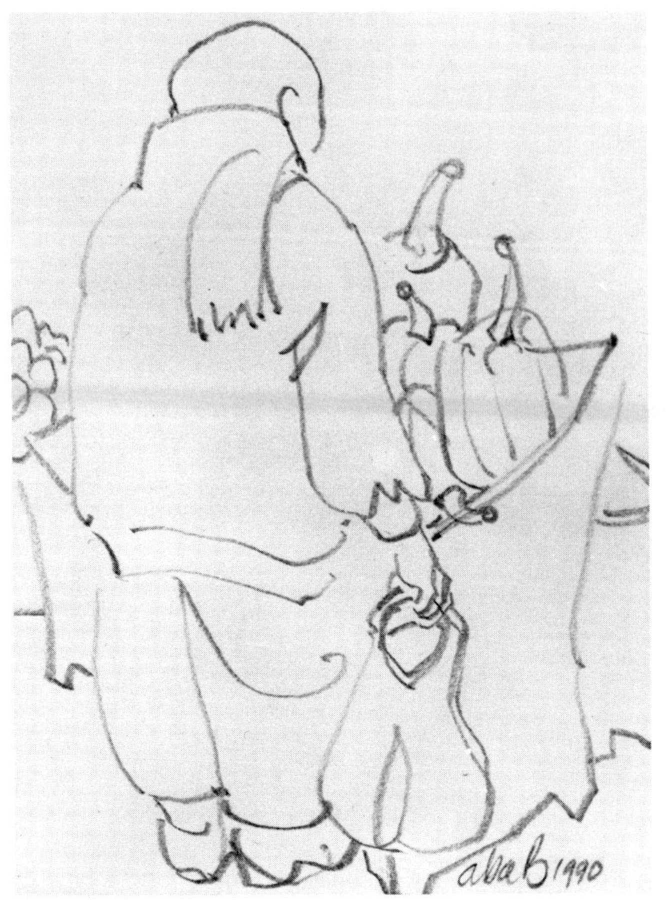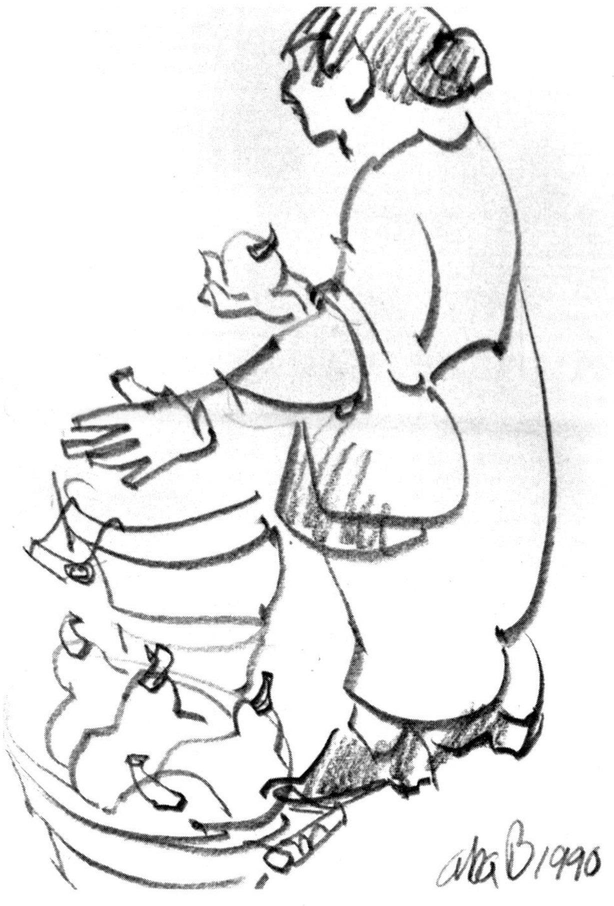

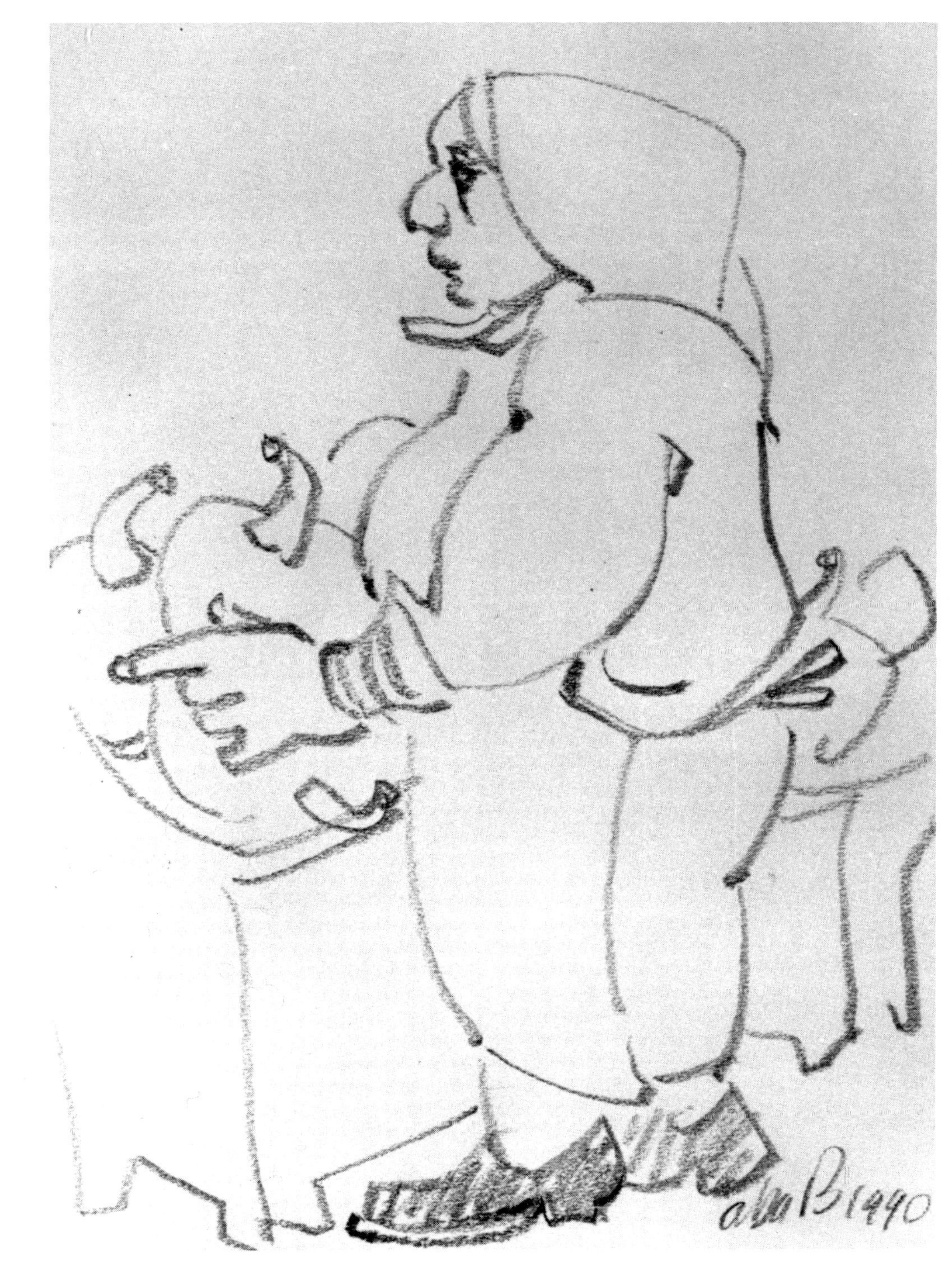

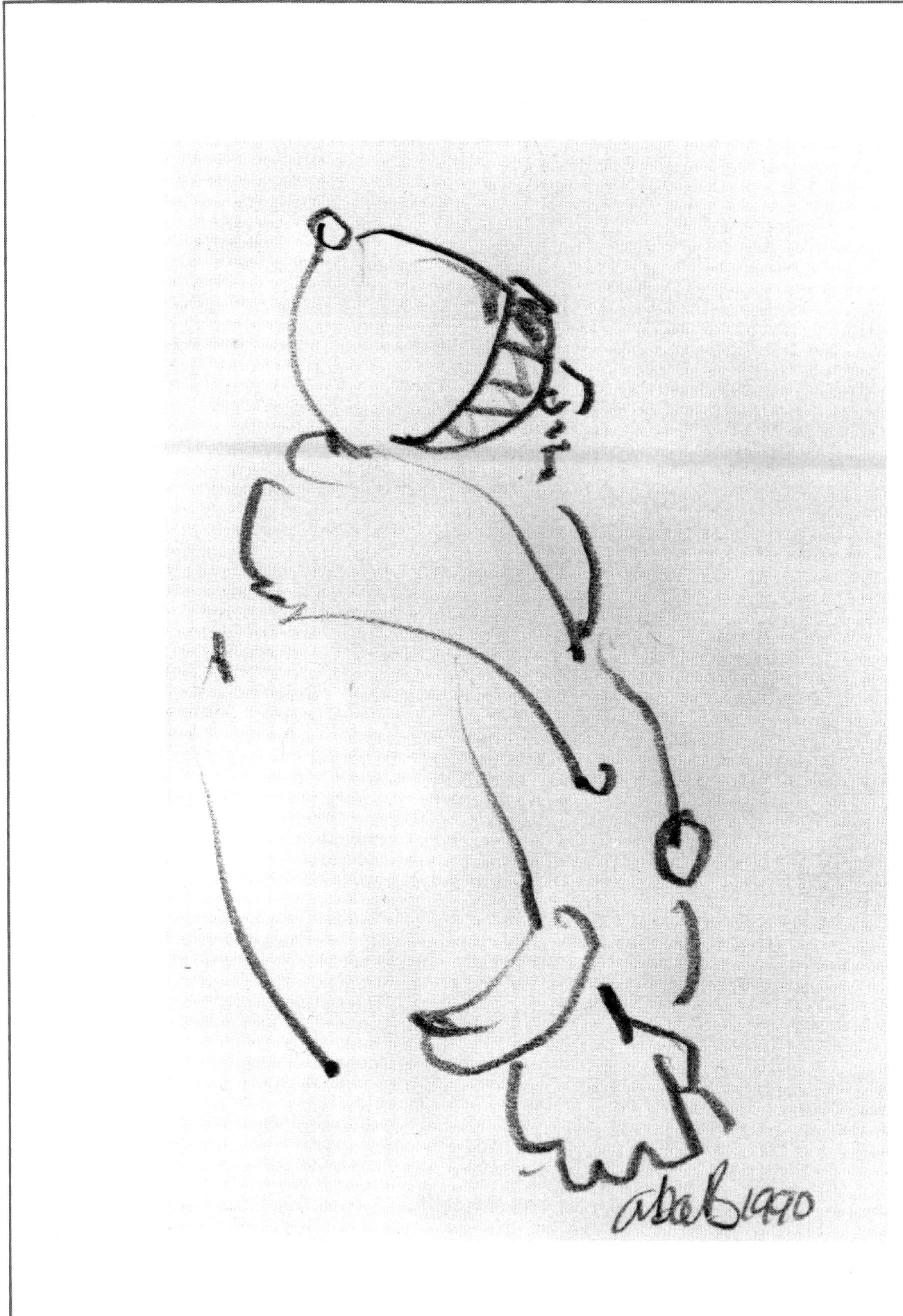

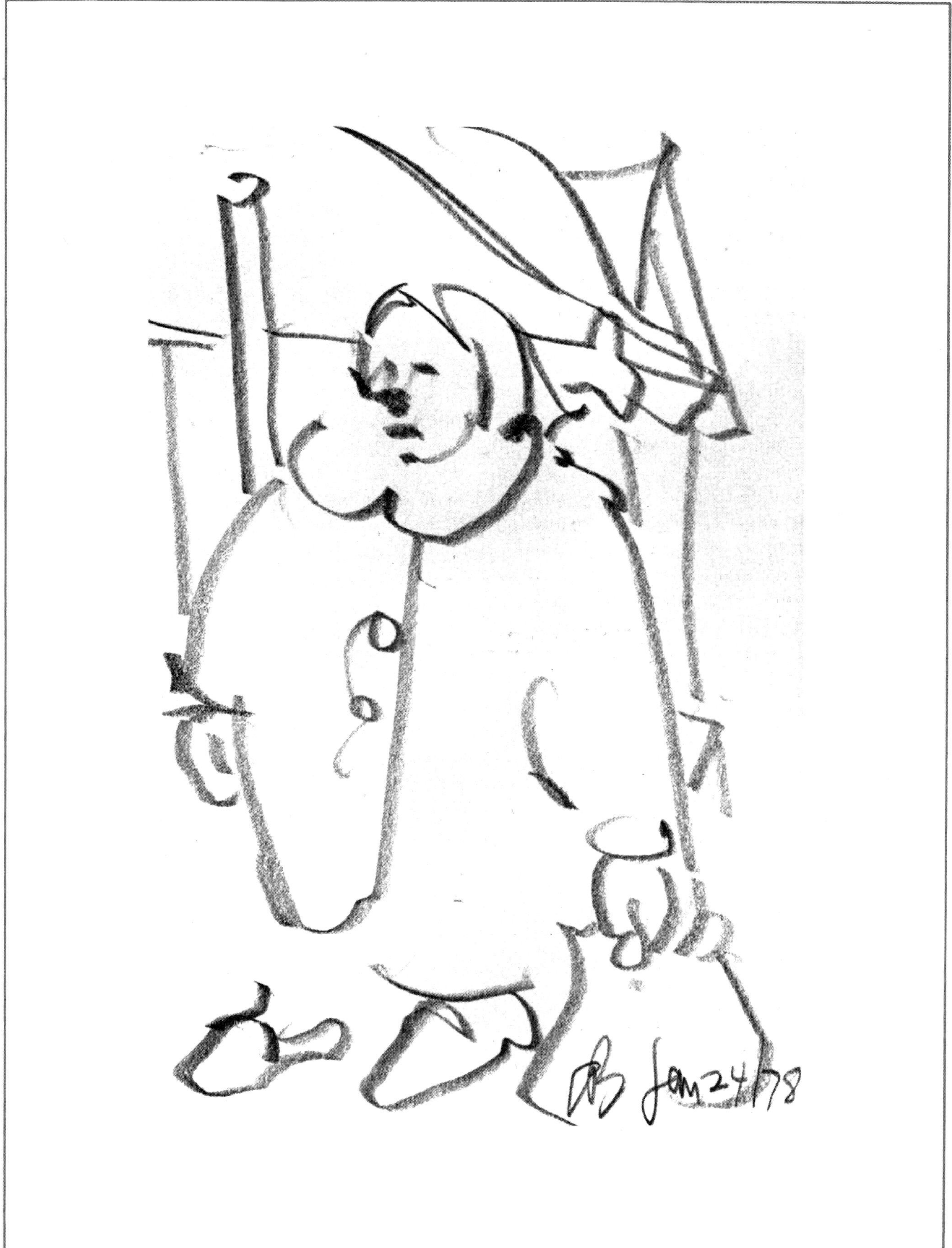

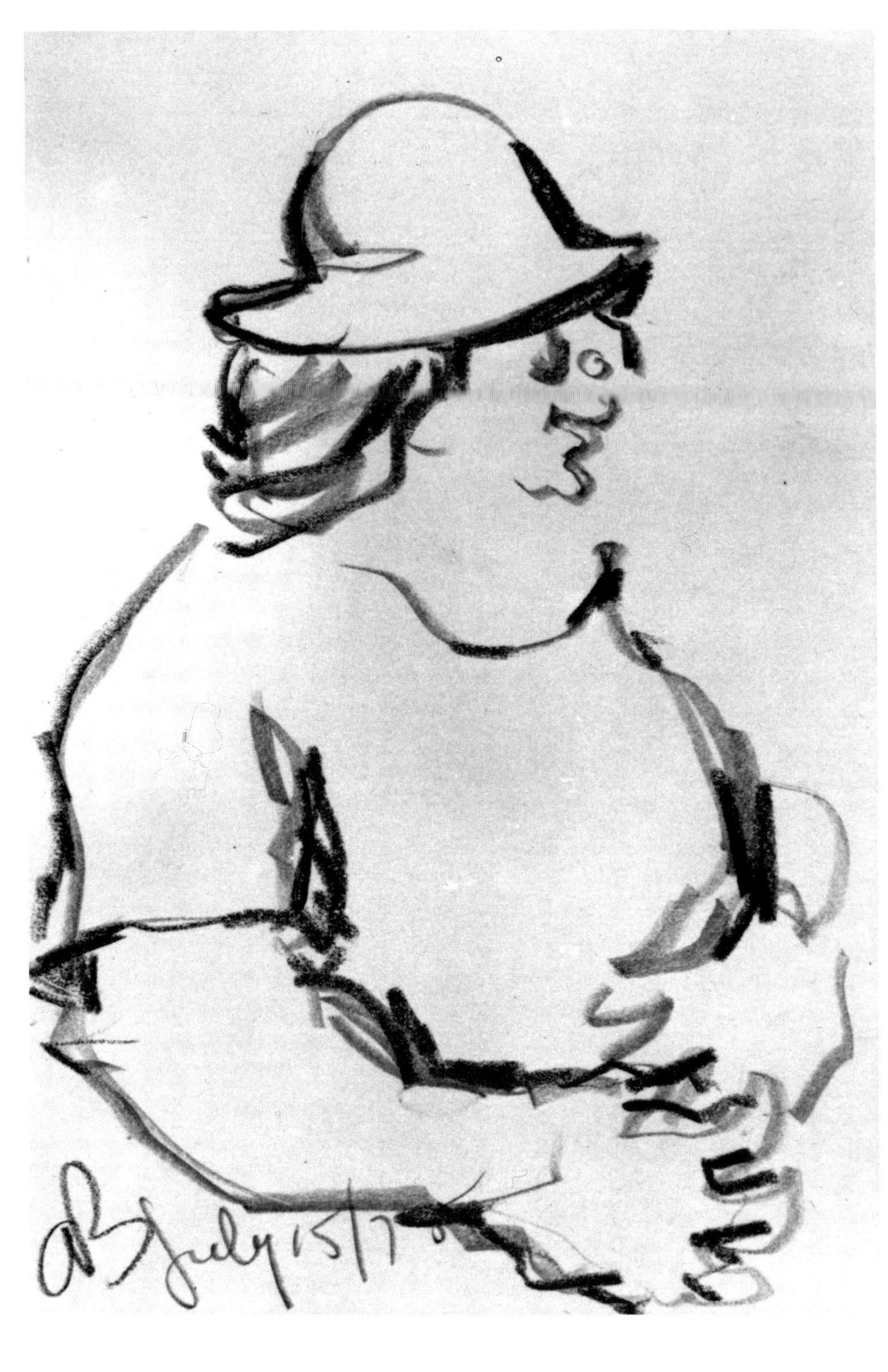

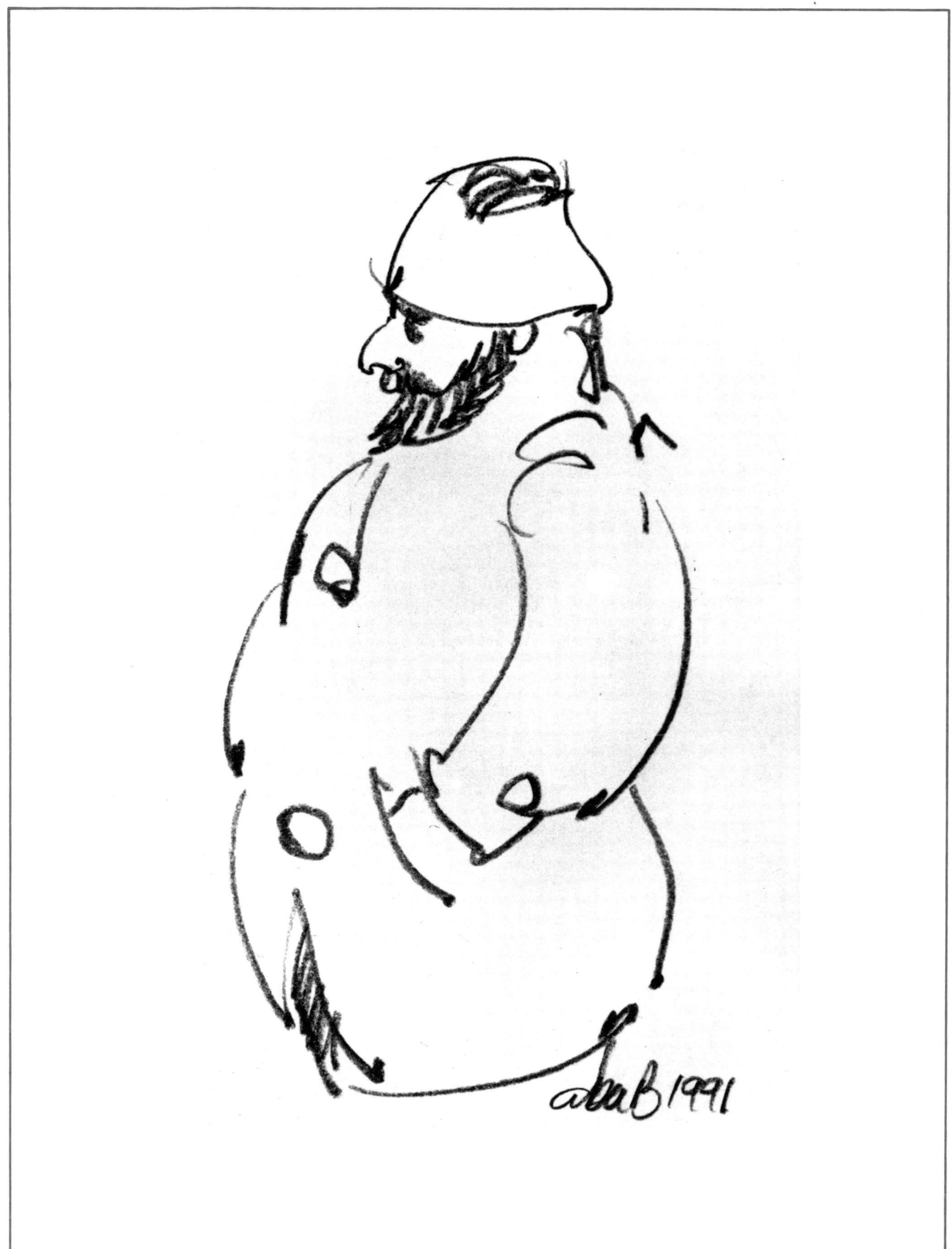

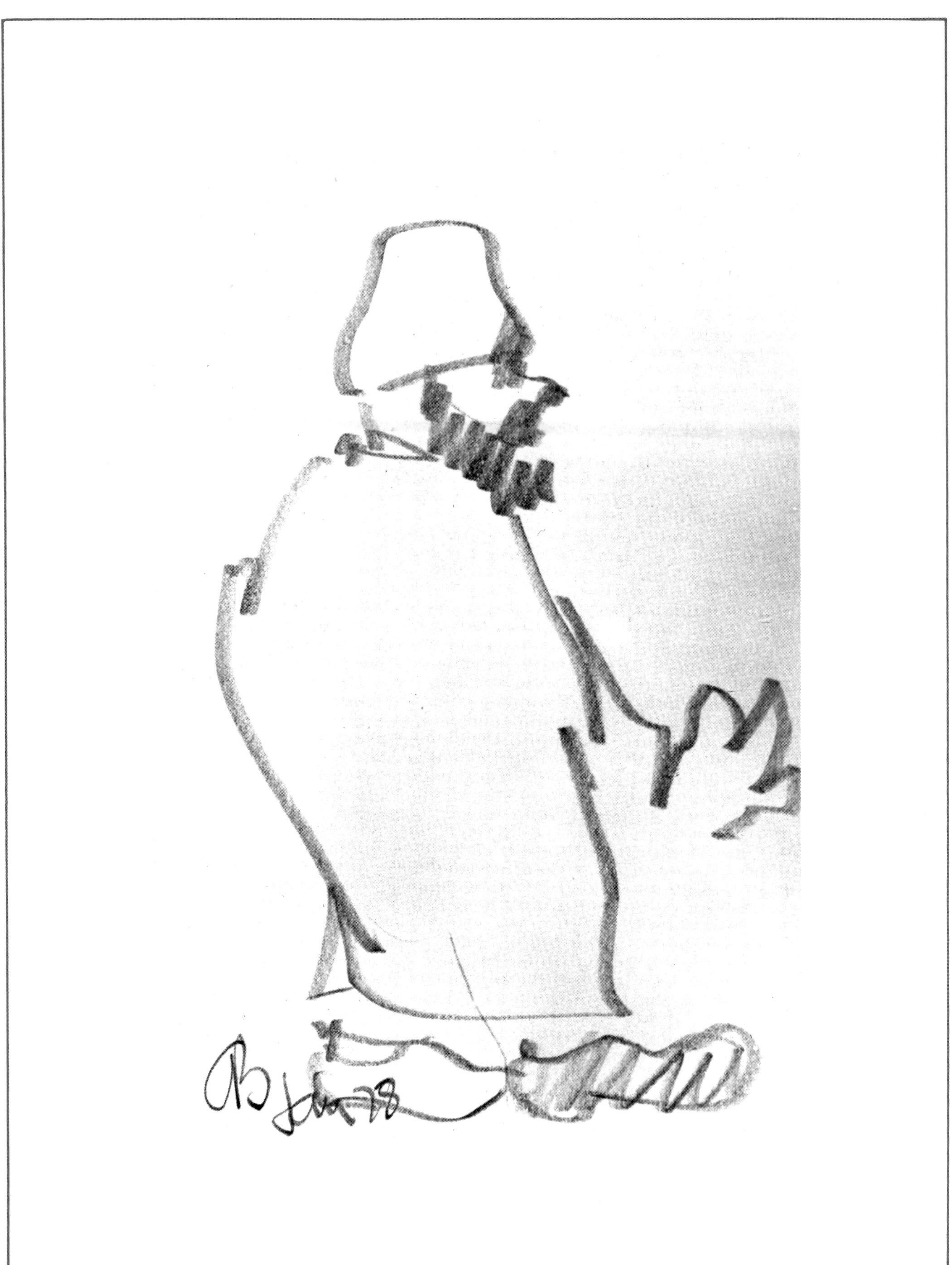

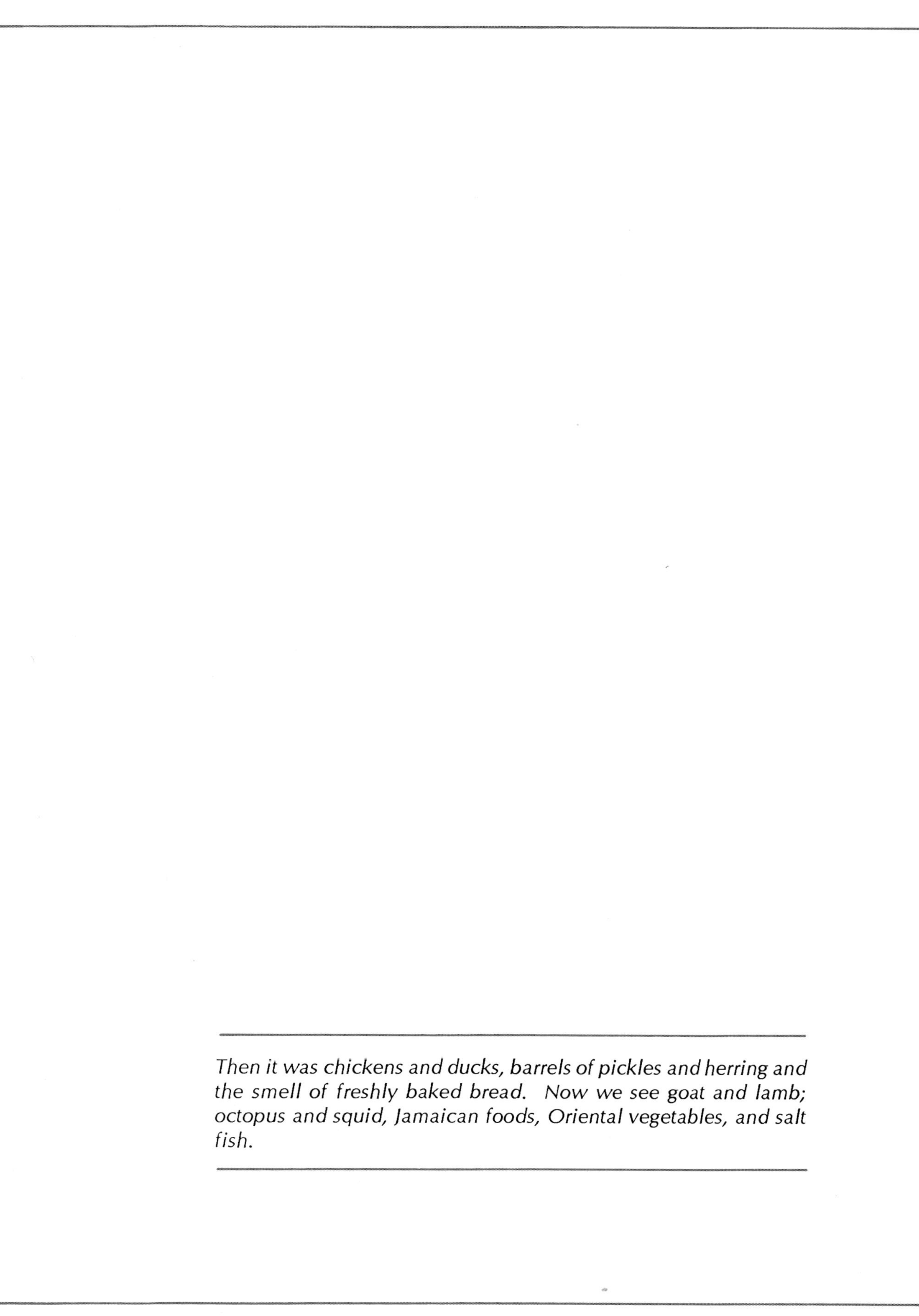

Then it was chickens and ducks, barrels of pickles and herring and the smell of freshly baked bread. Now we see goat and lamb; octopus and squid, Jamaican foods, Oriental vegetables, and salt fish.

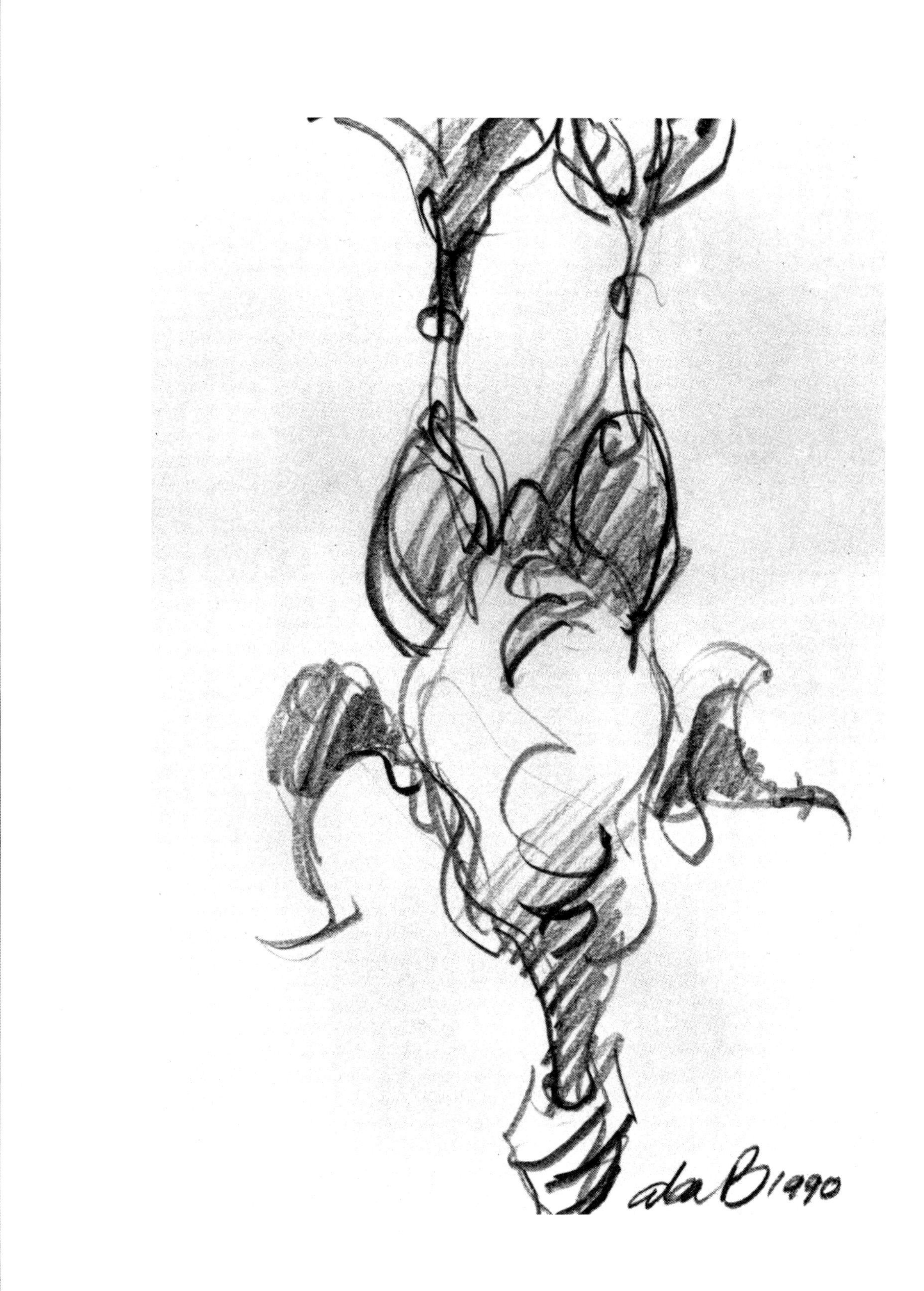

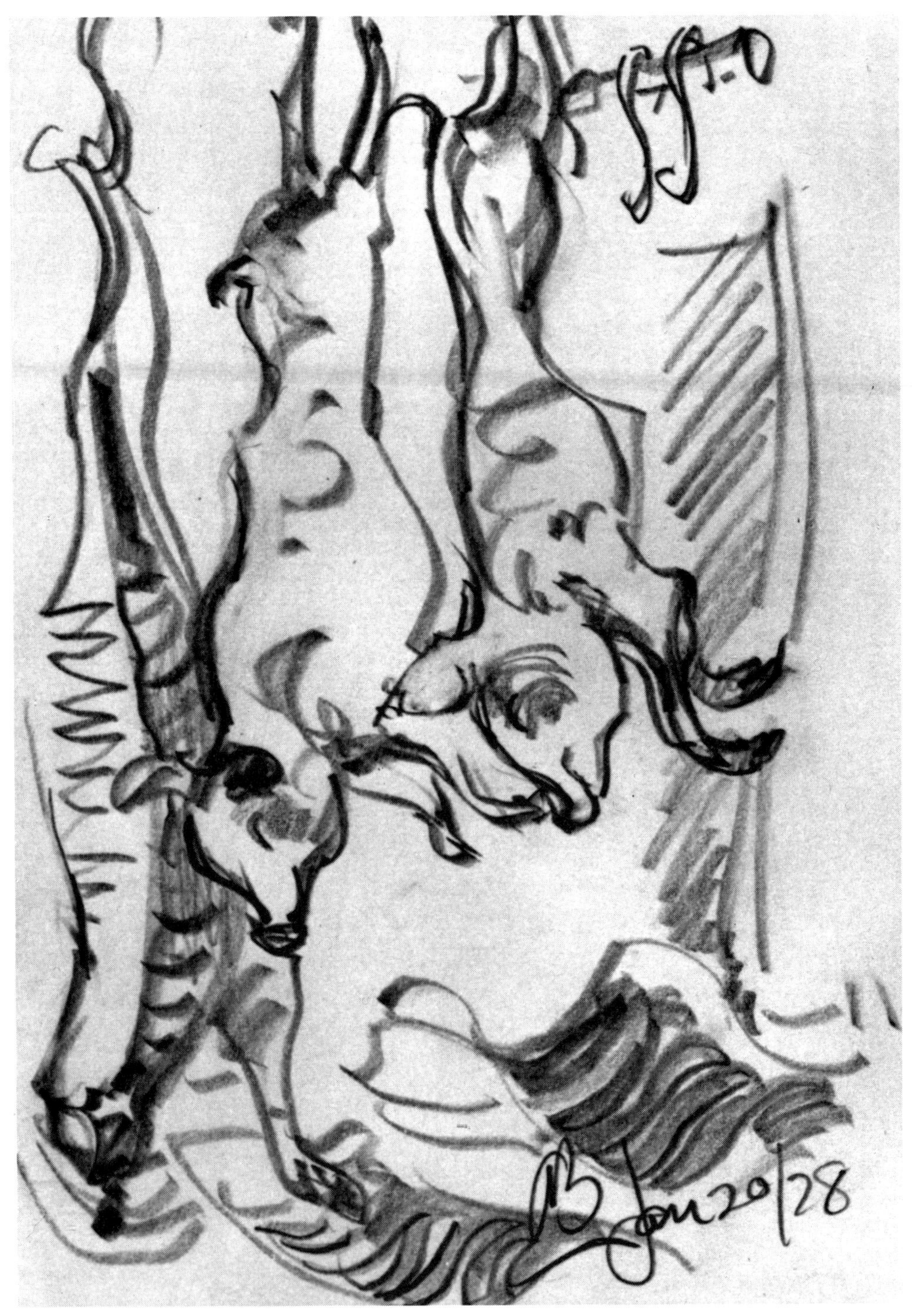

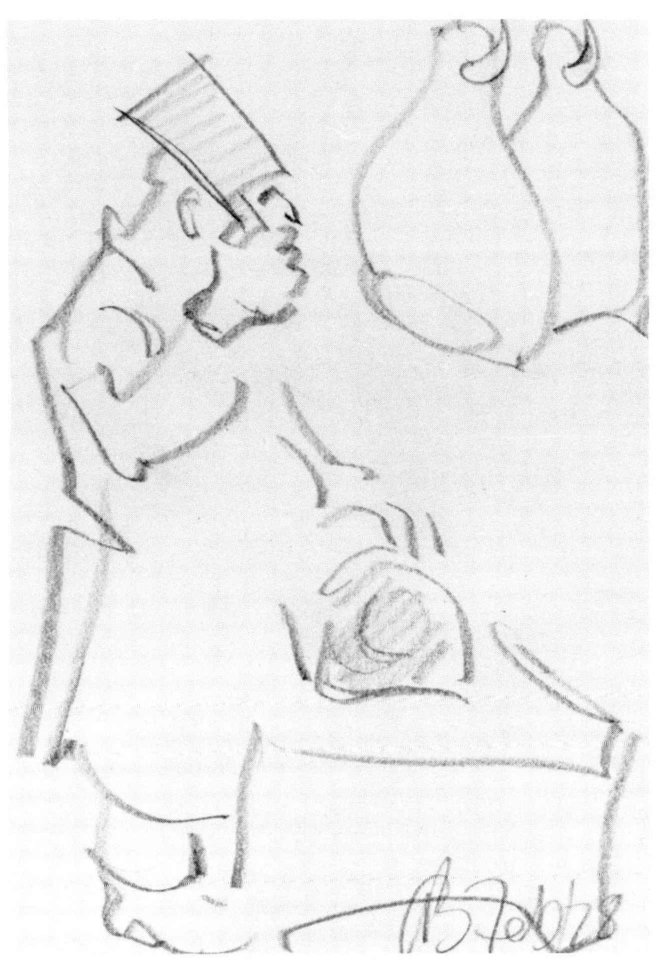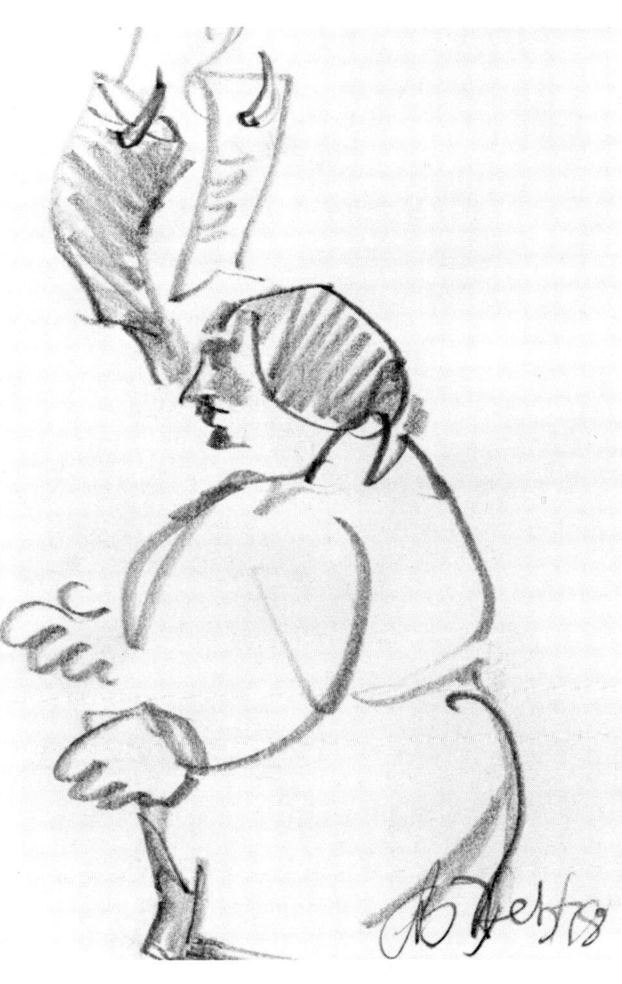

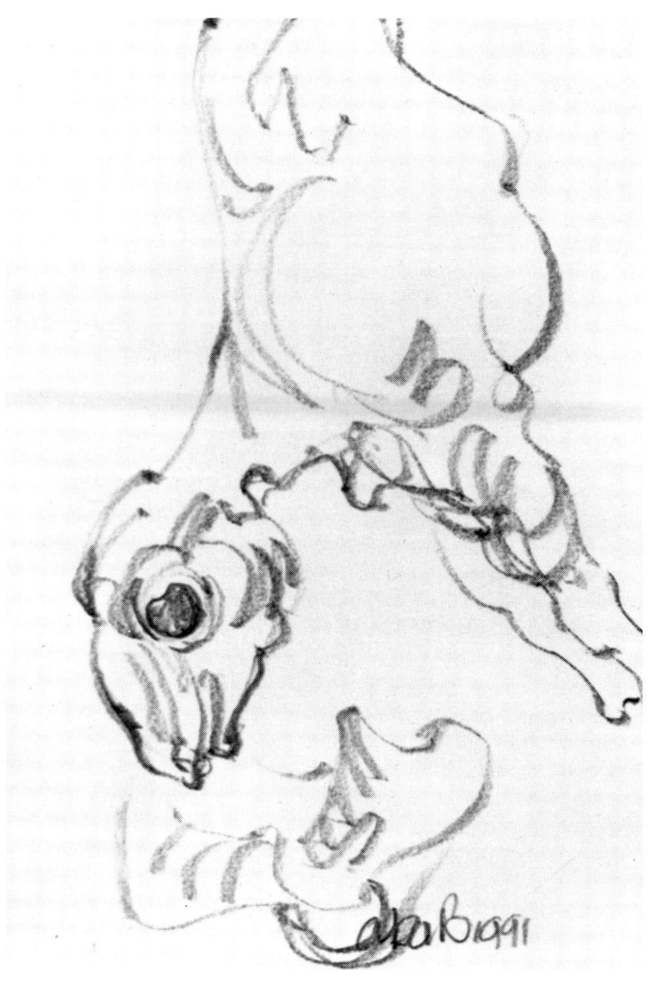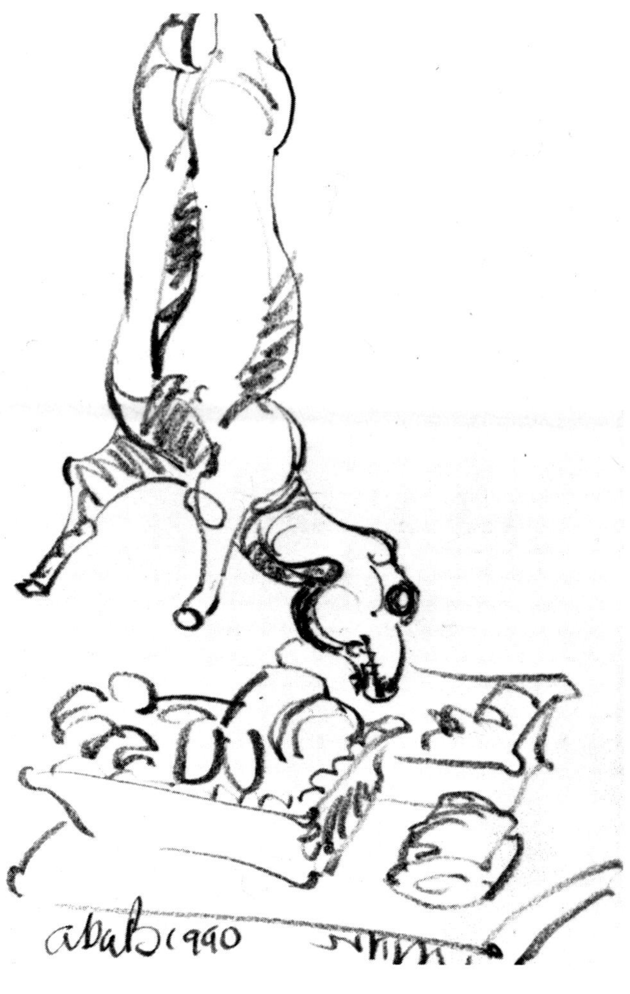

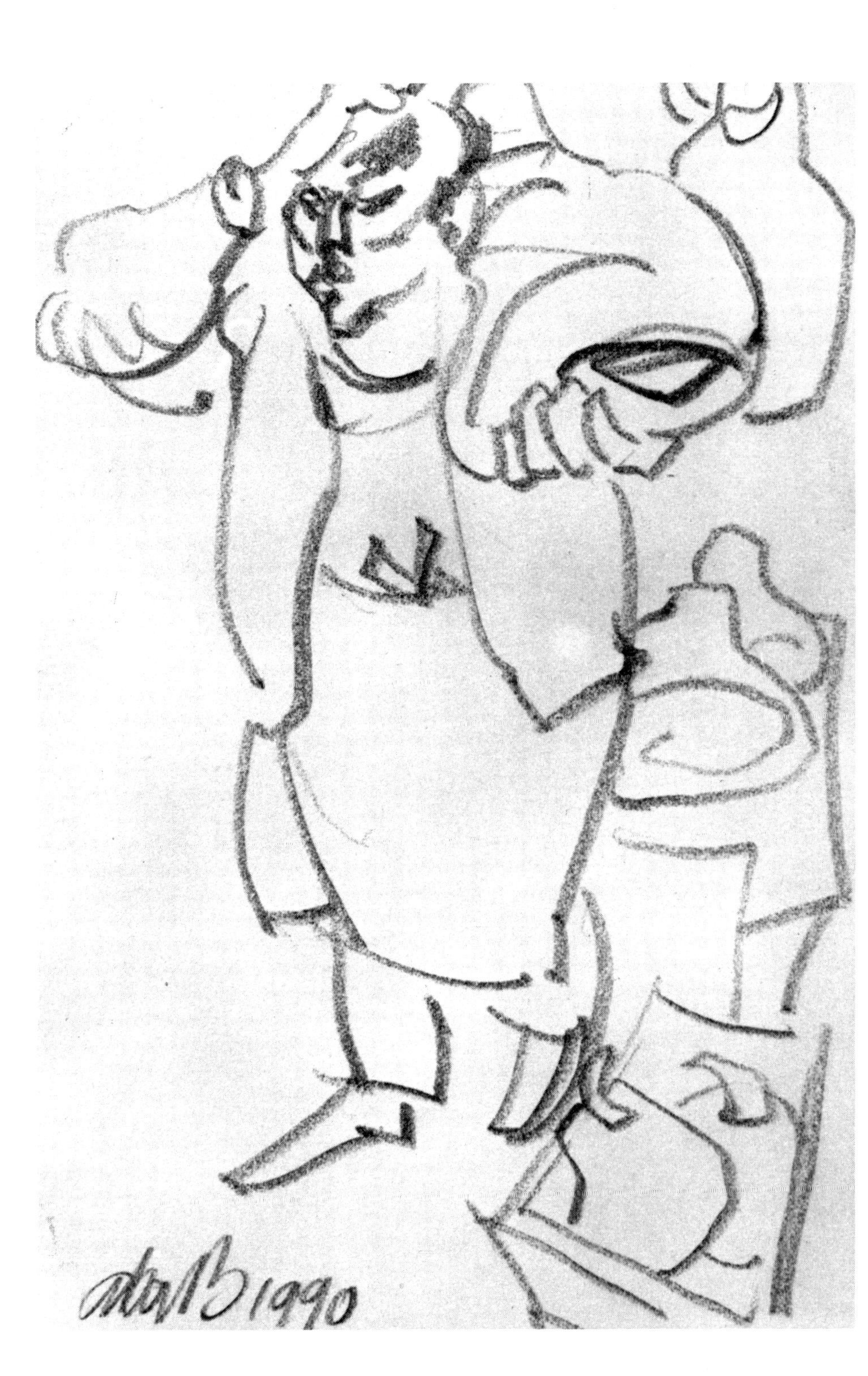

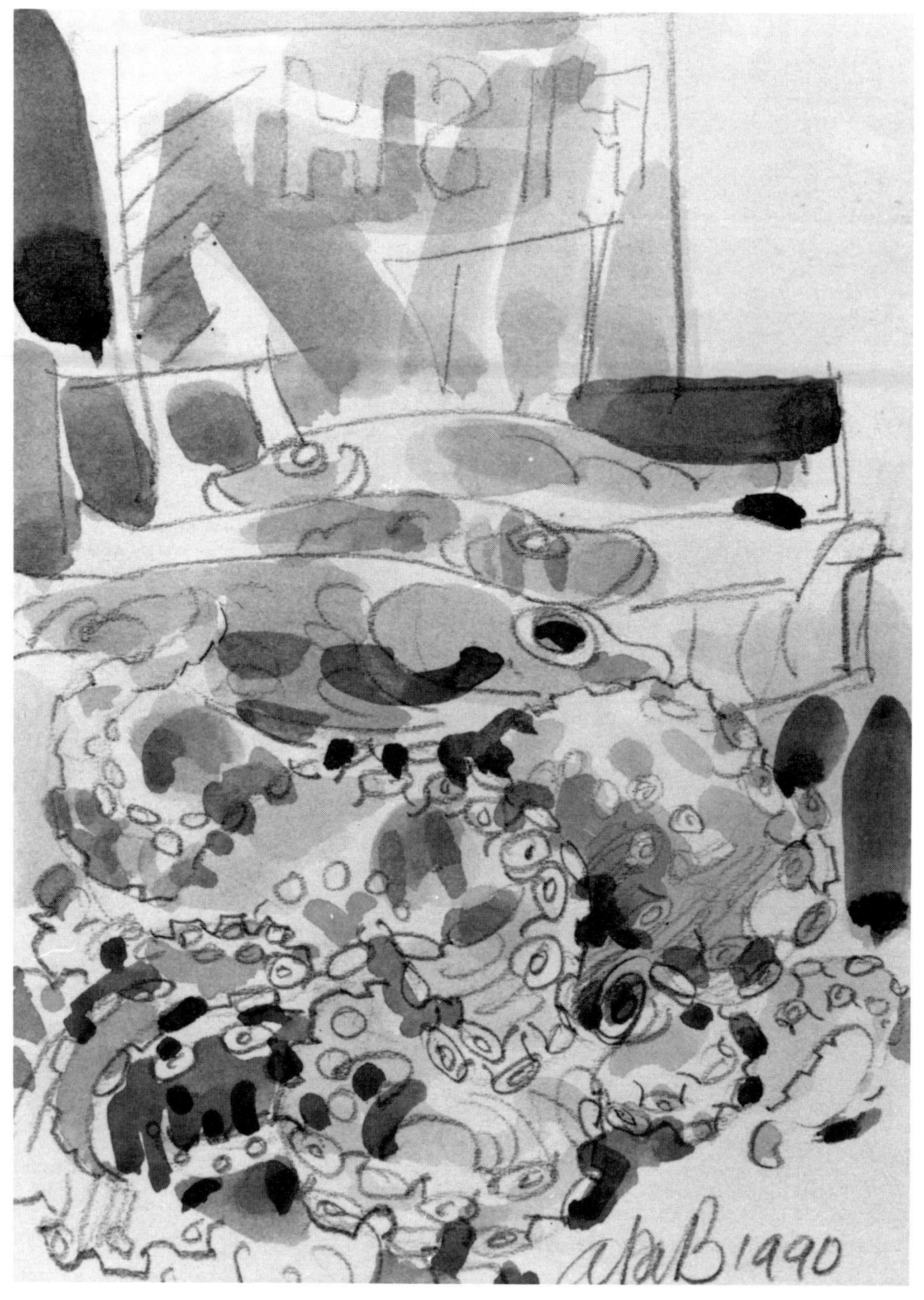

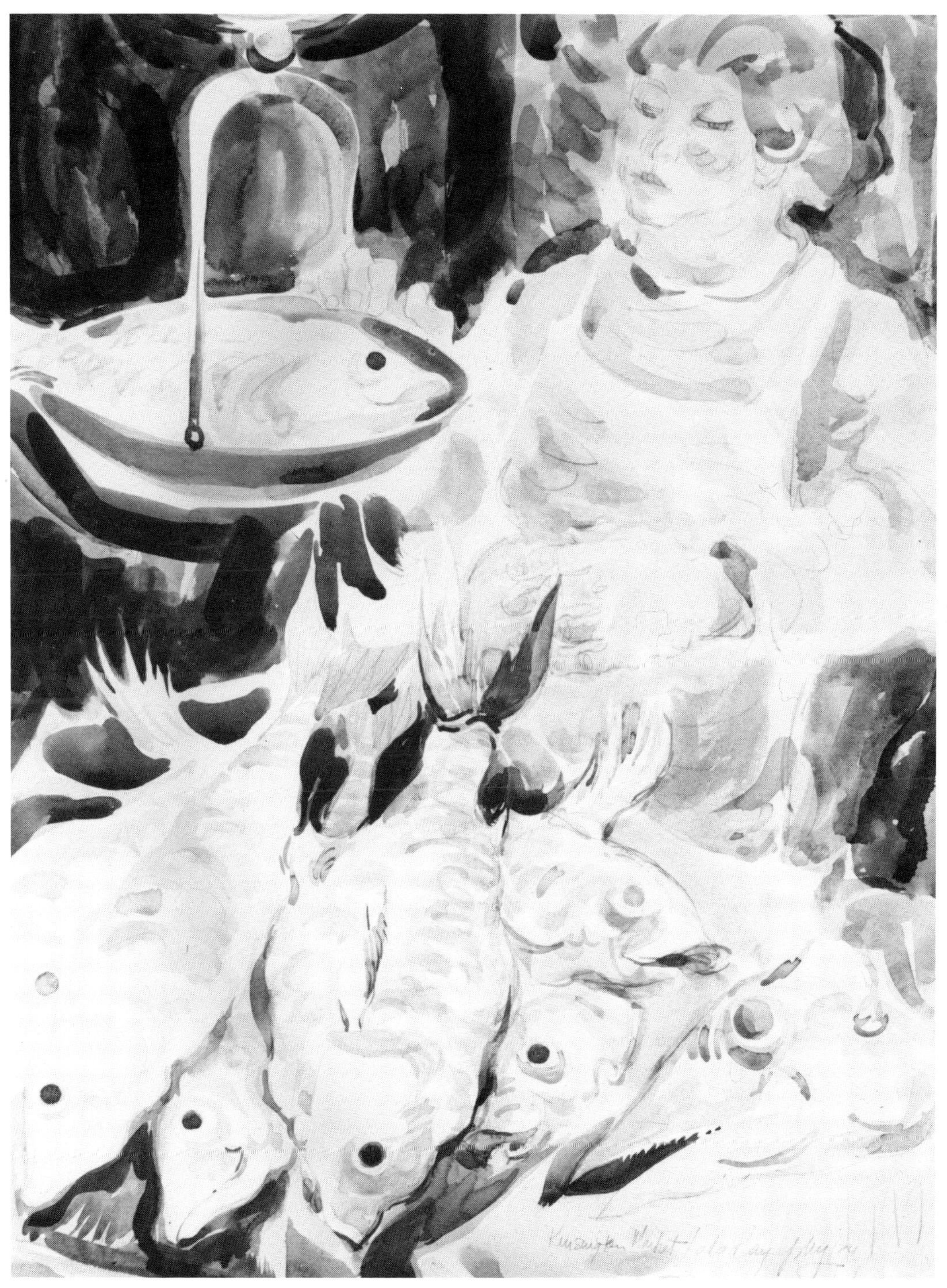

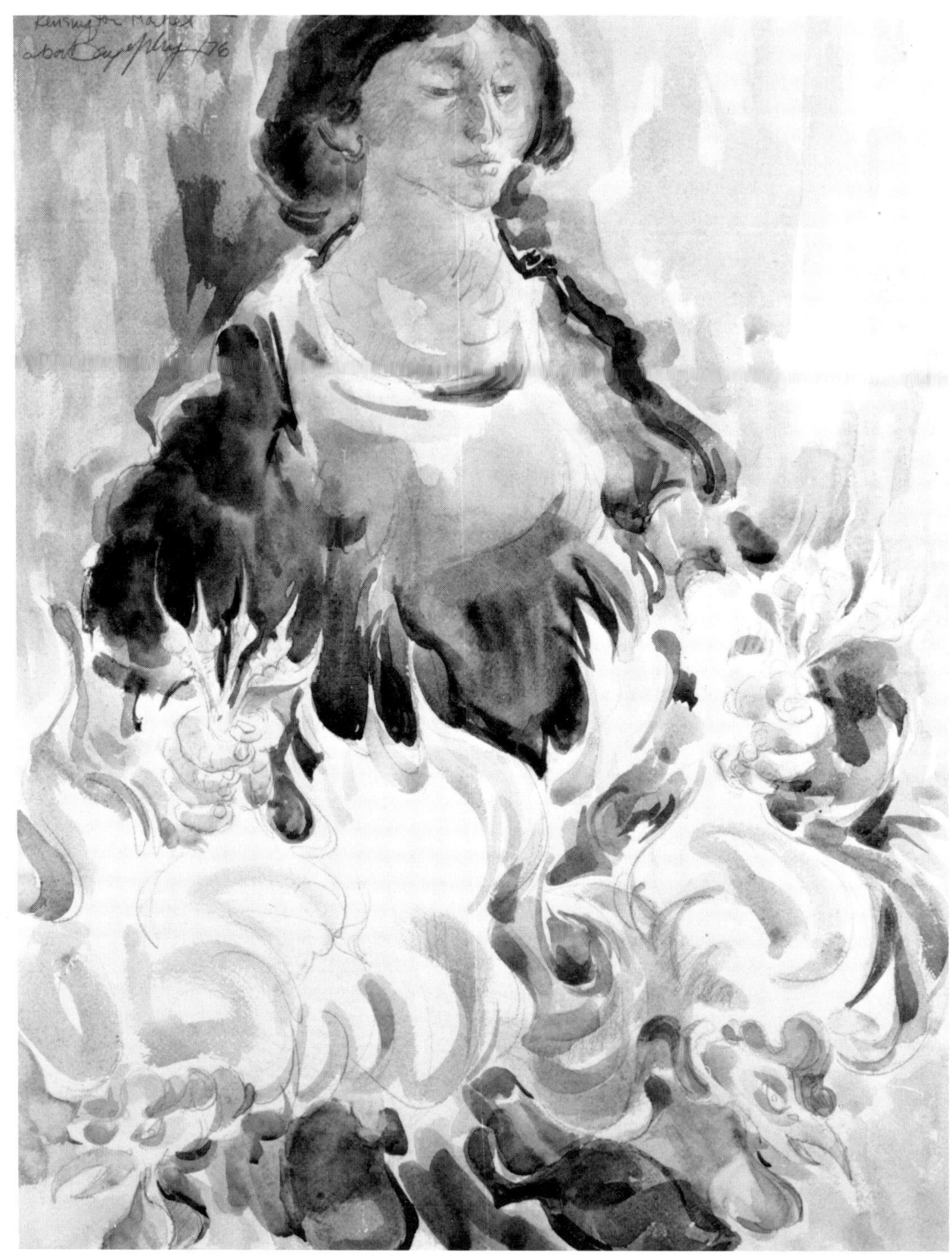

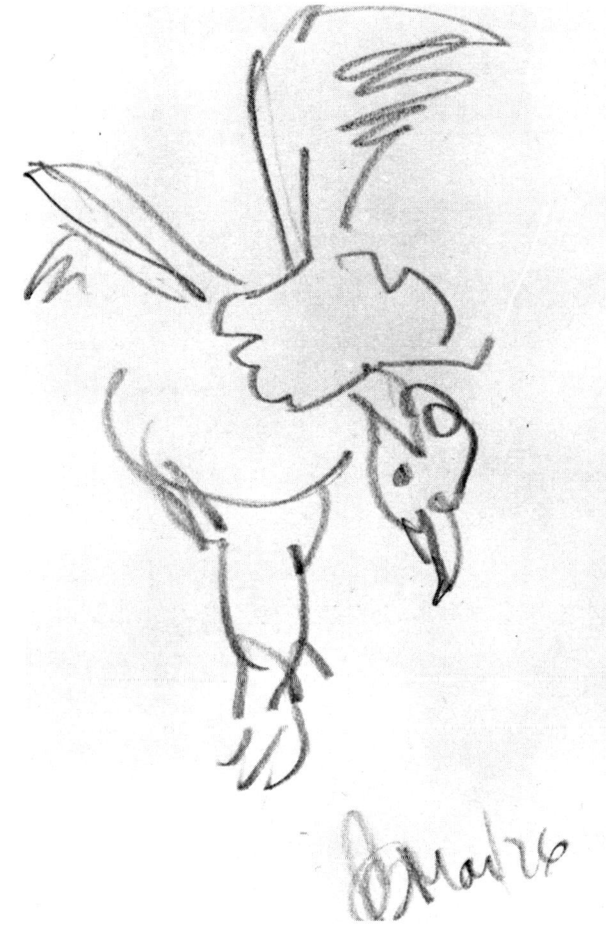

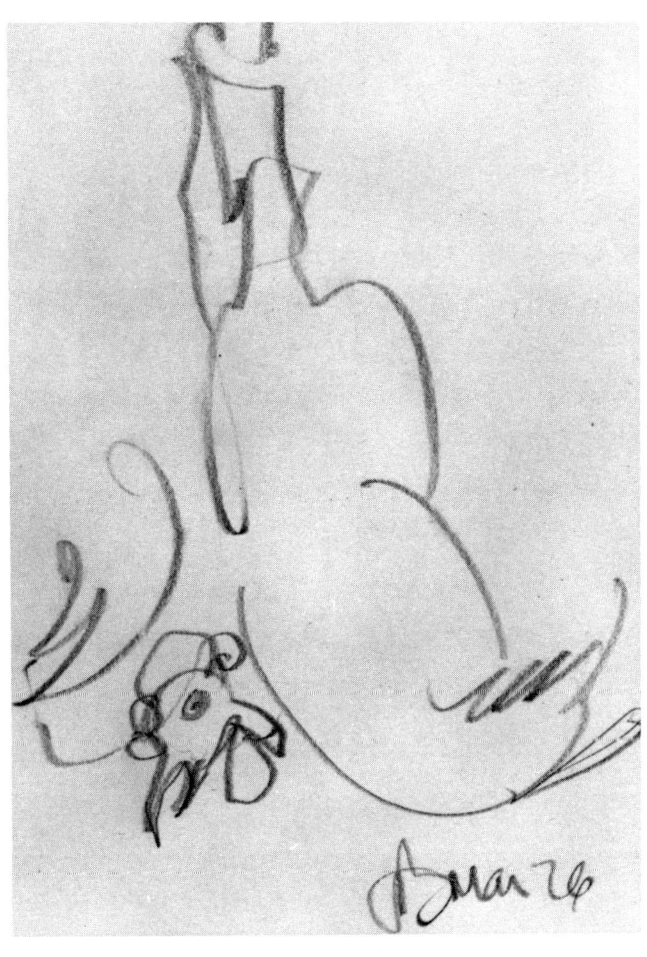

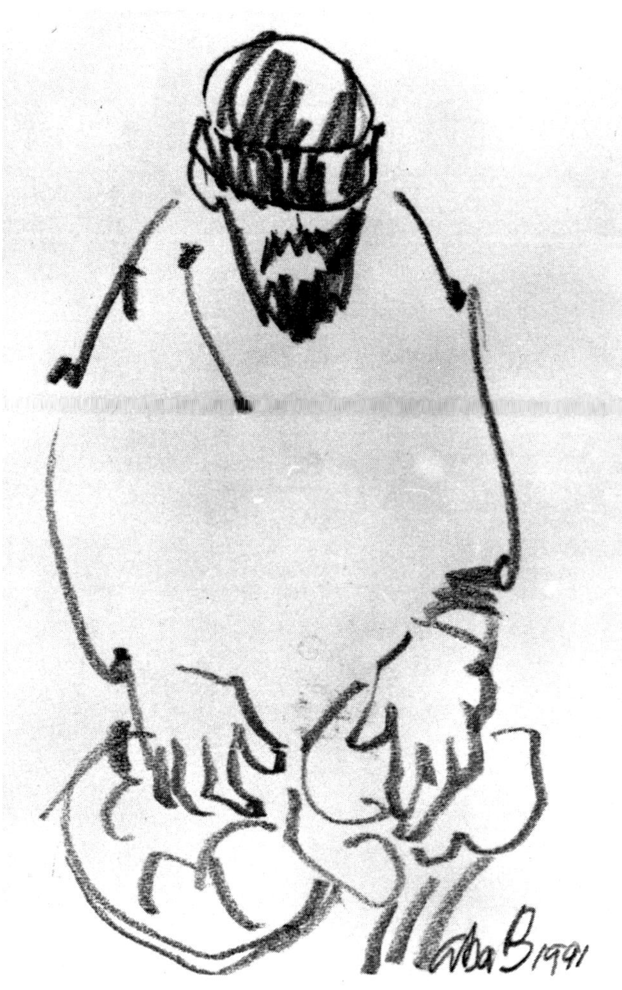

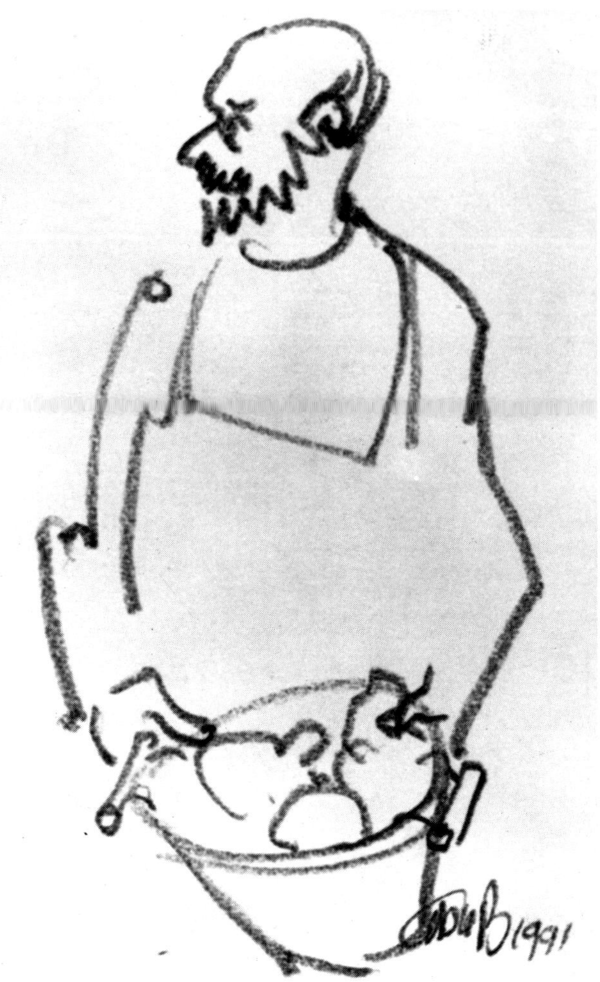

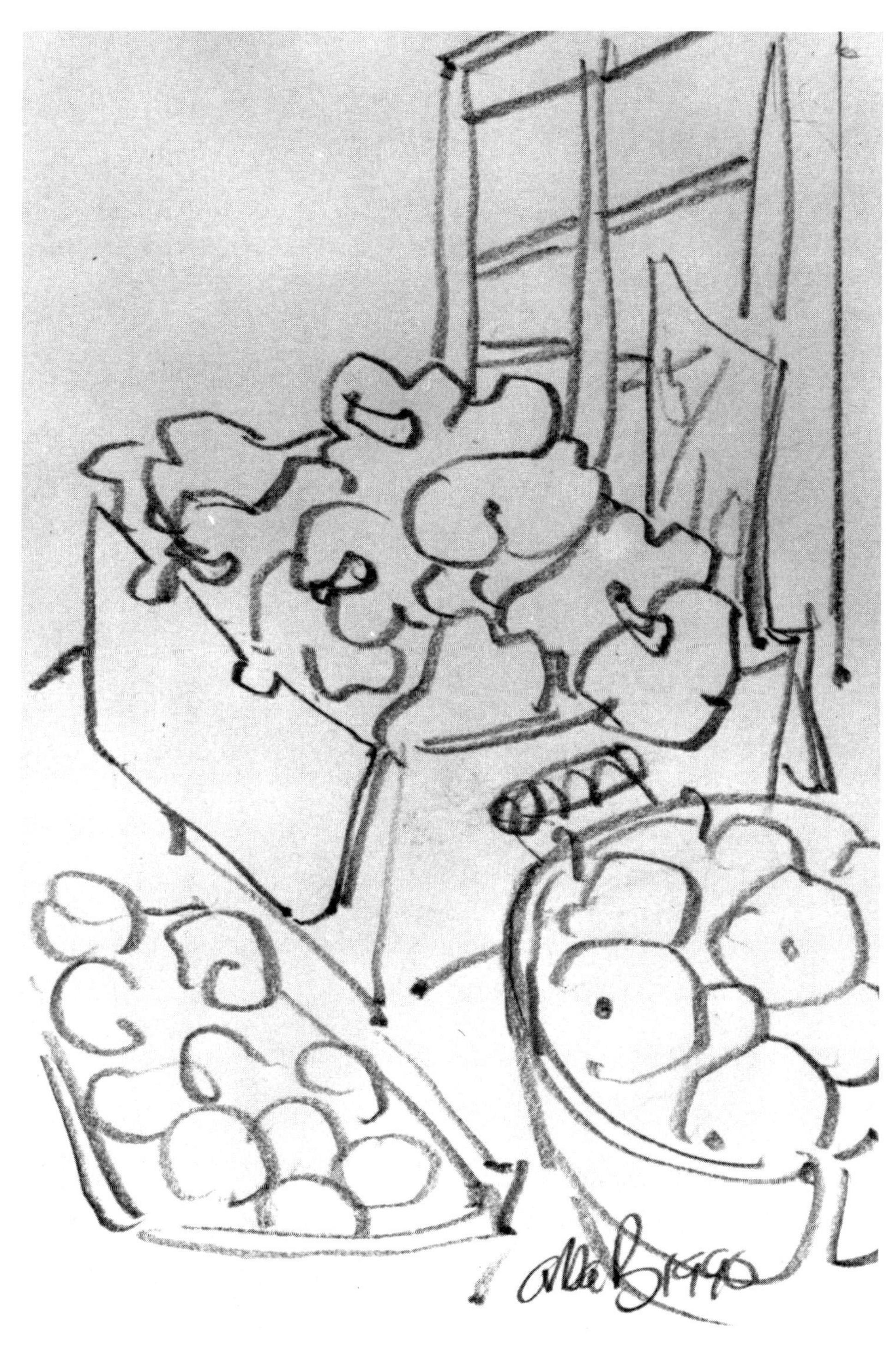

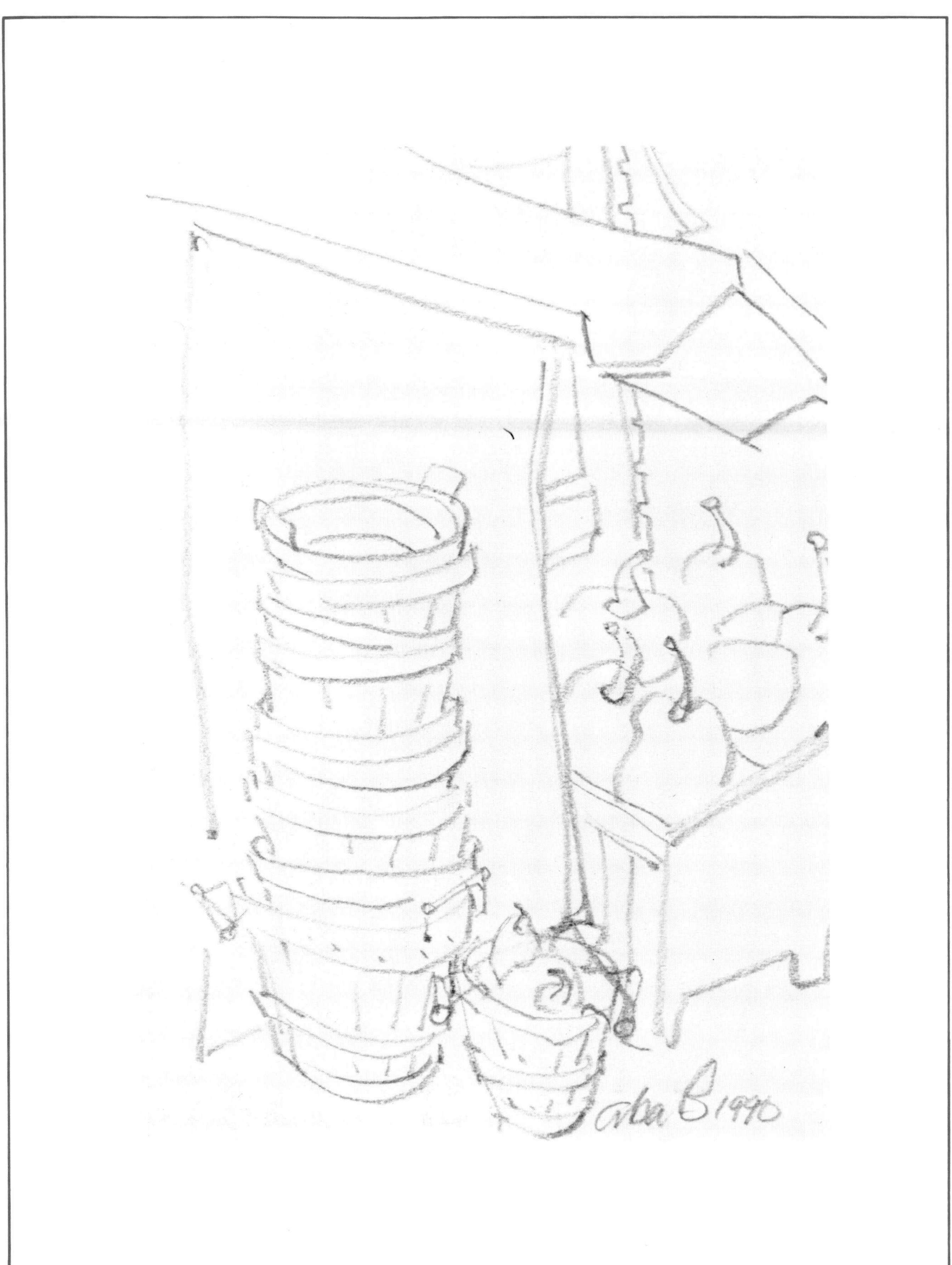

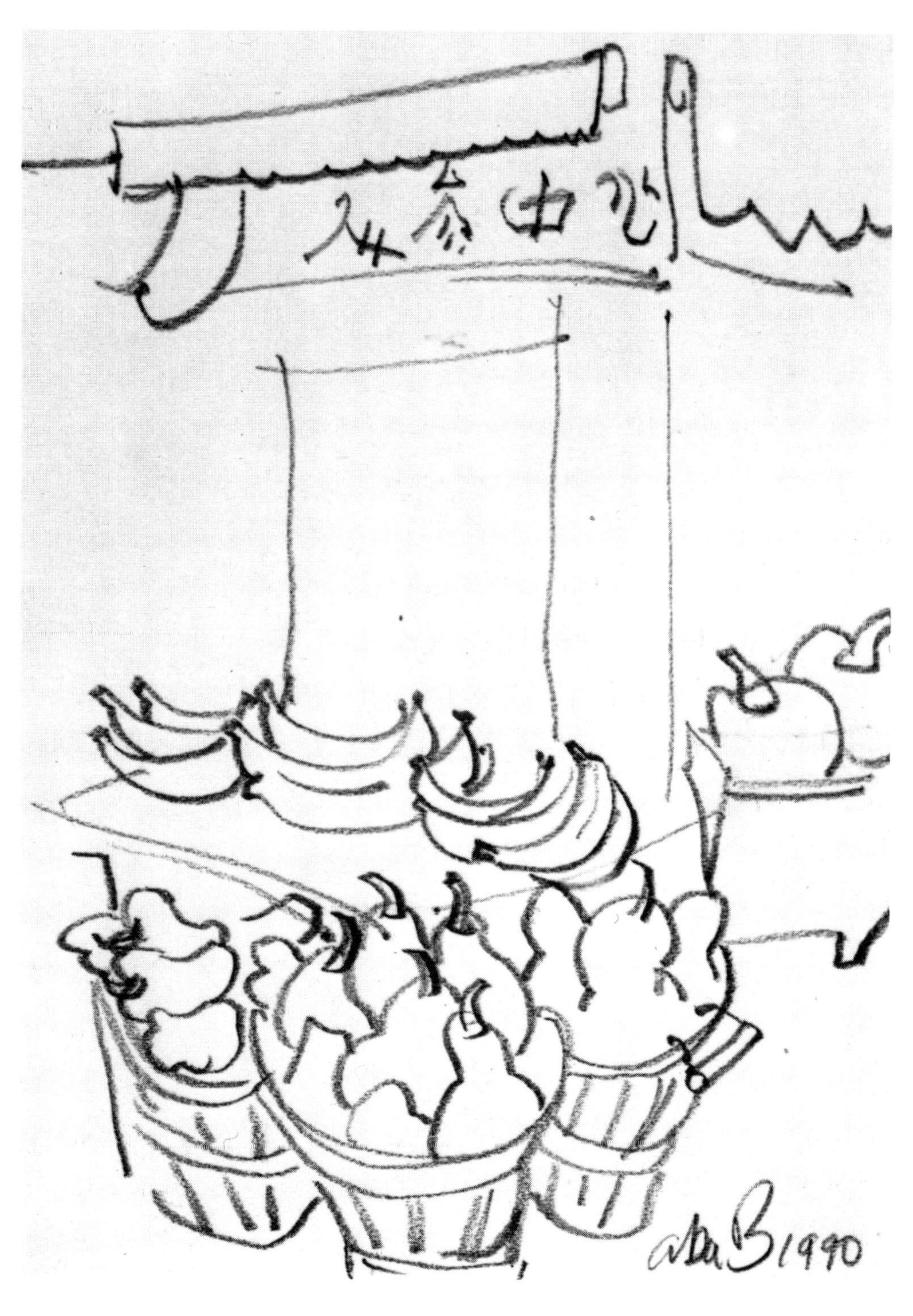

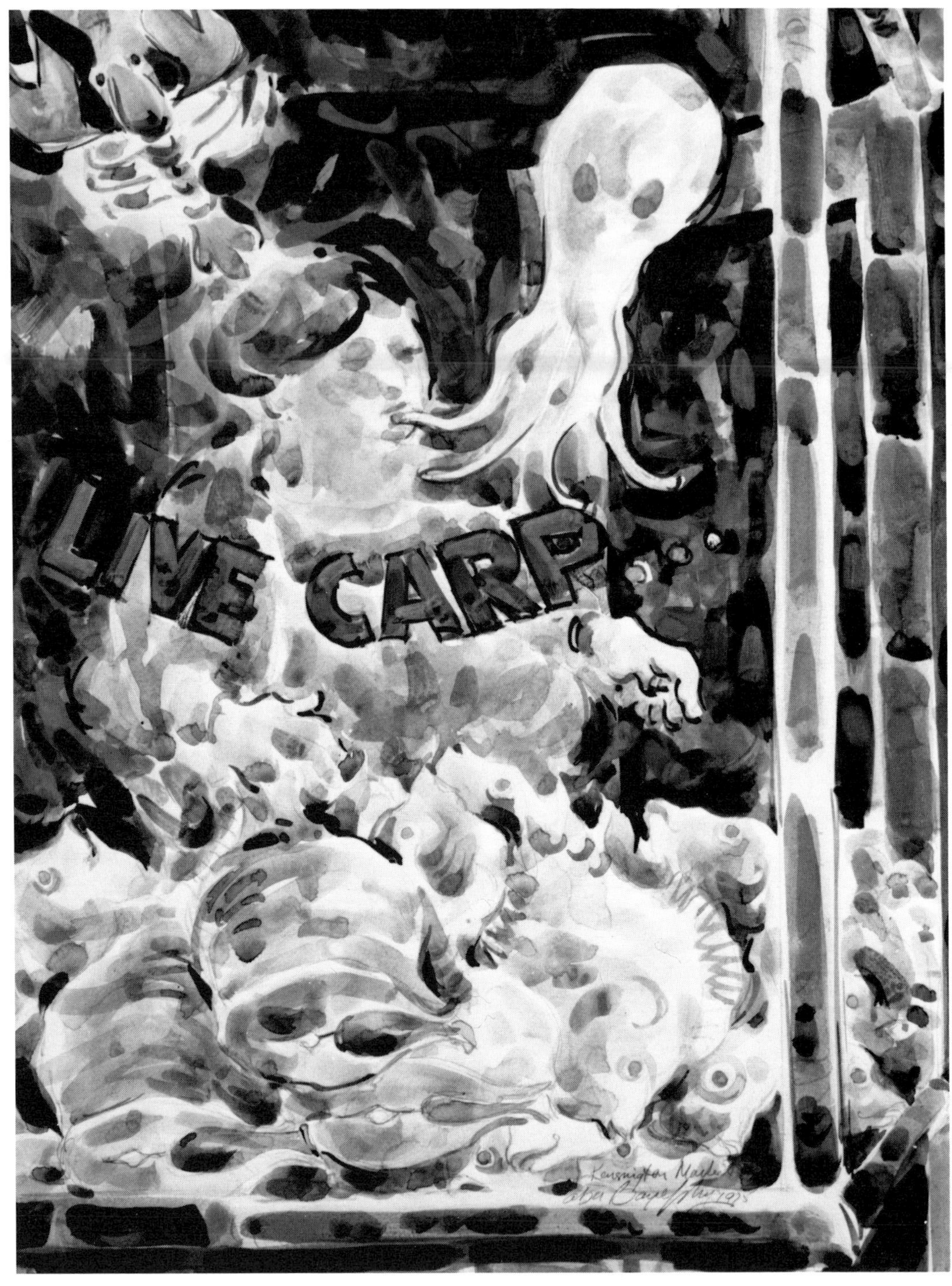

LIVE CARP

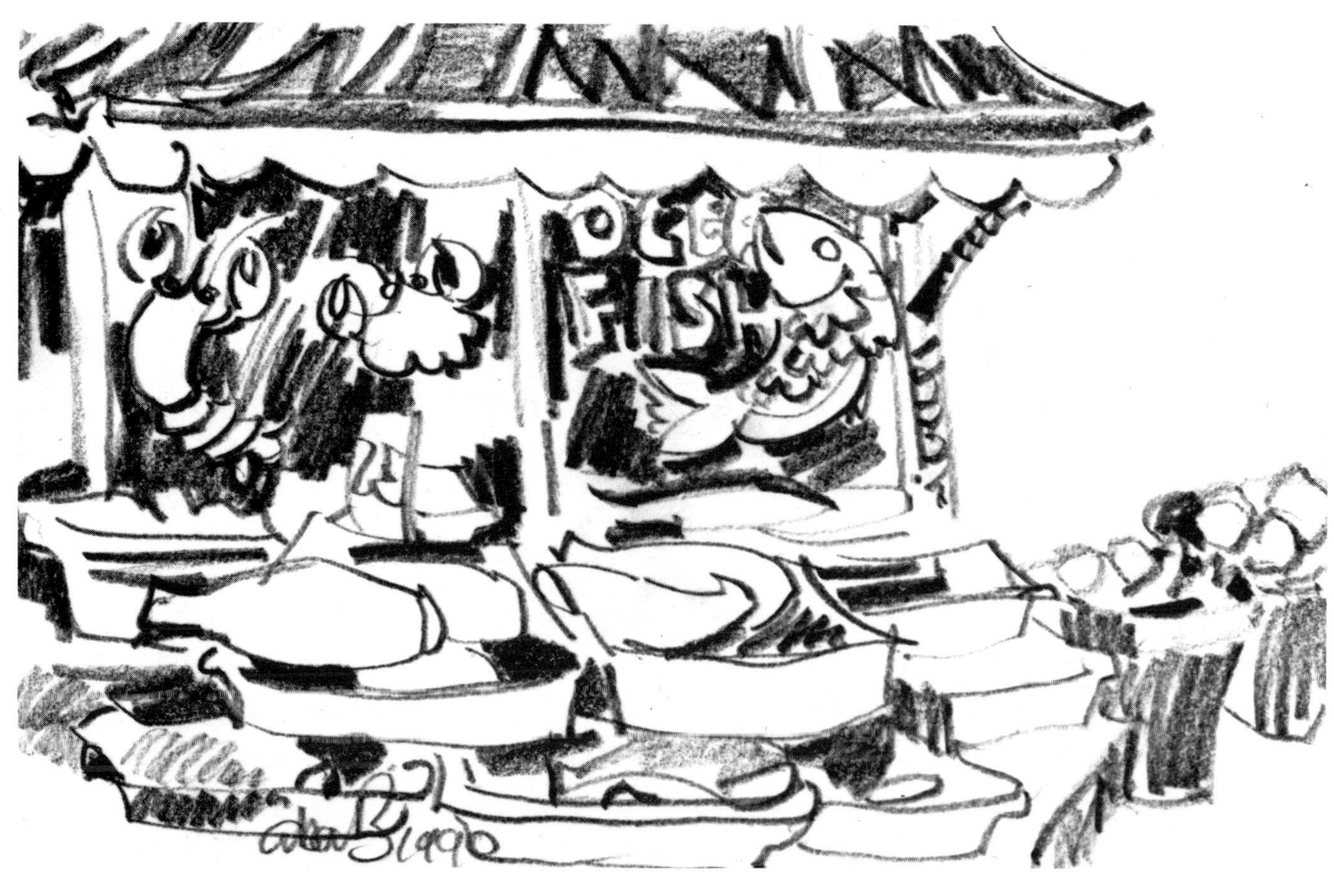
FISH

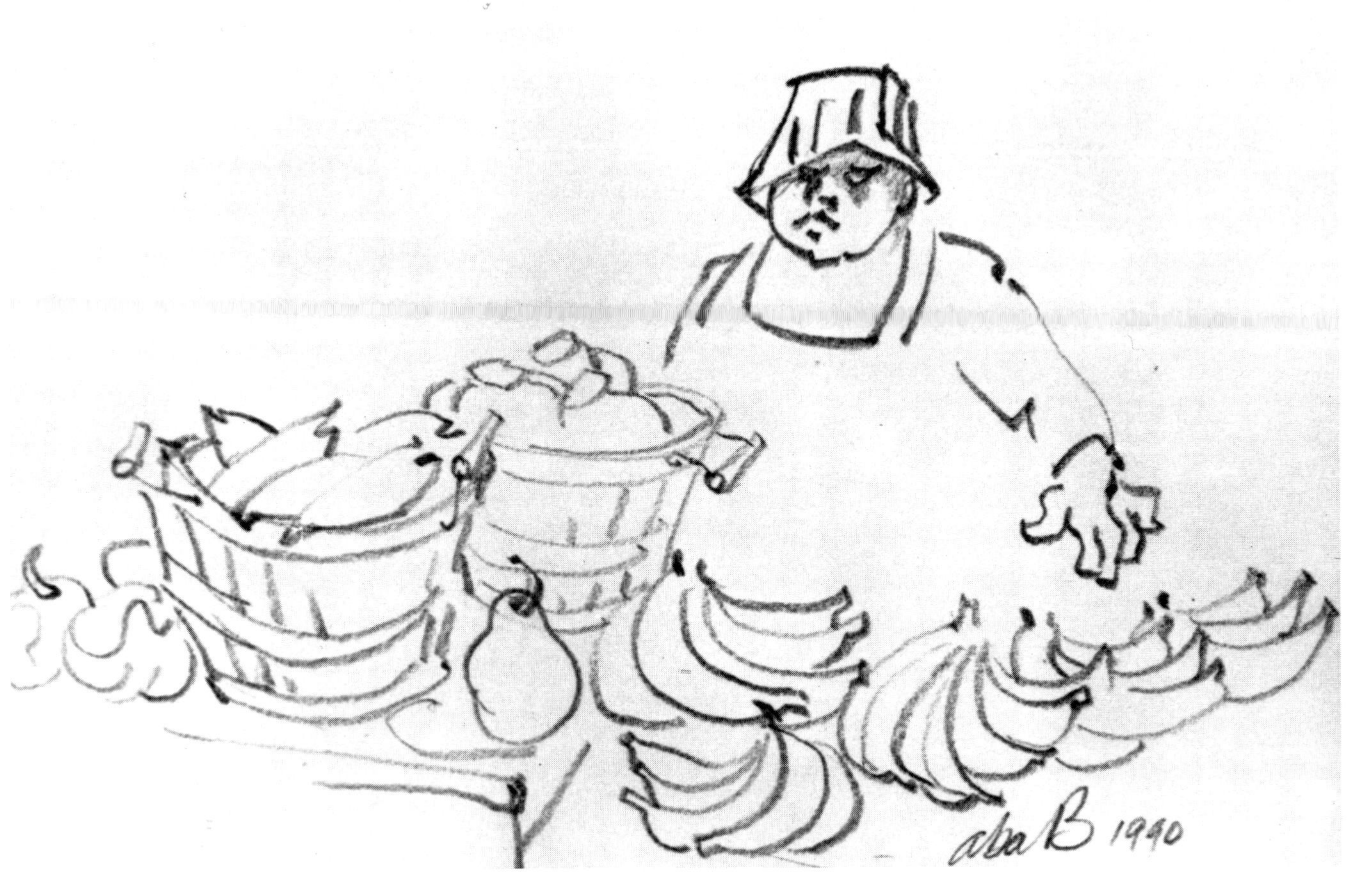

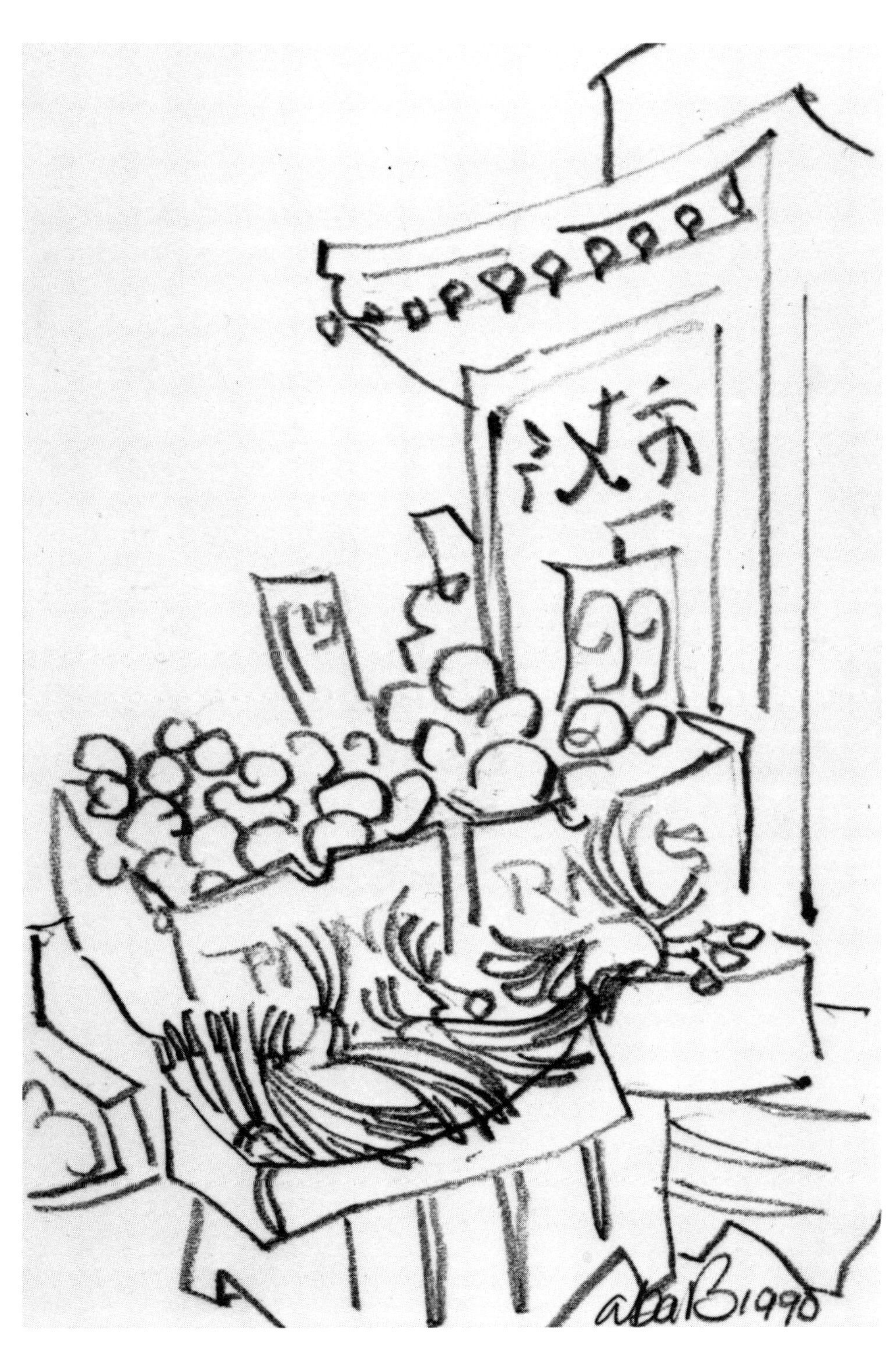

aBaB 1990

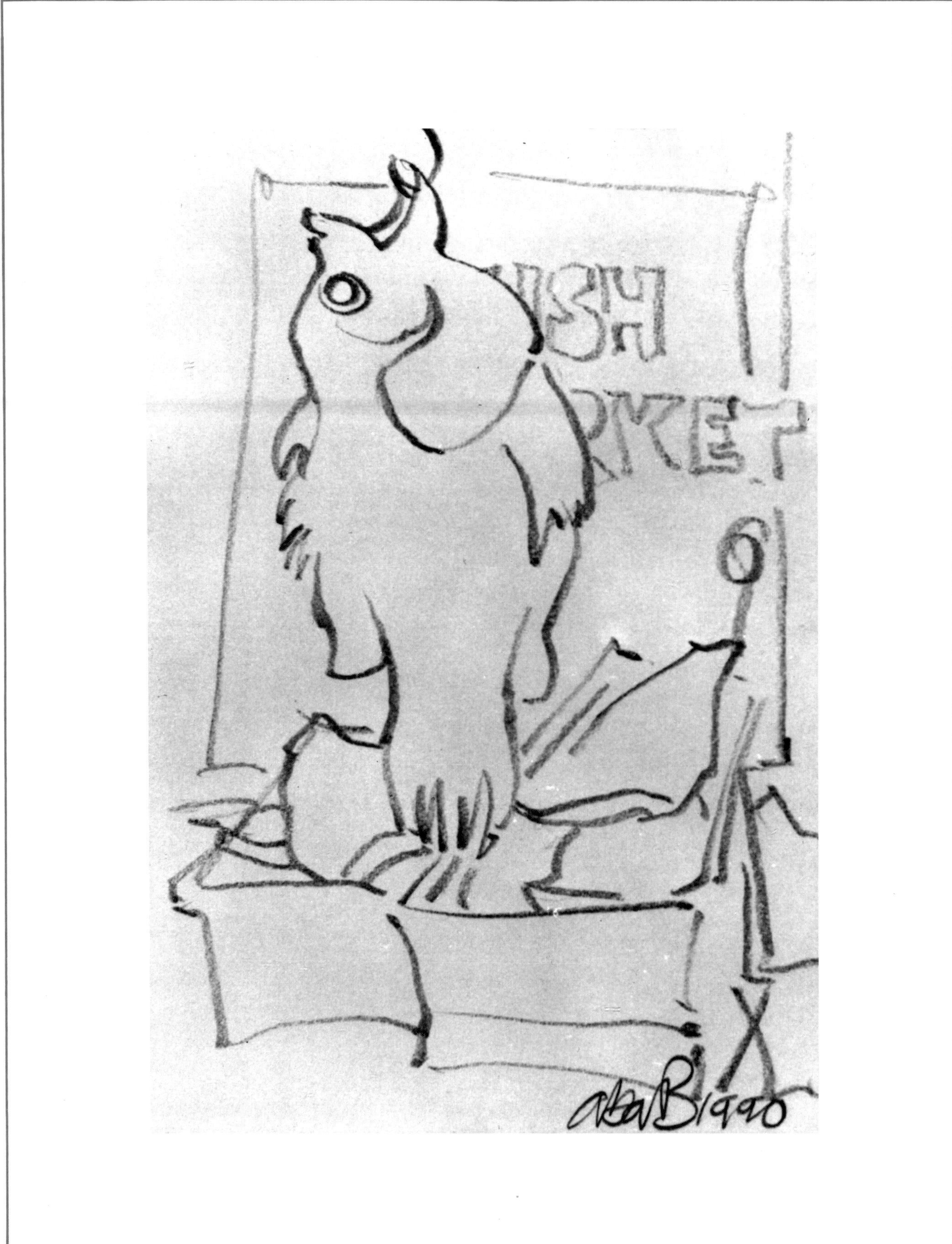
ISH
RKET
6

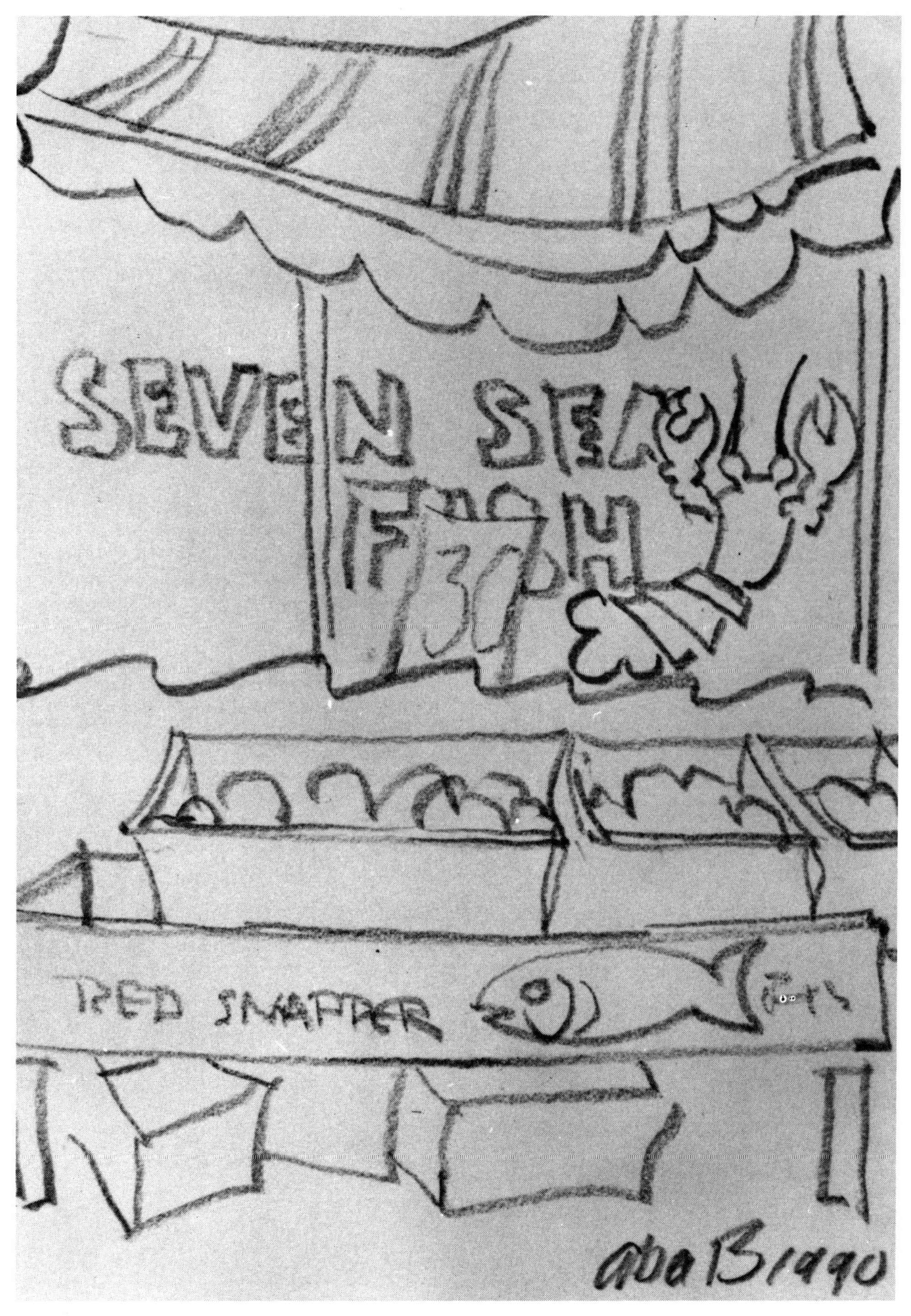
SEVEN SEAS
FISH
FRESH
RED SNAPPER
aba B 1990

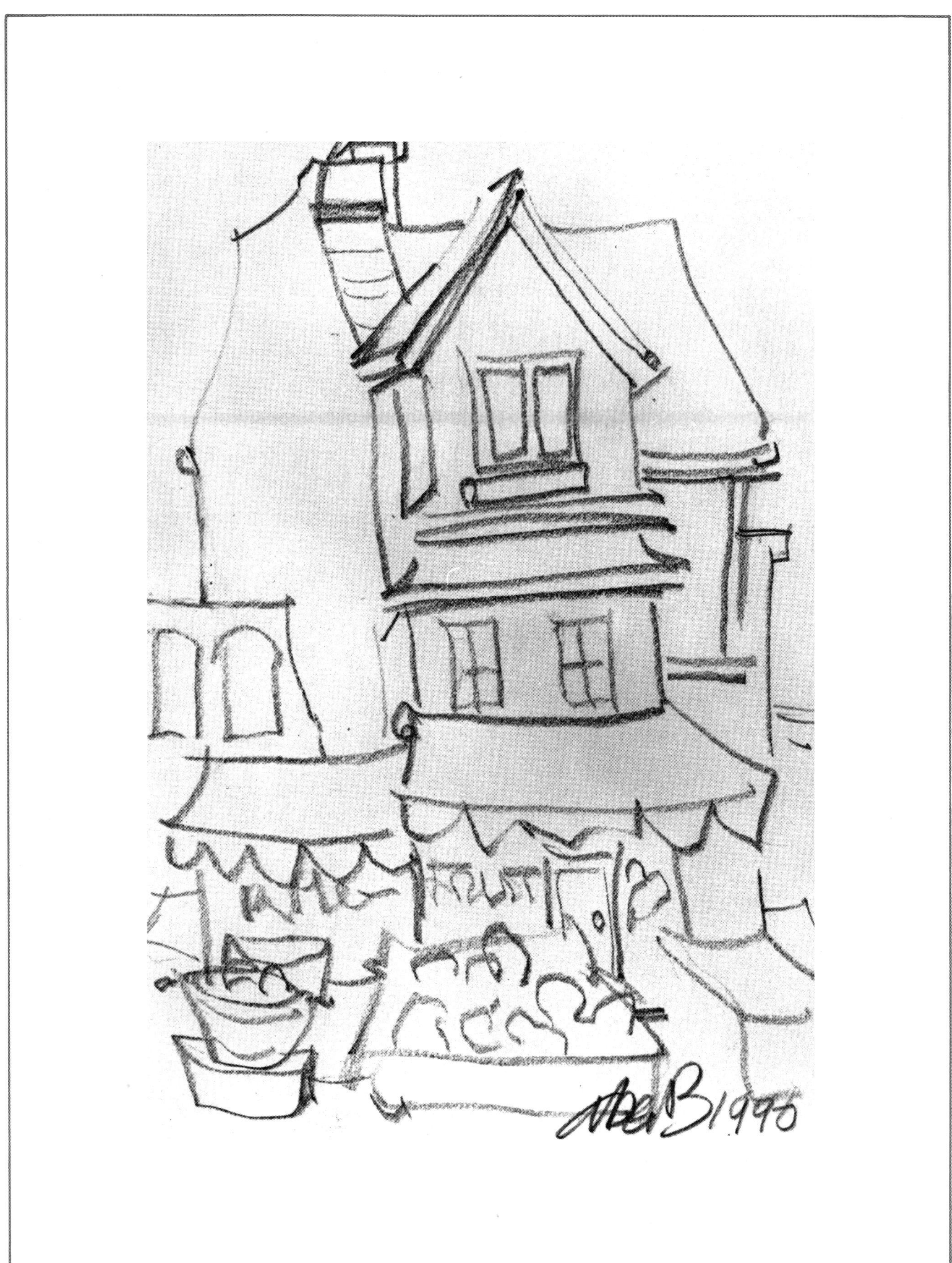

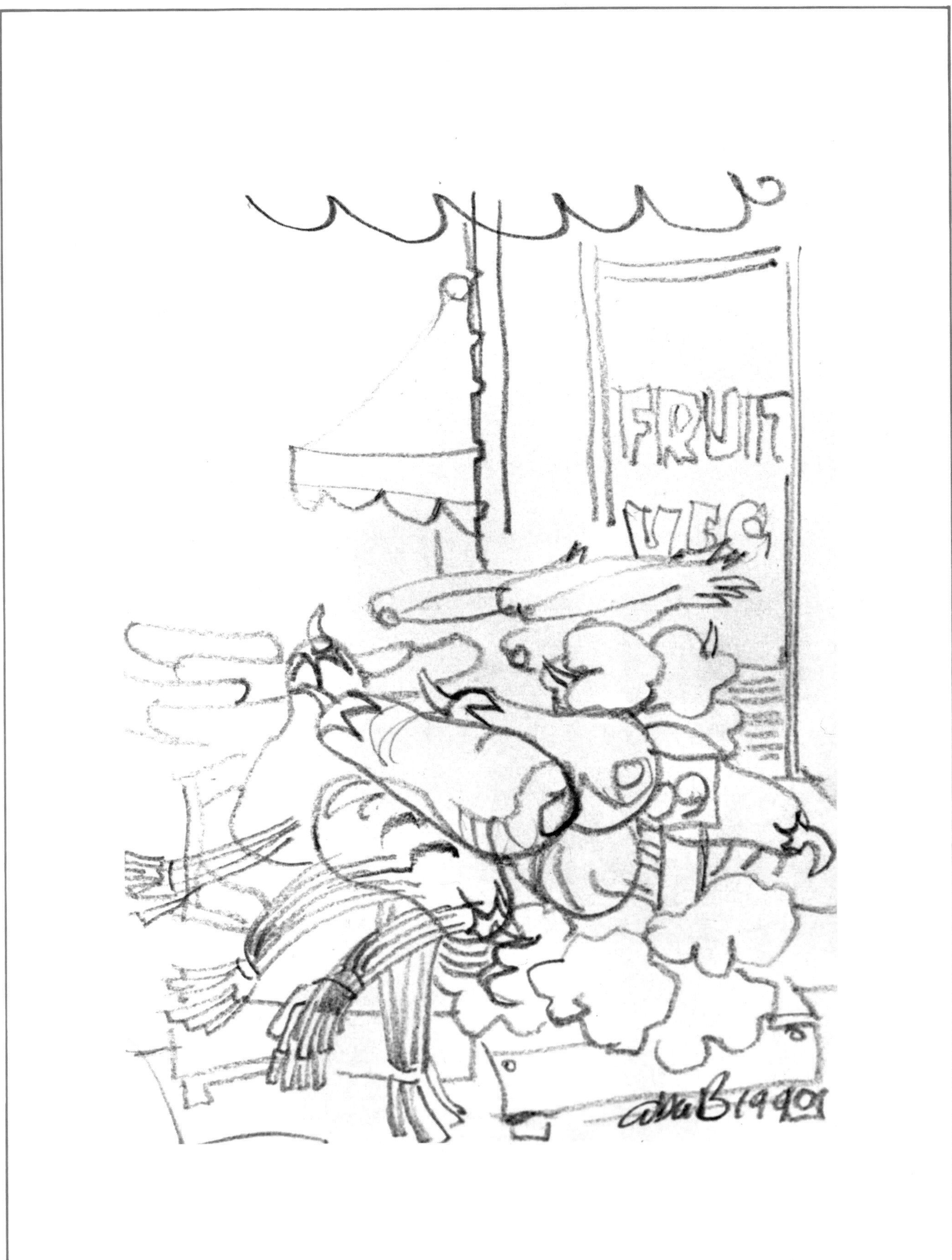

FRUIT
VEG

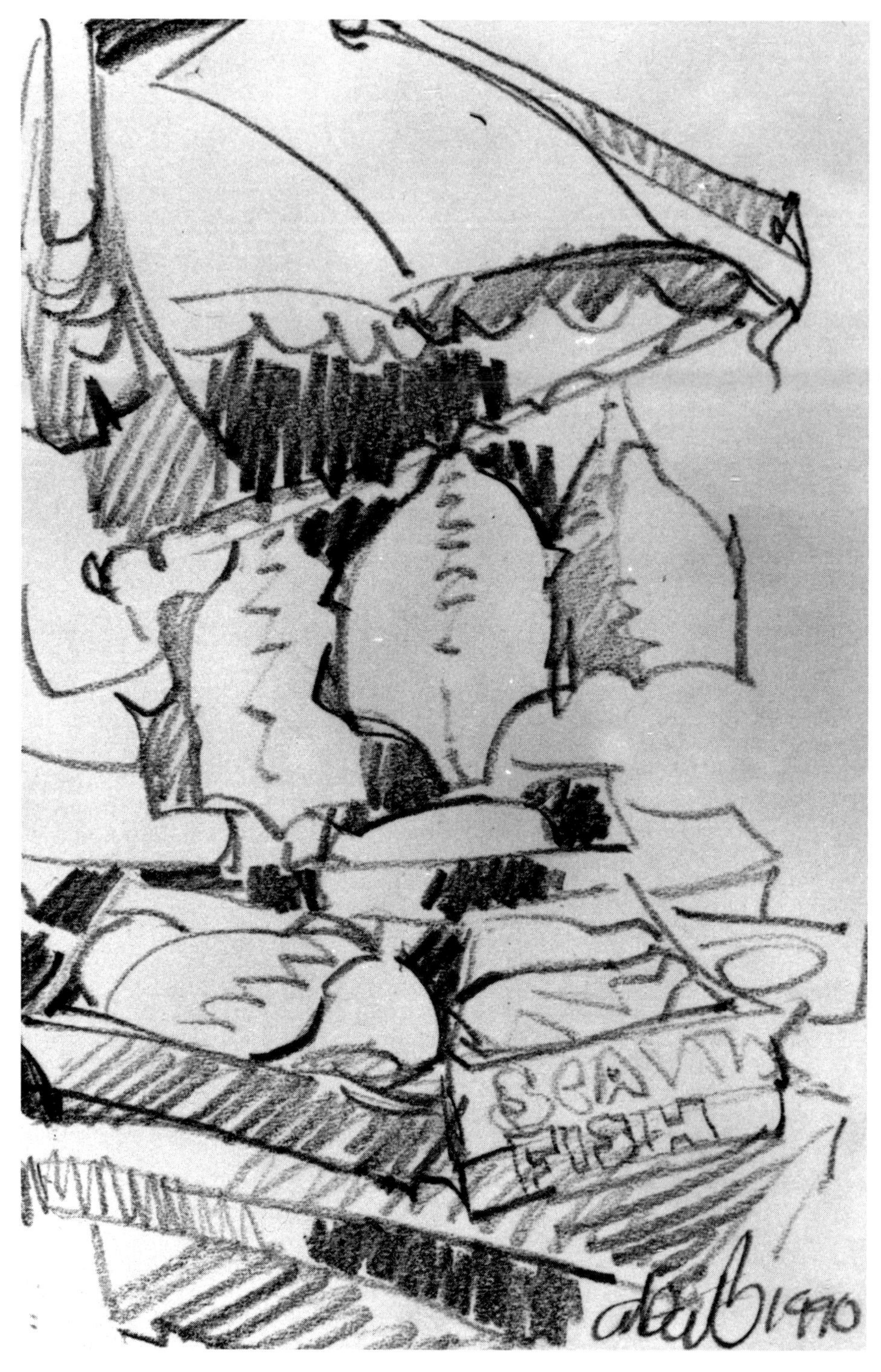

SEAVIEW
FISH

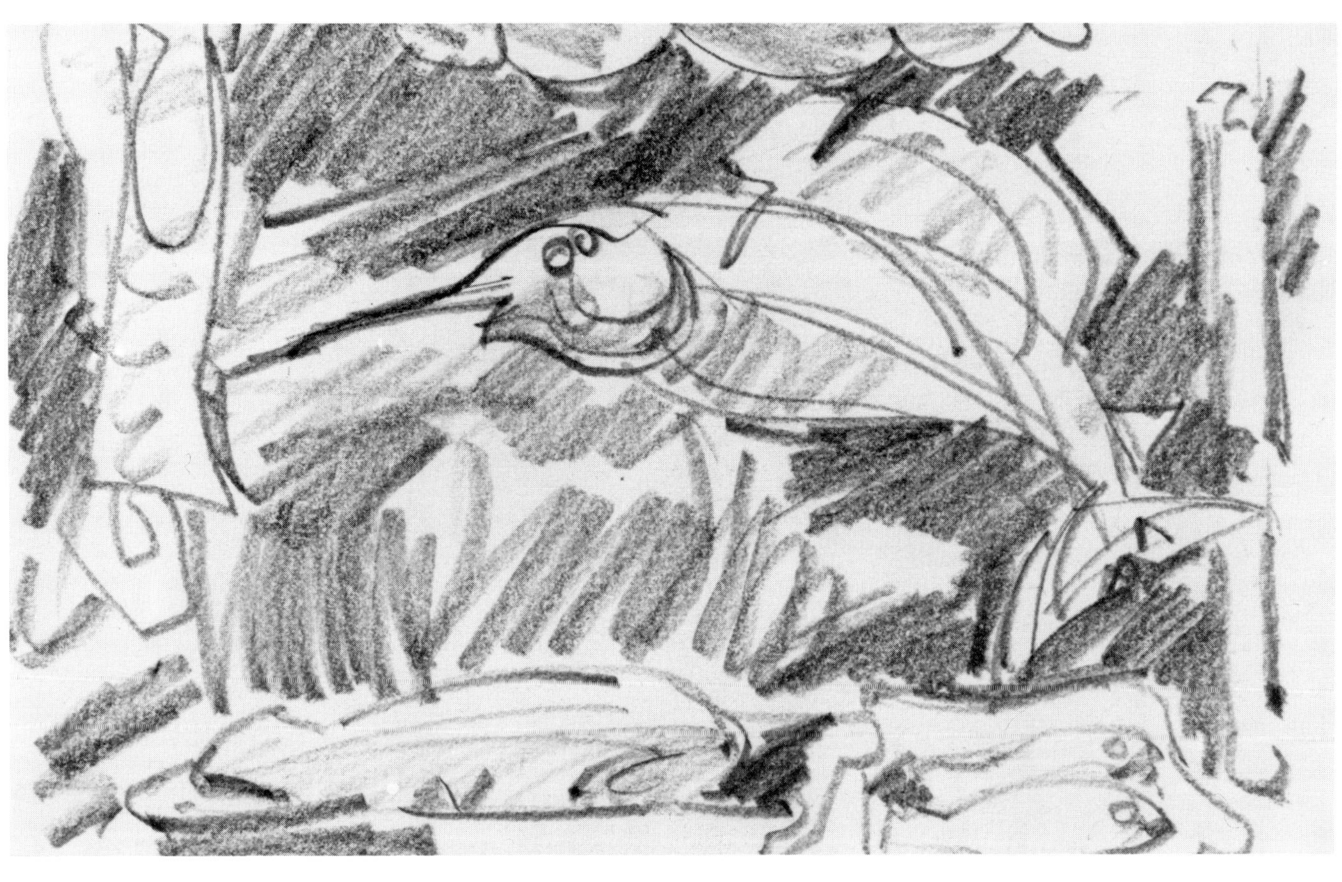

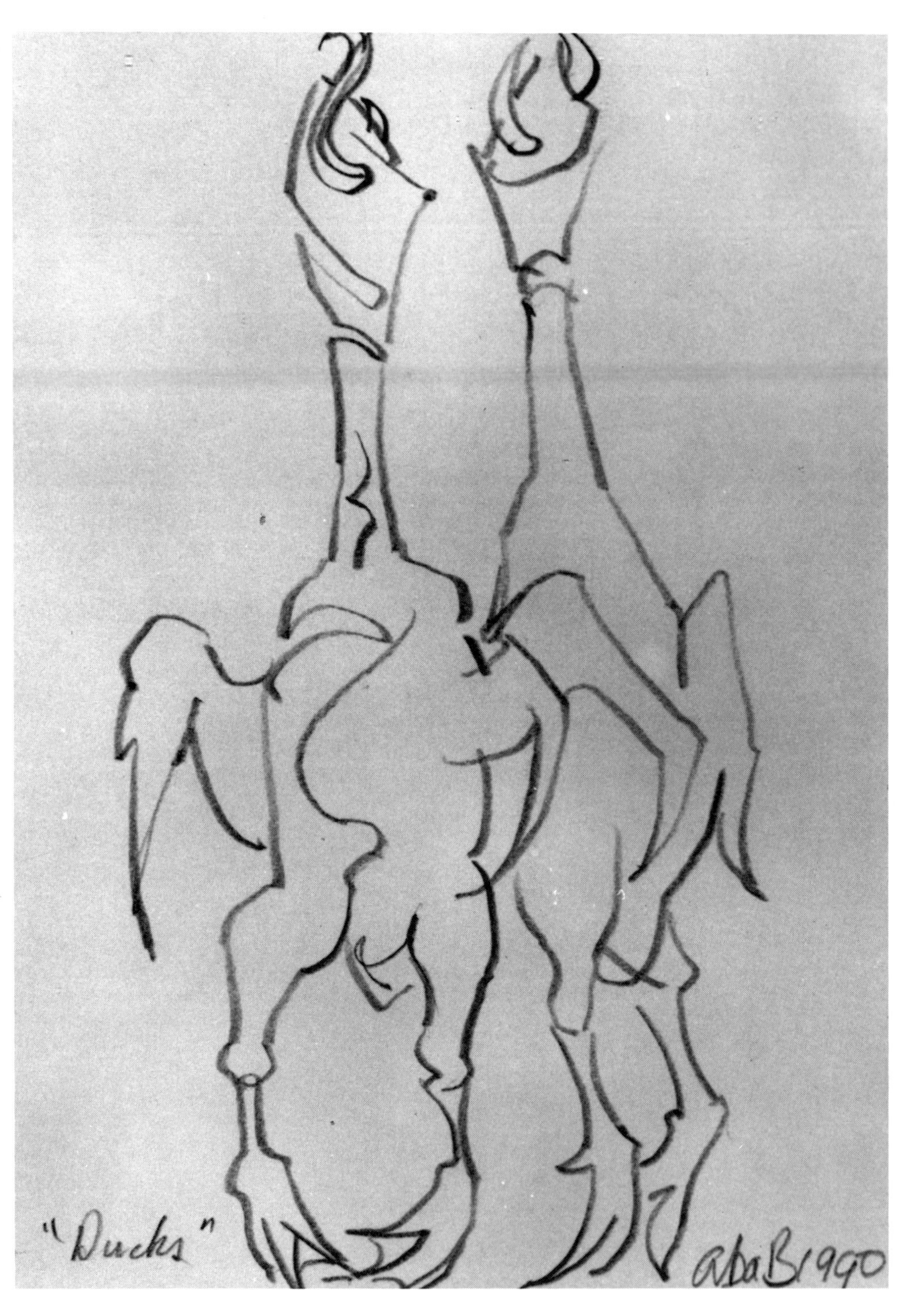

"Ducks"
AdaB 1990

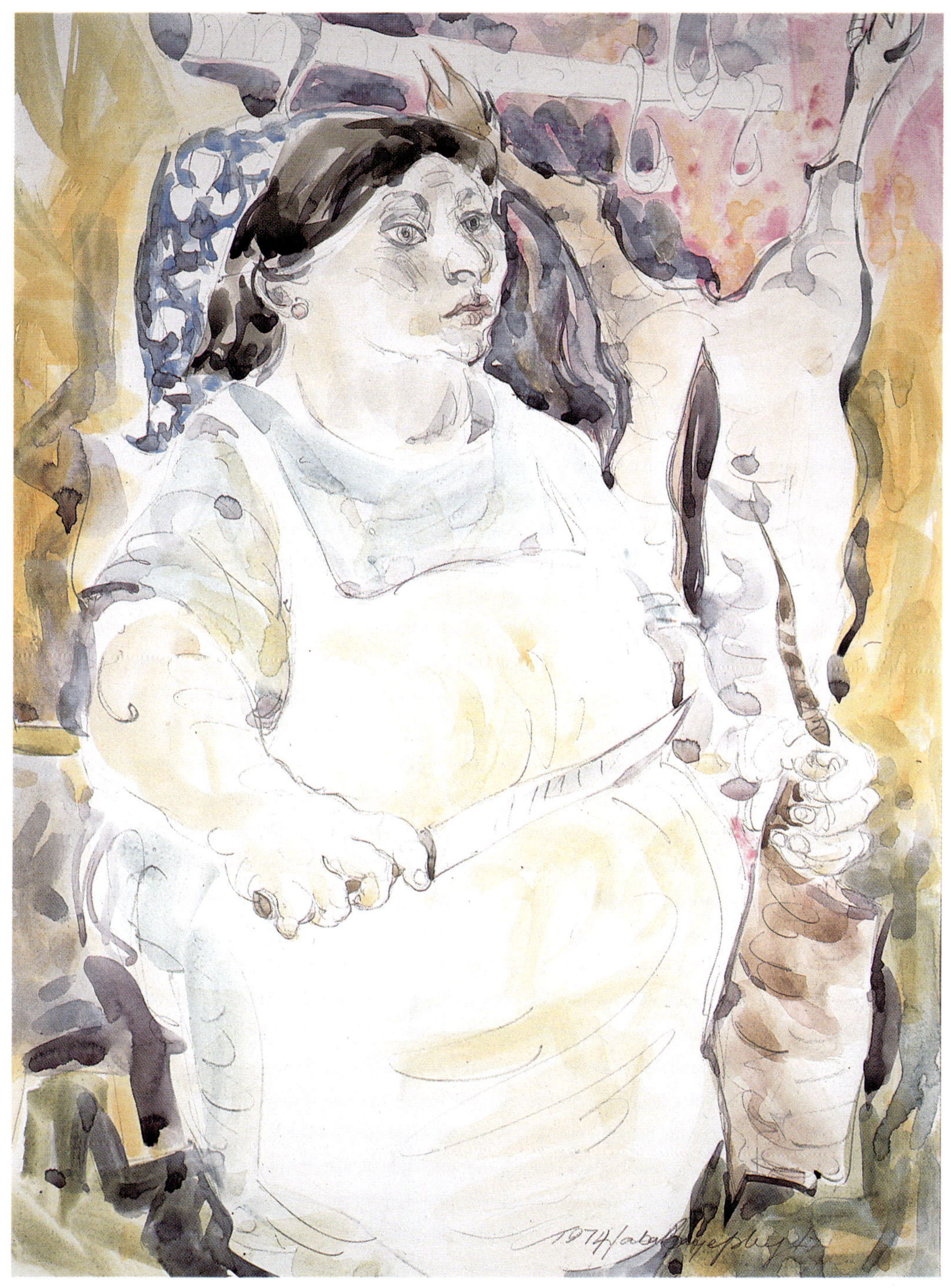

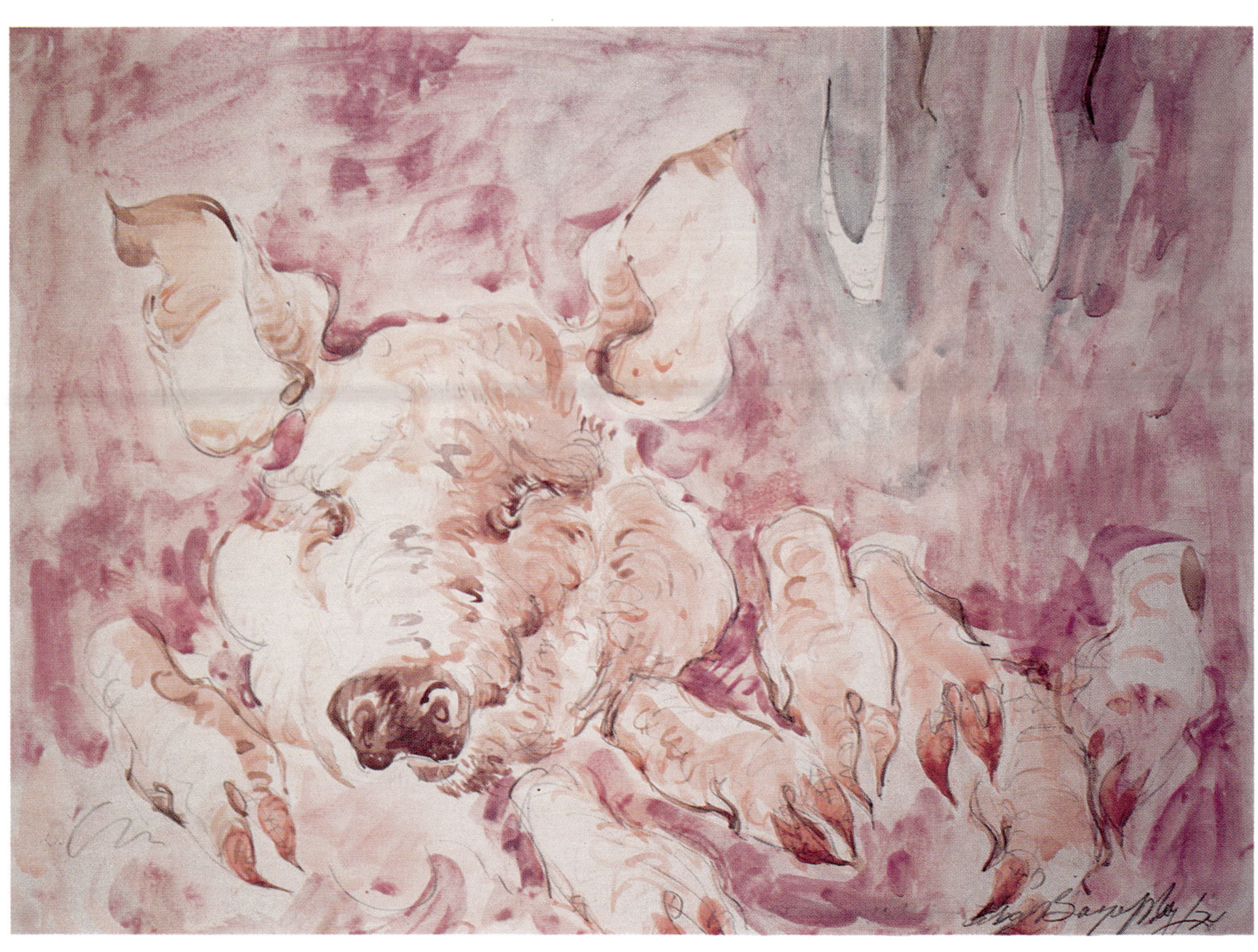

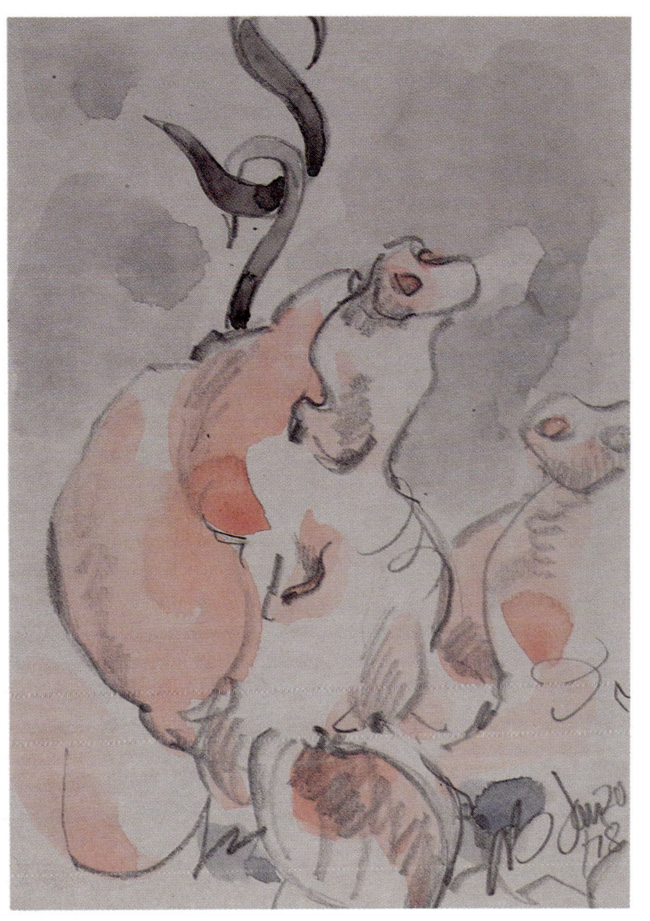 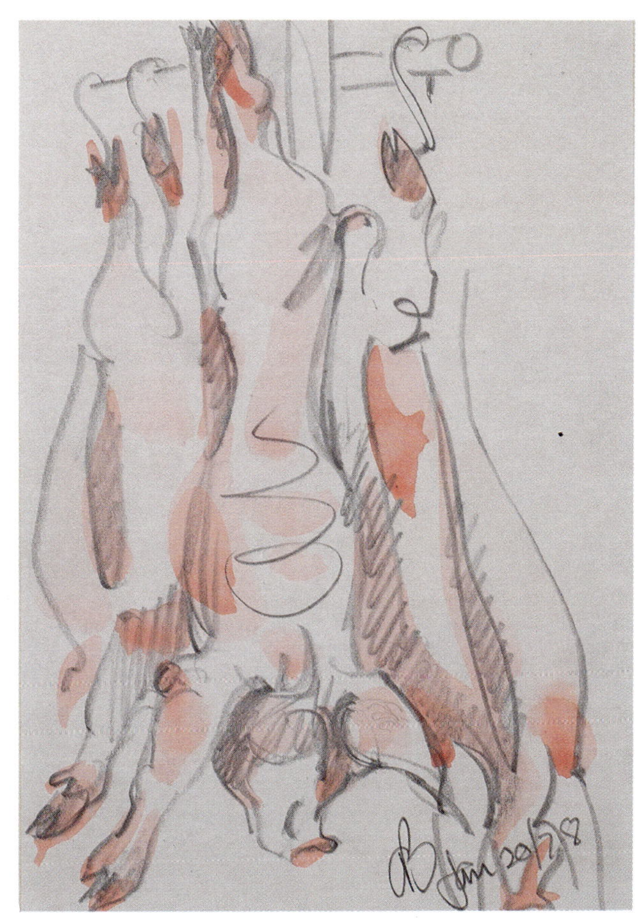

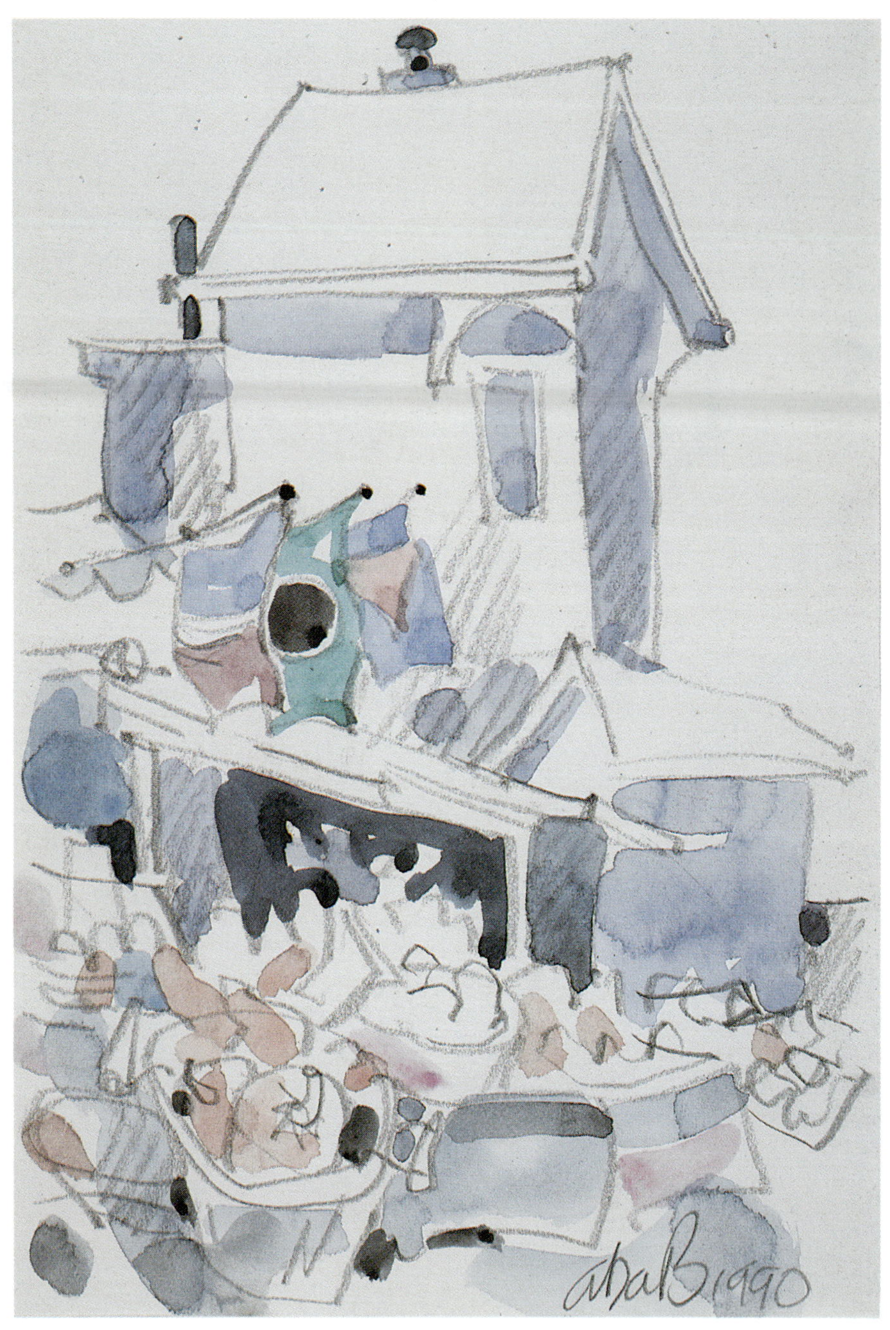

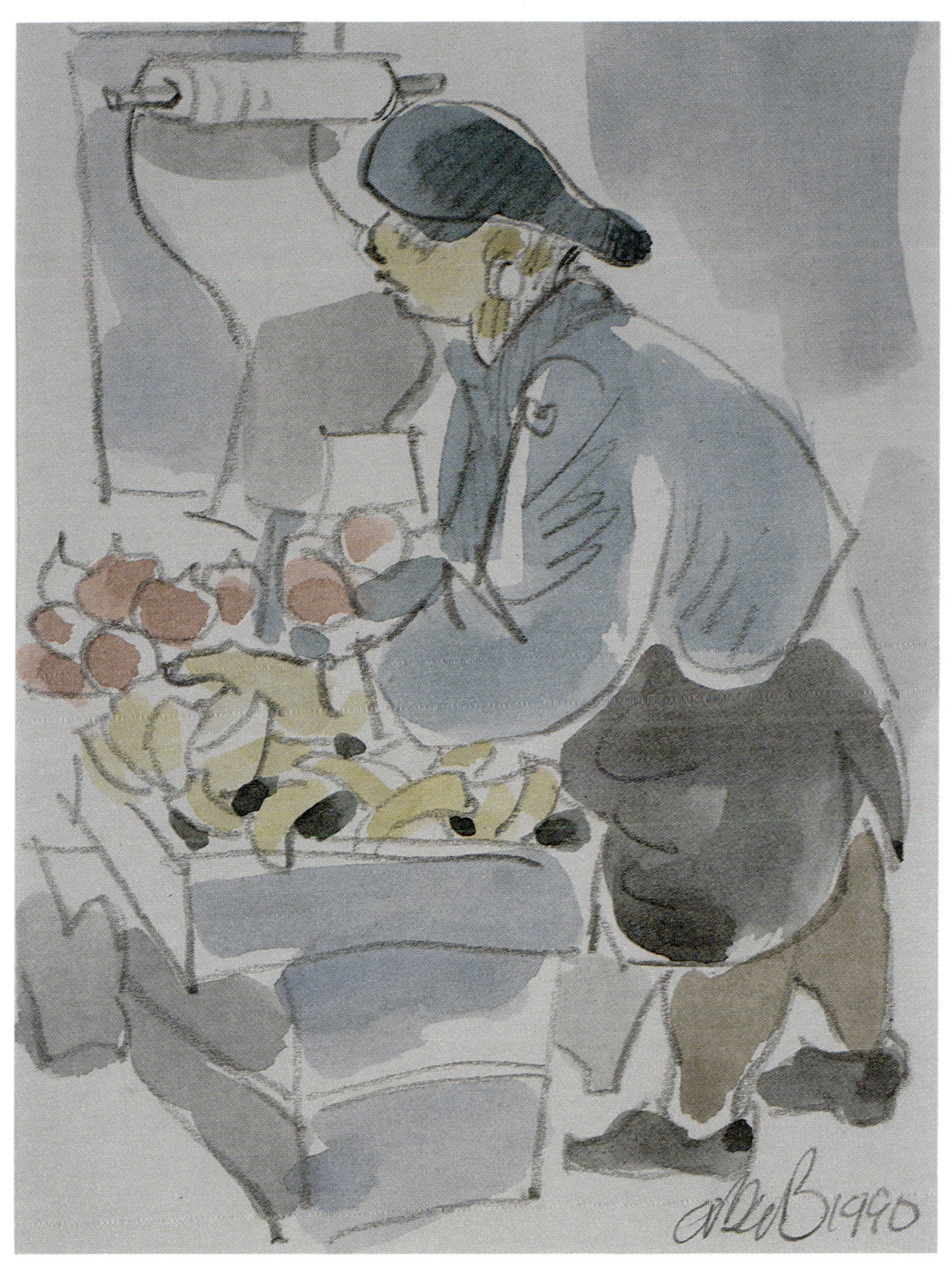

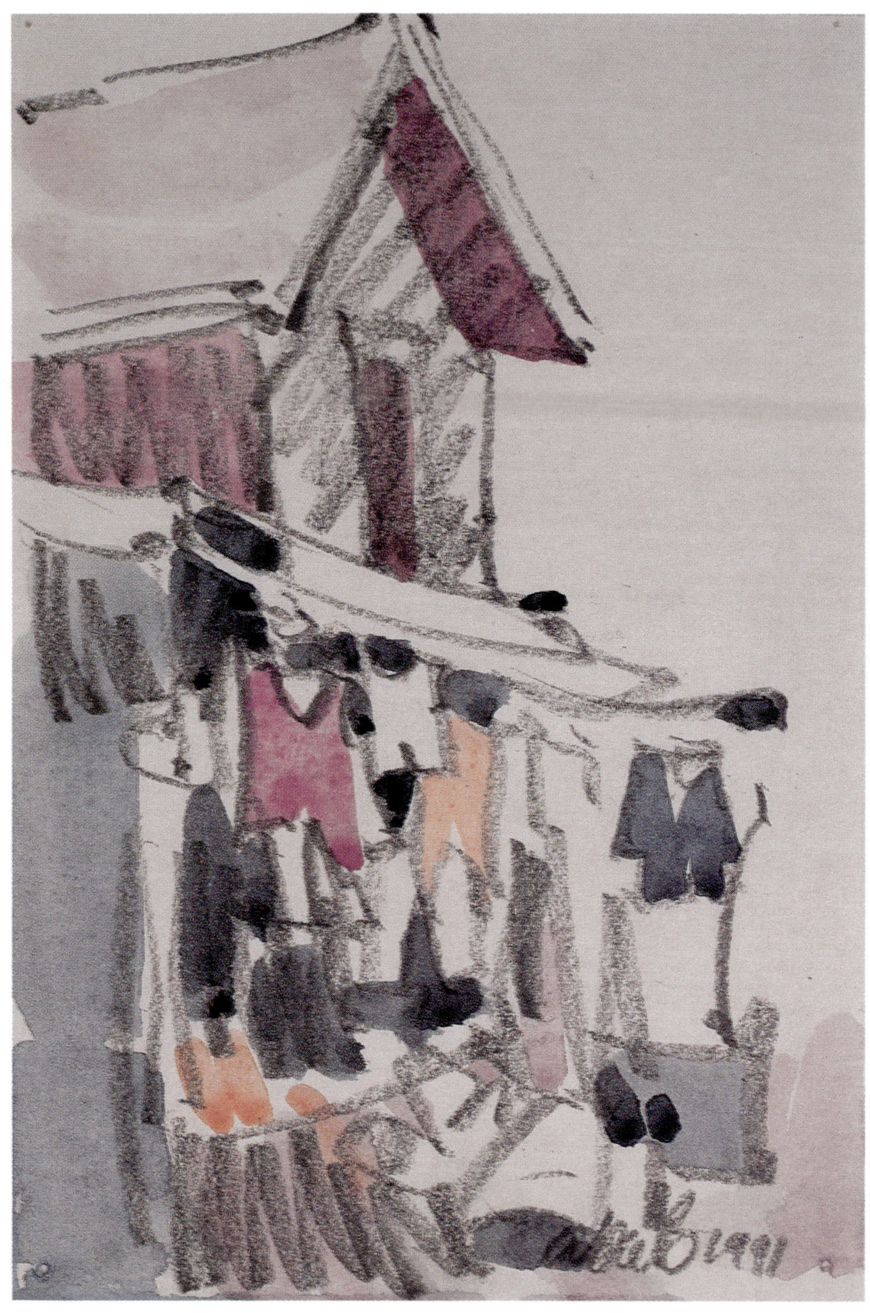

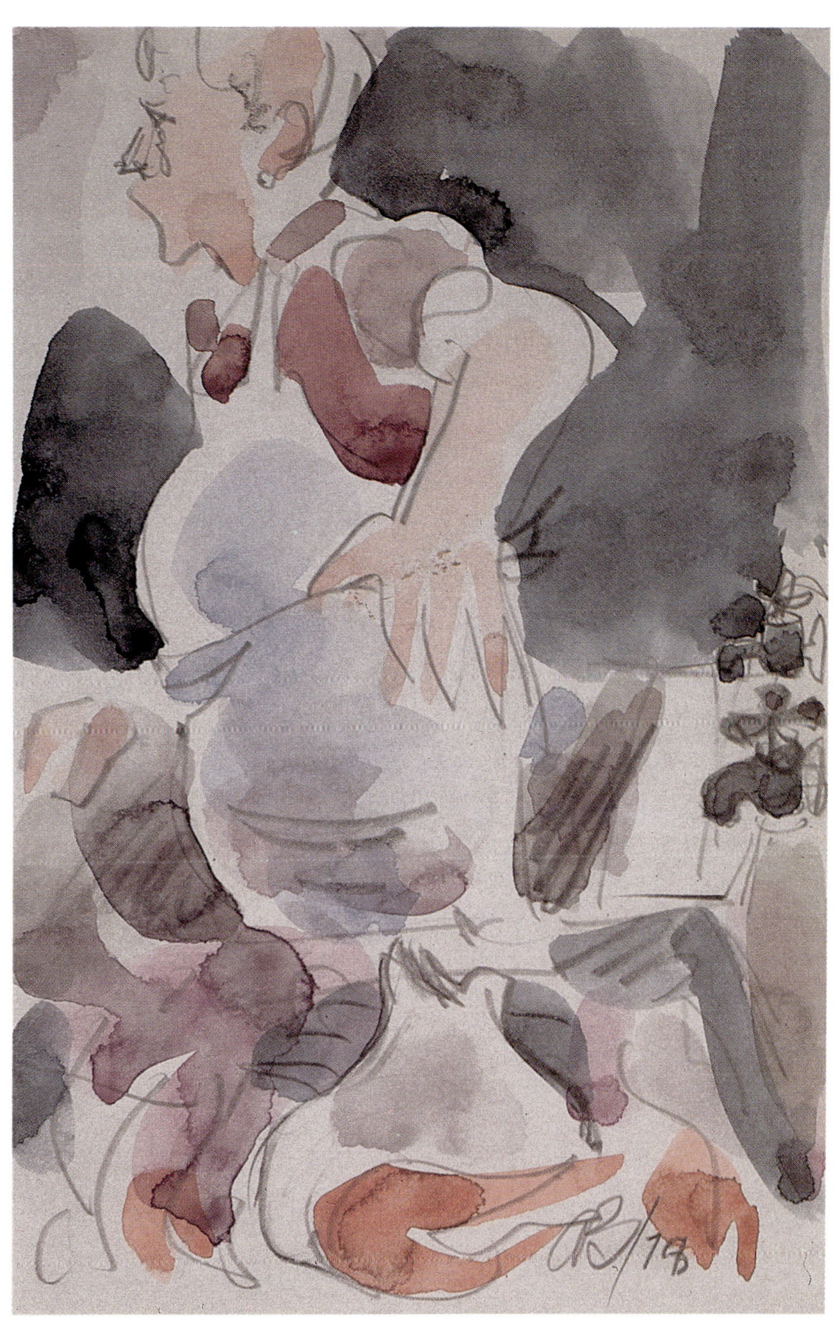

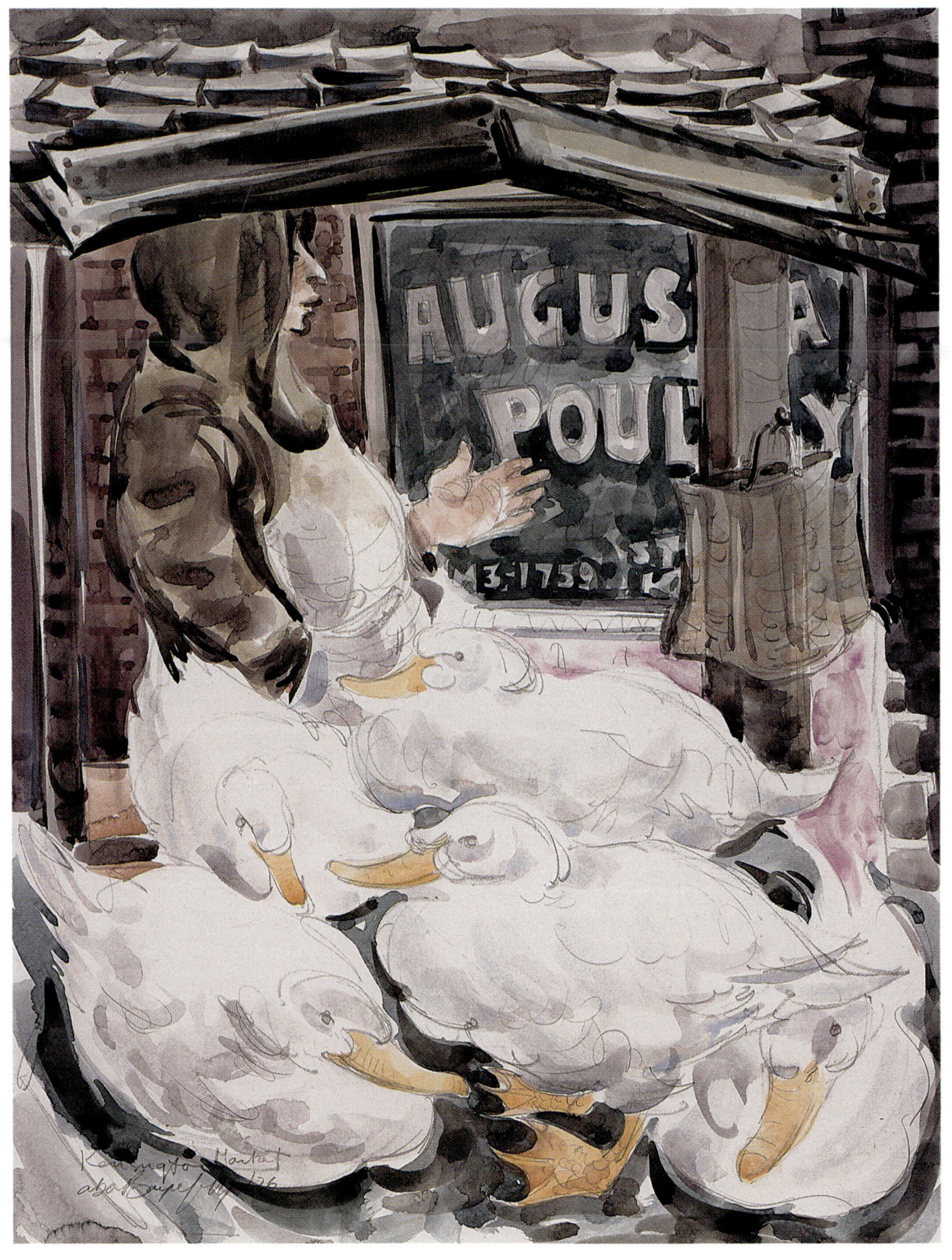

AUGUSTA
POULTRY
3-1759

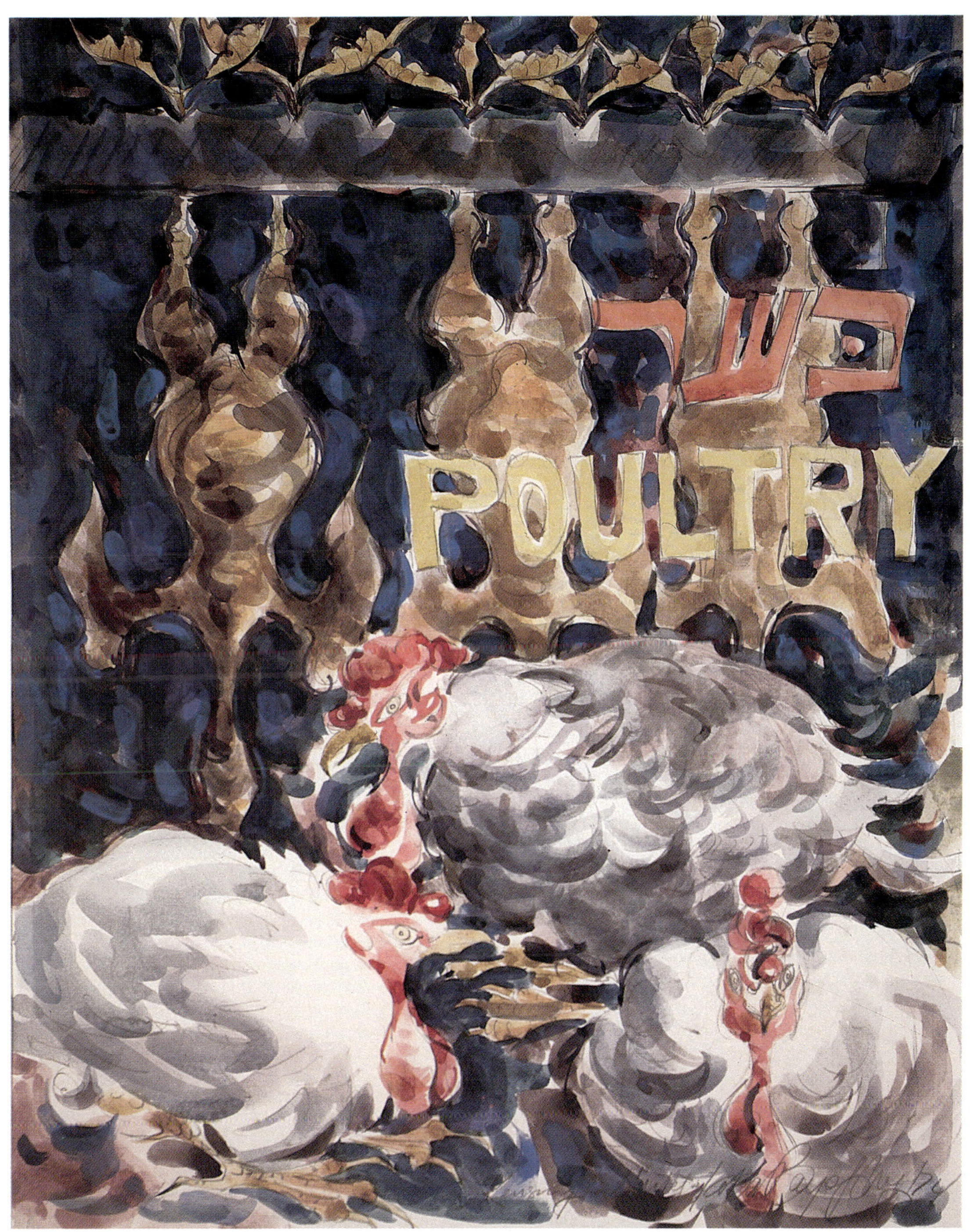
פסשר
POULTRY

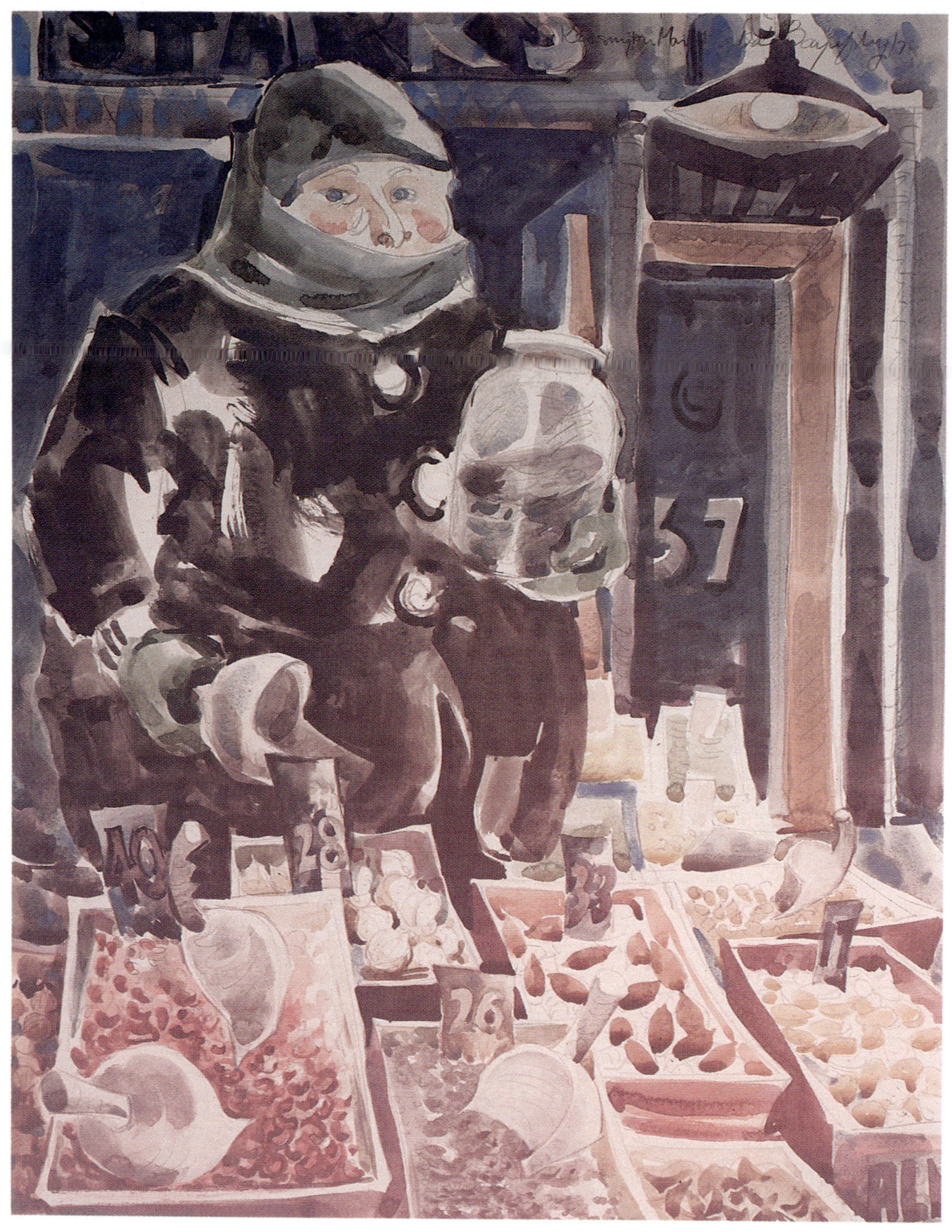

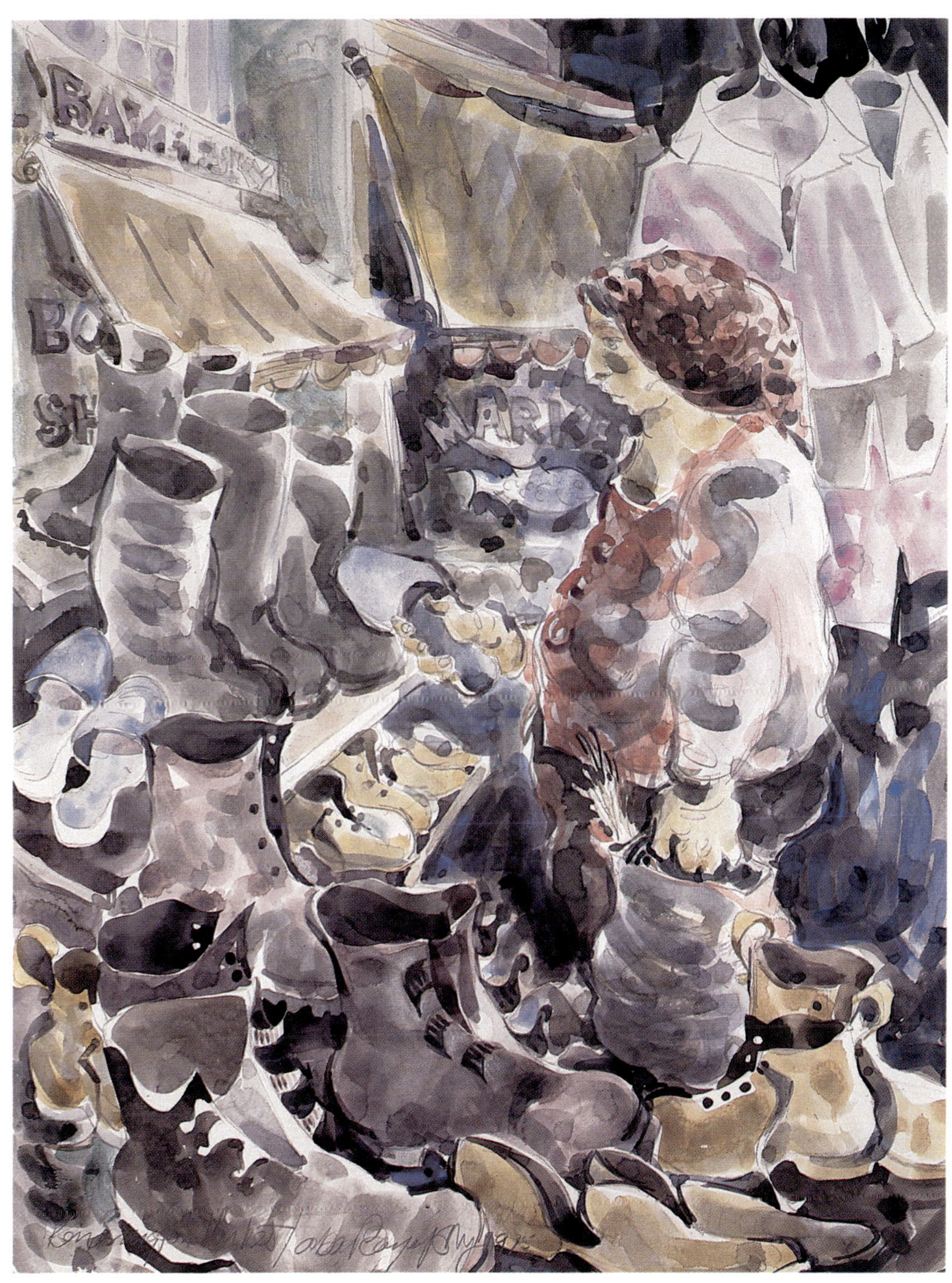

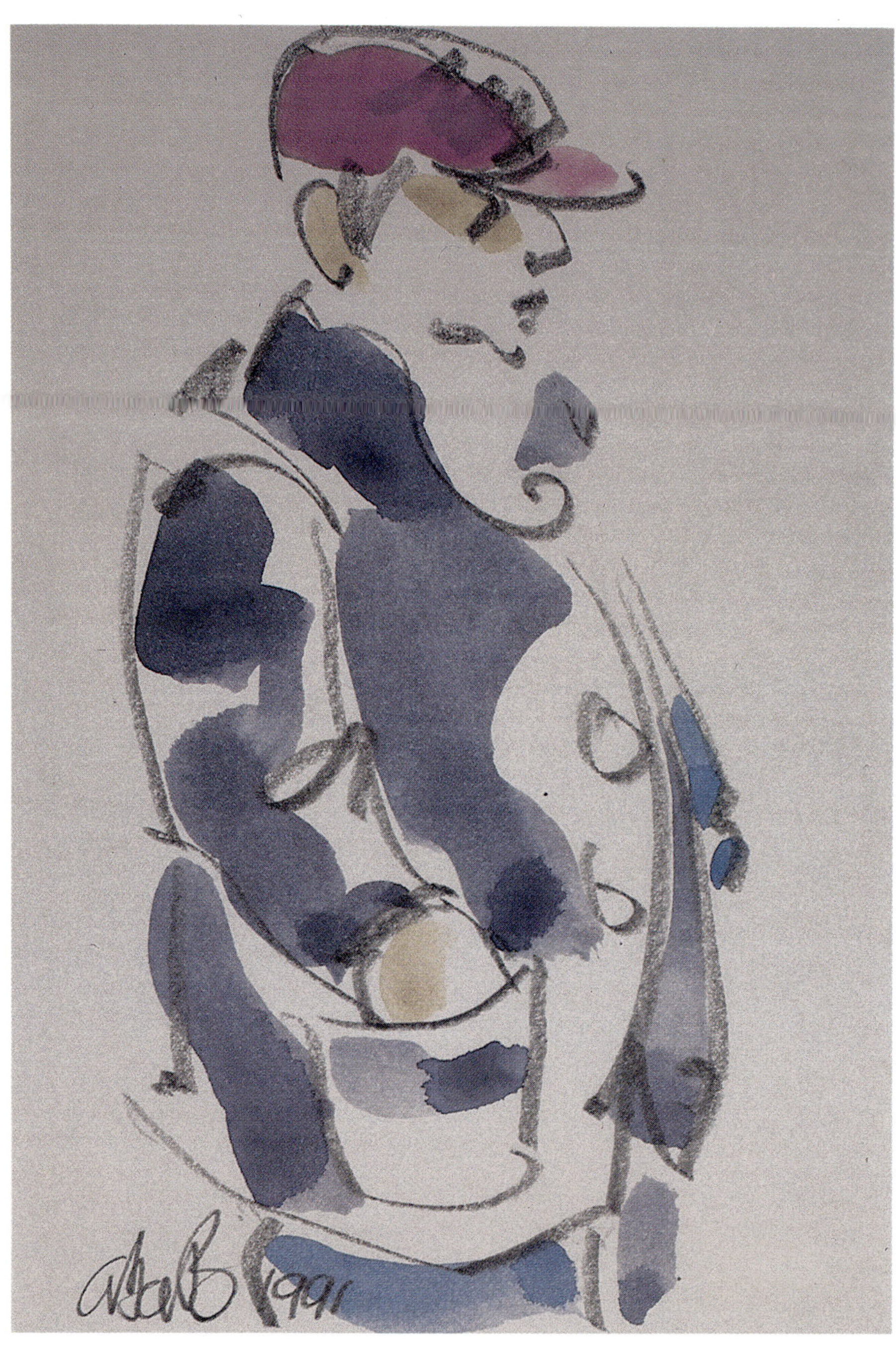

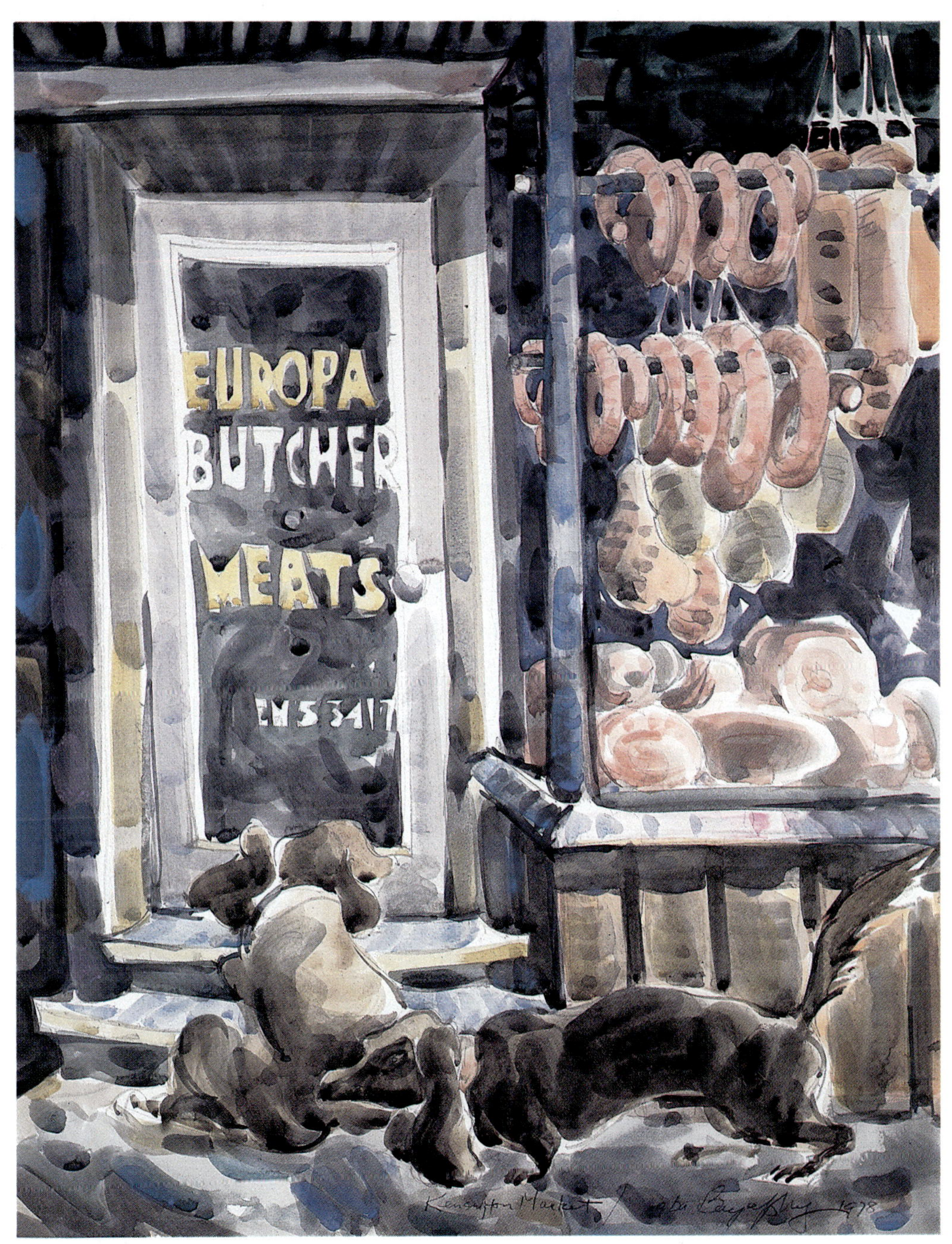

EUROPA
BUTCHER
MEATS

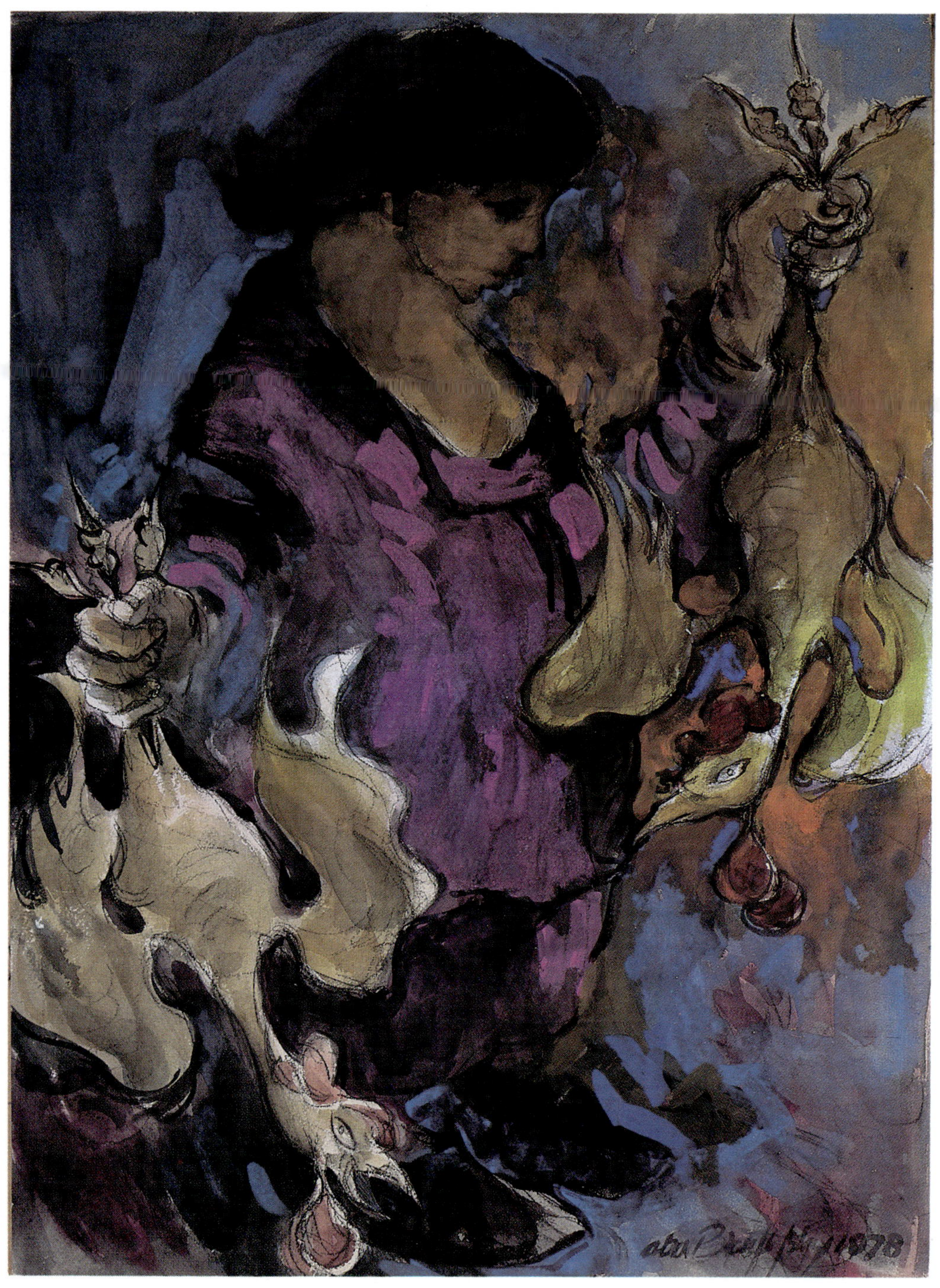

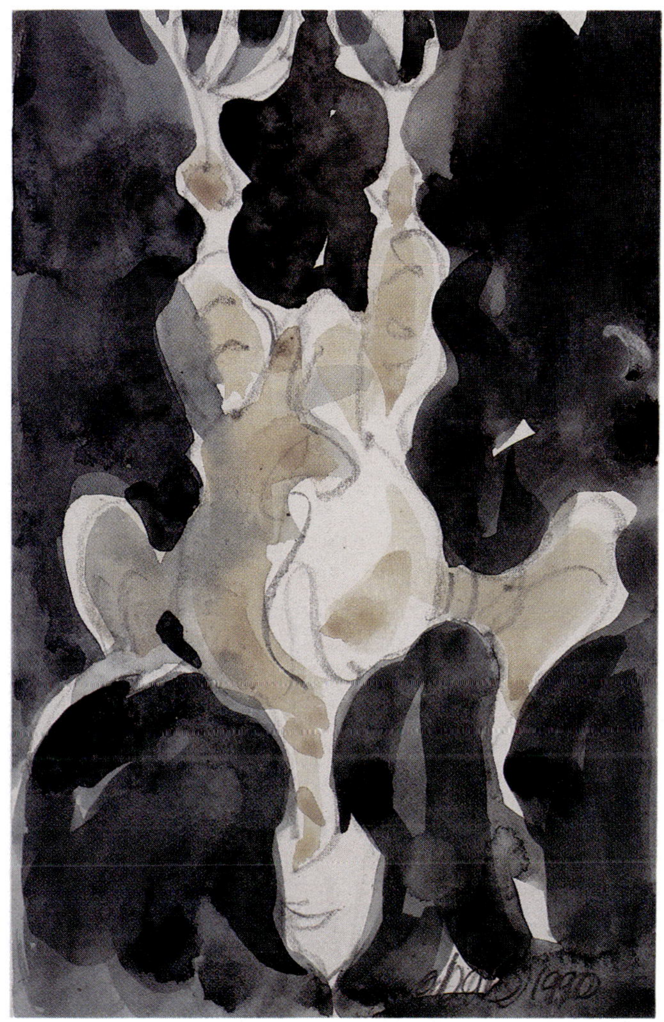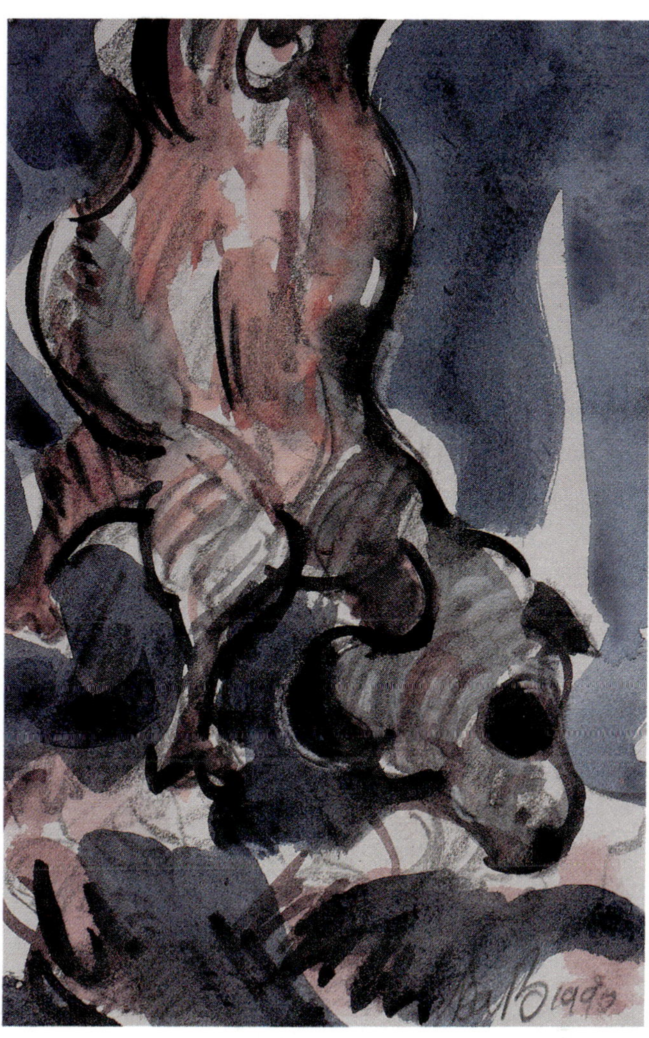

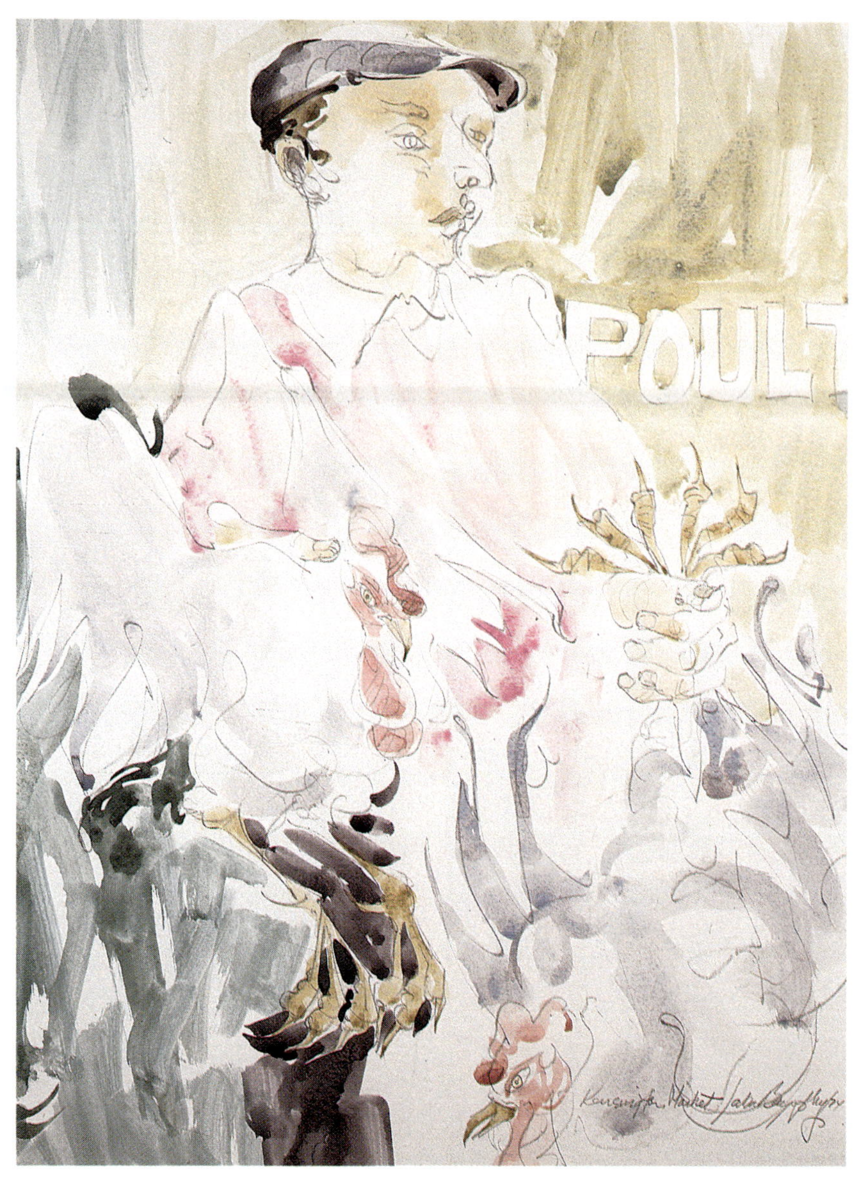

POULT

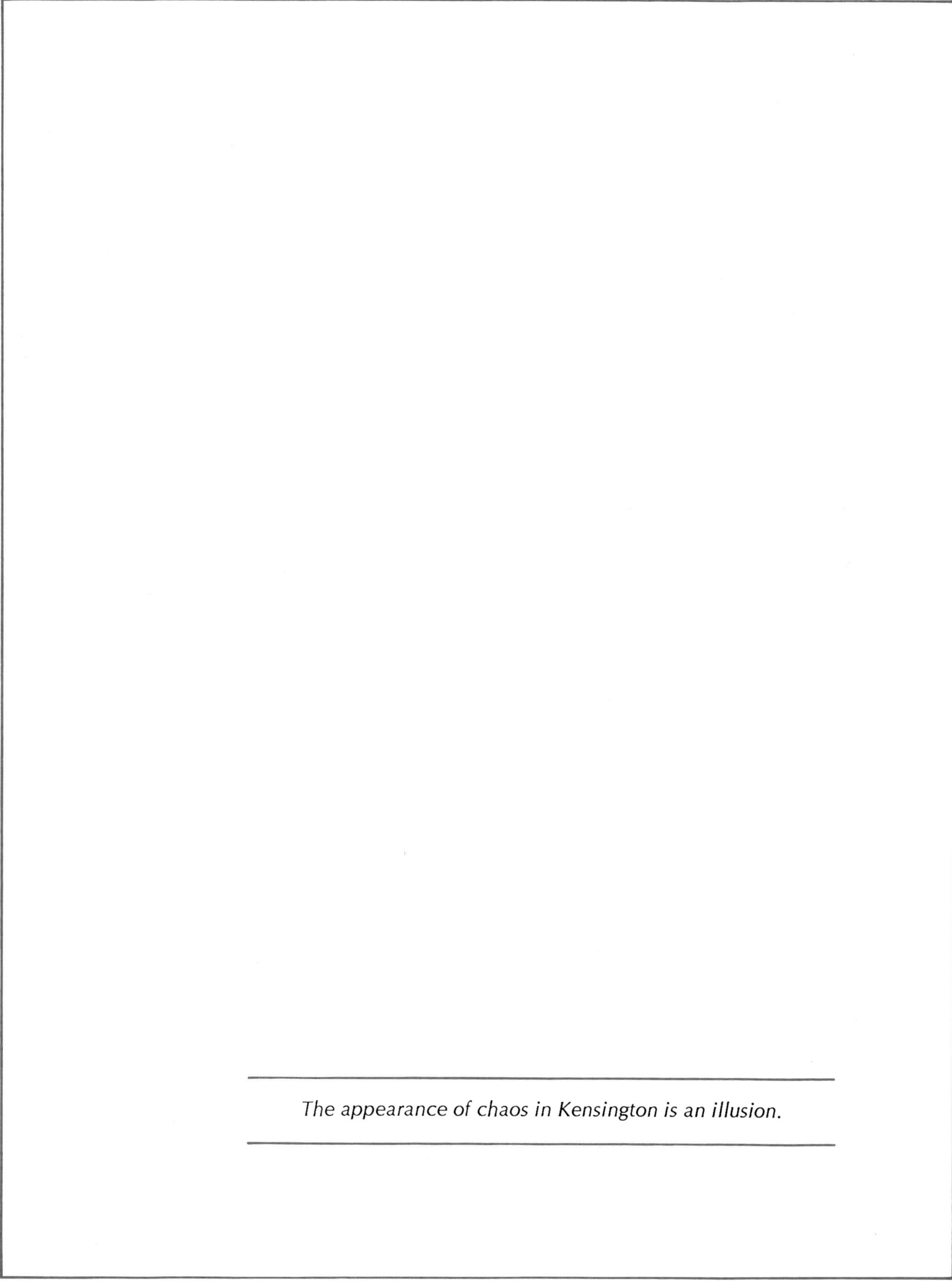

The appearance of chaos in Kensington is an illusion.

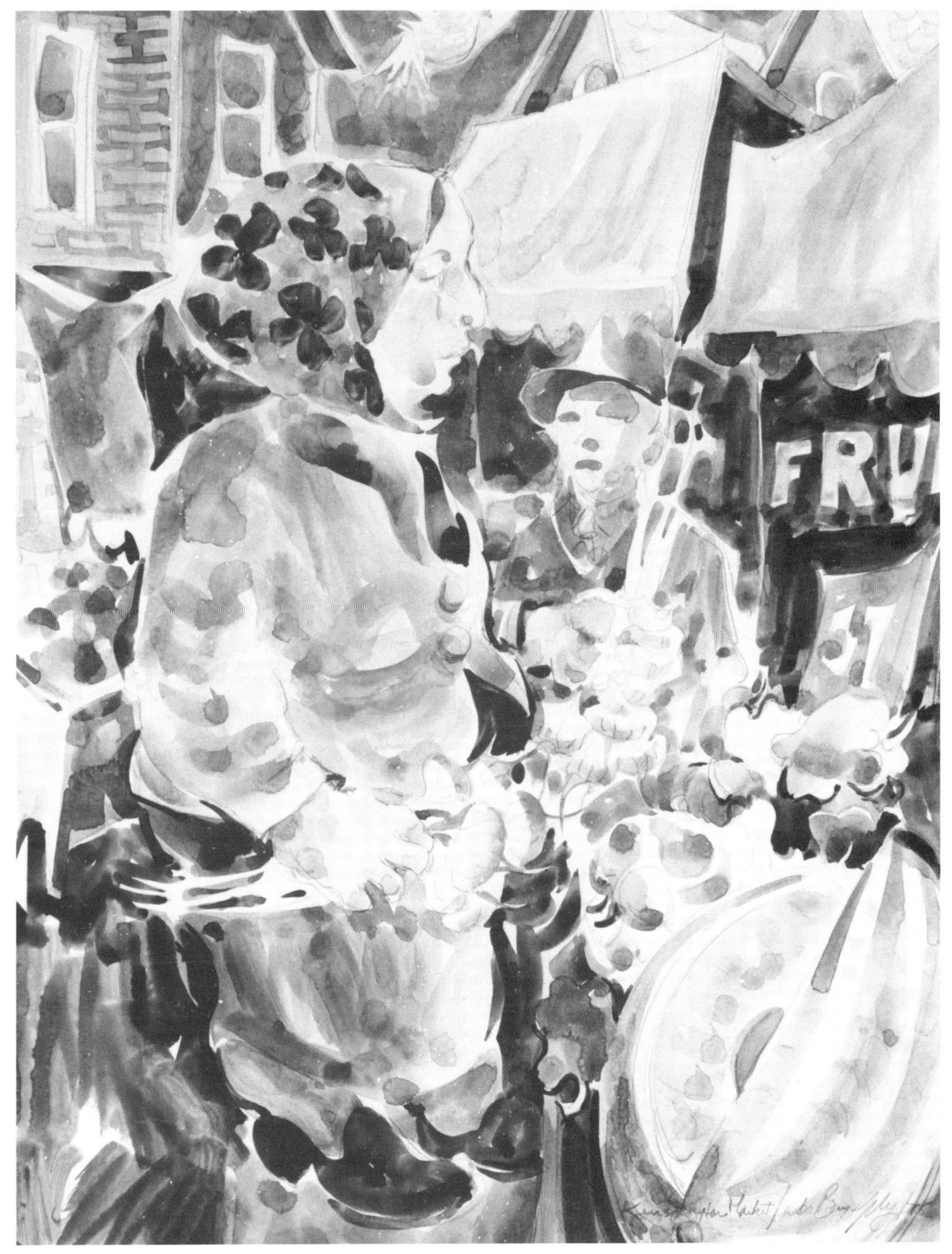

FRU

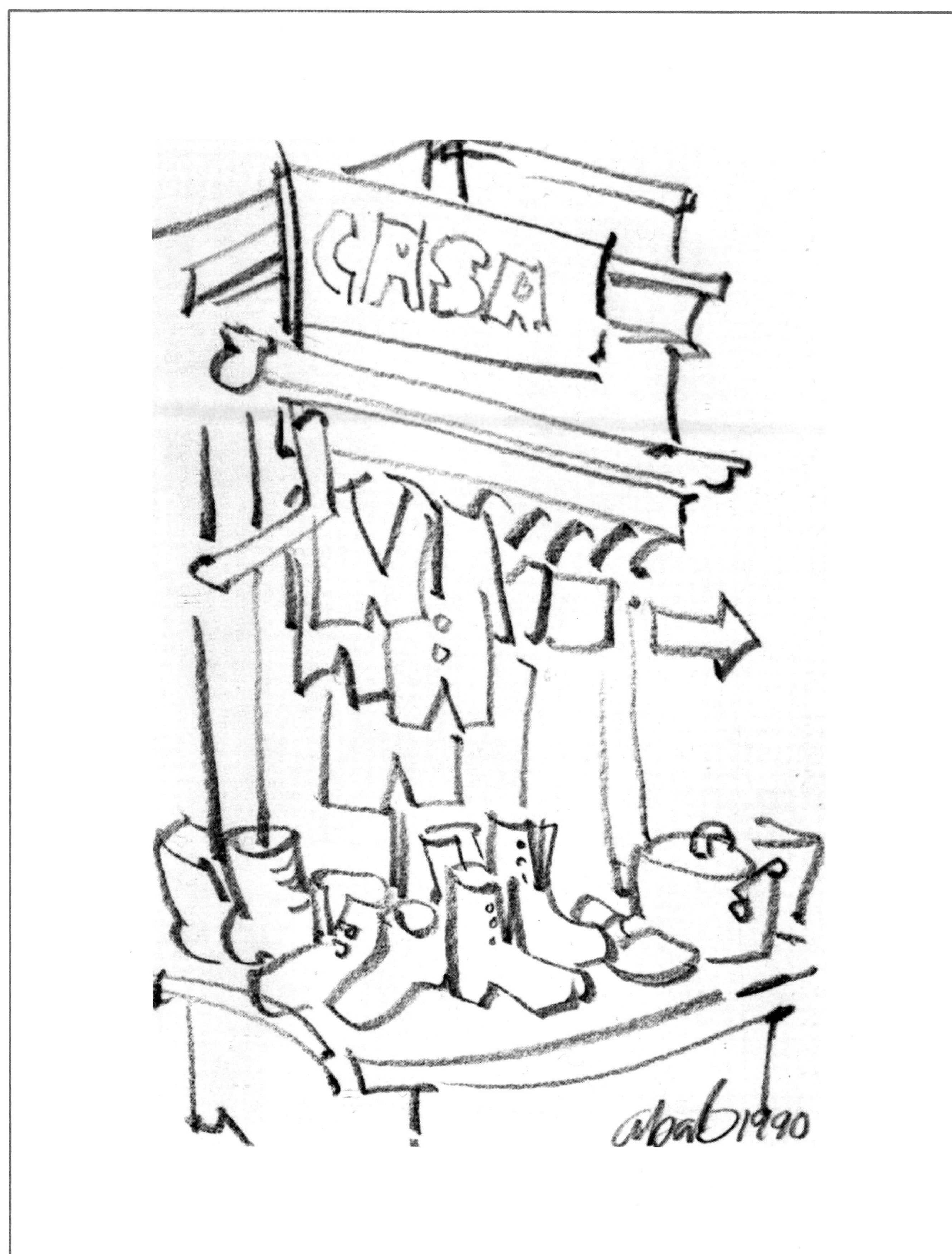
CASA

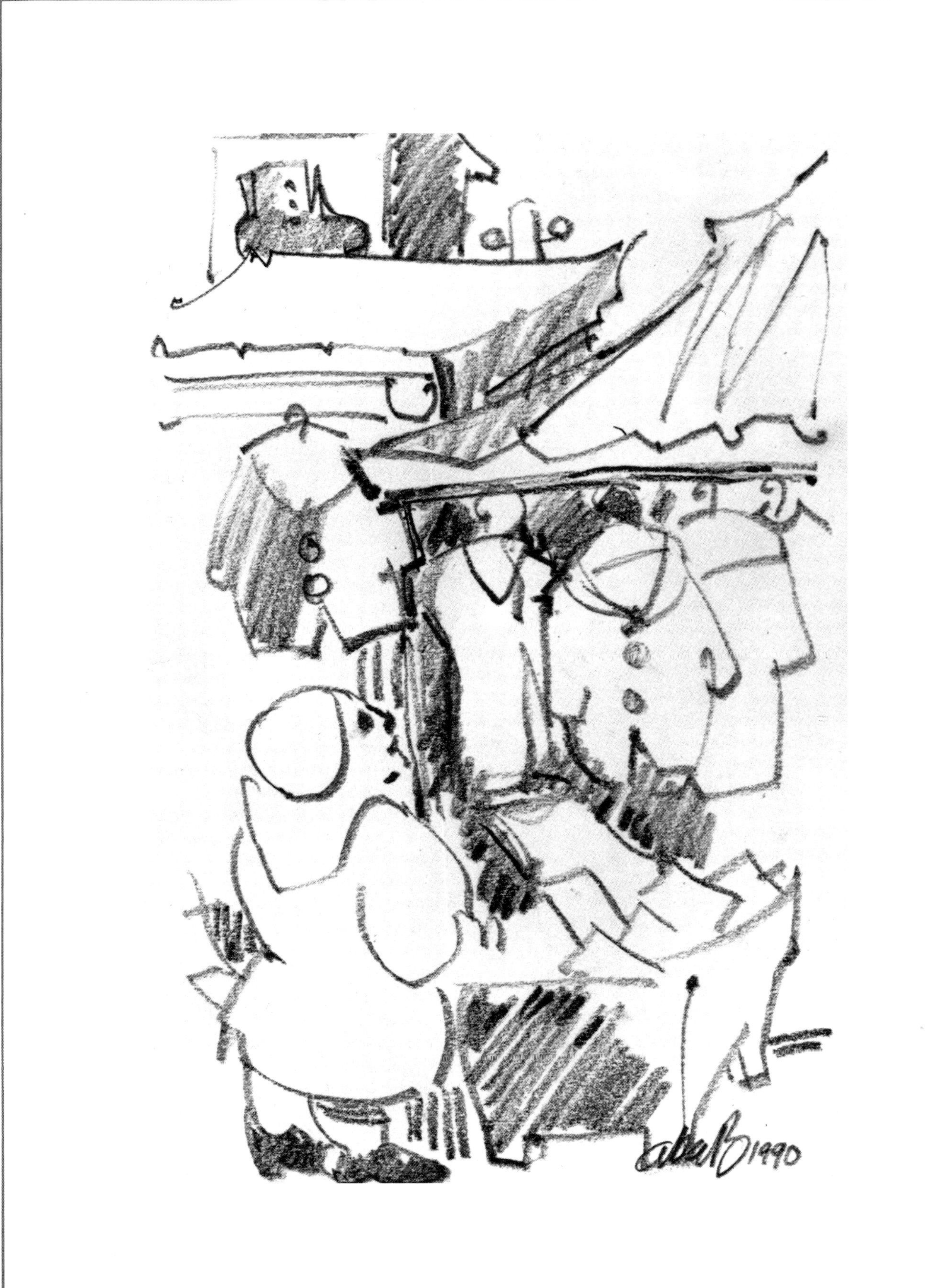

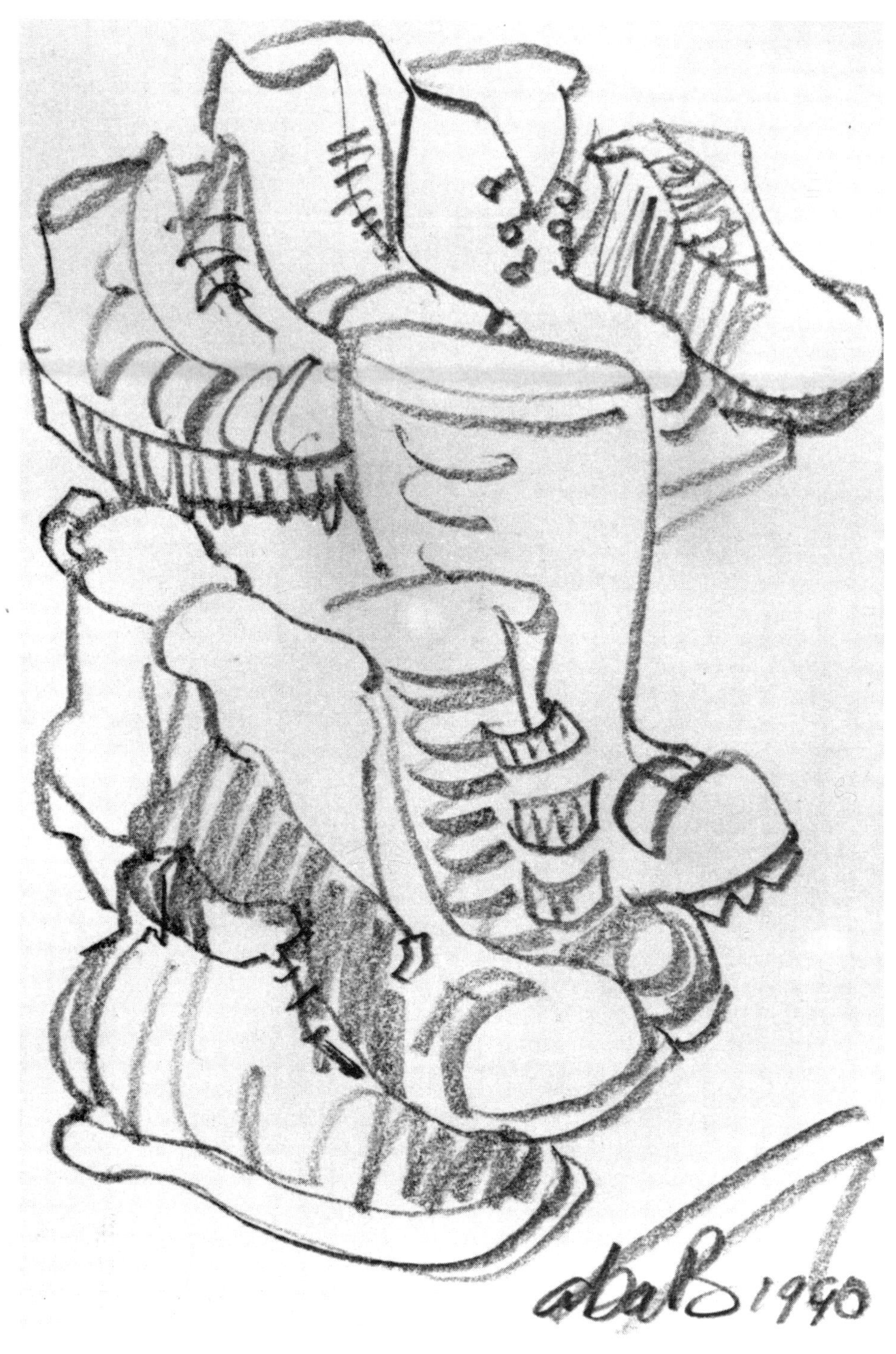

dal 1990

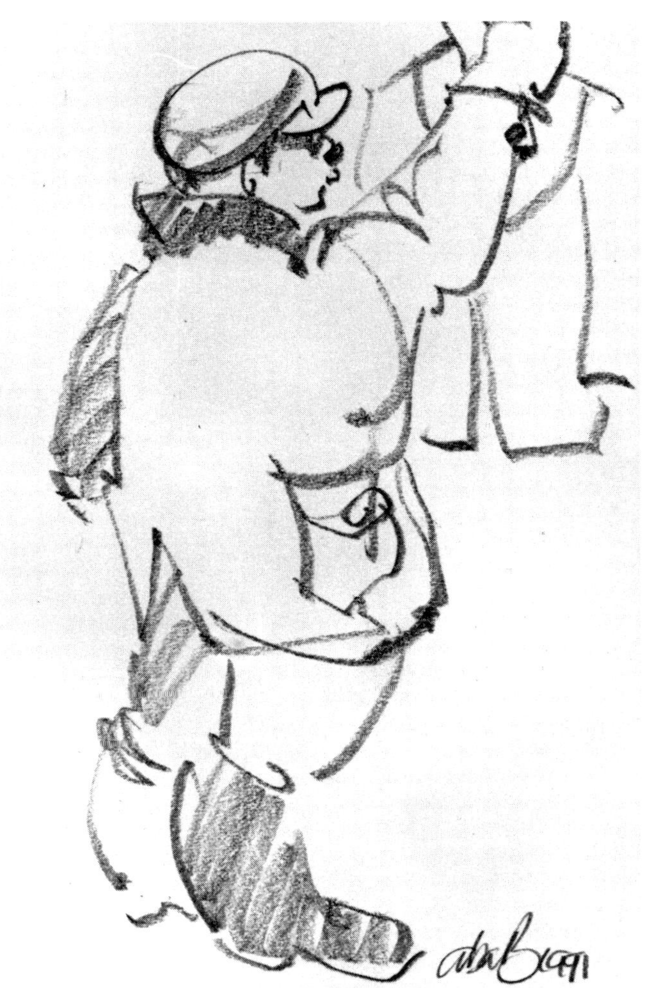

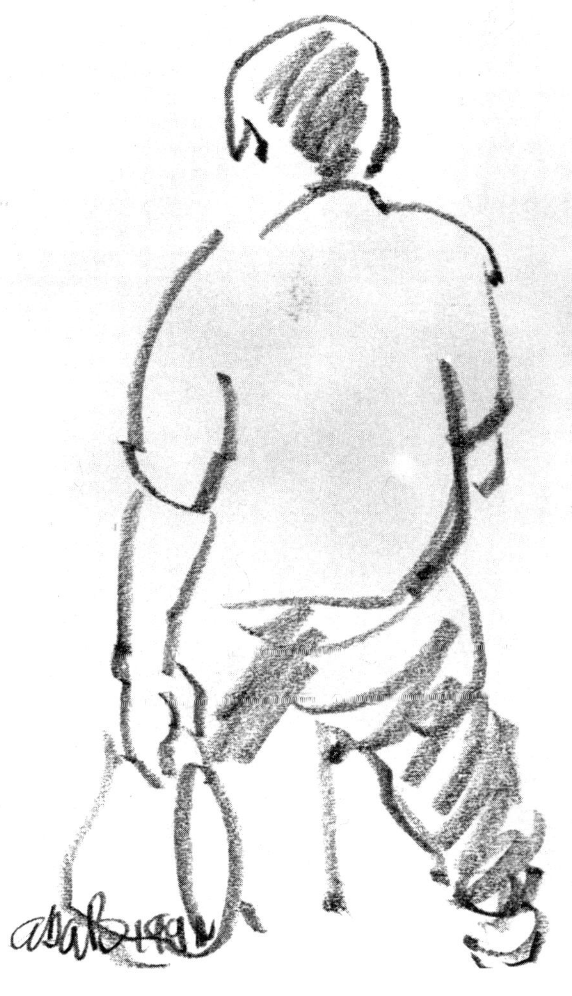

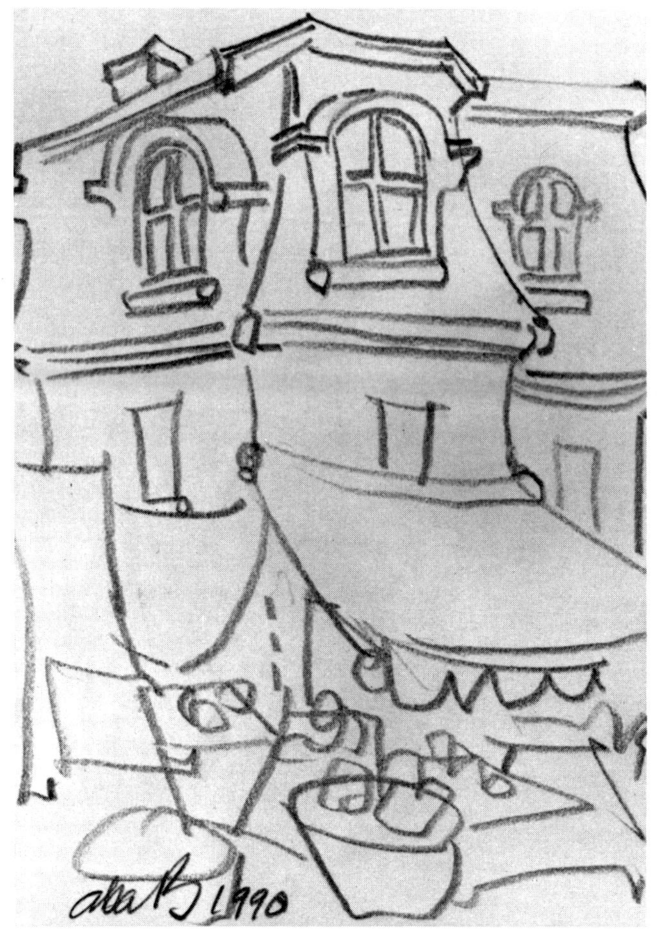

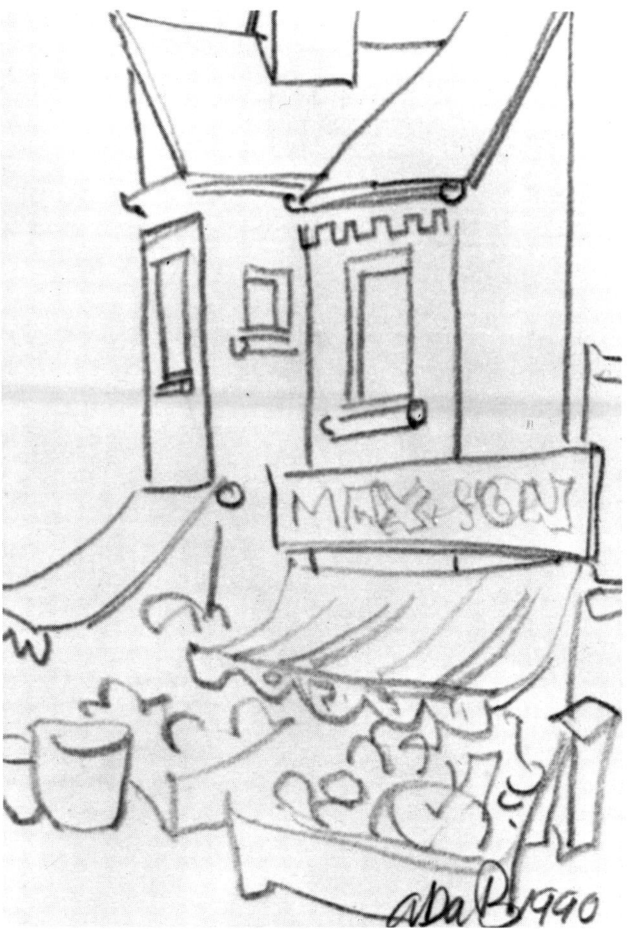
MAISON

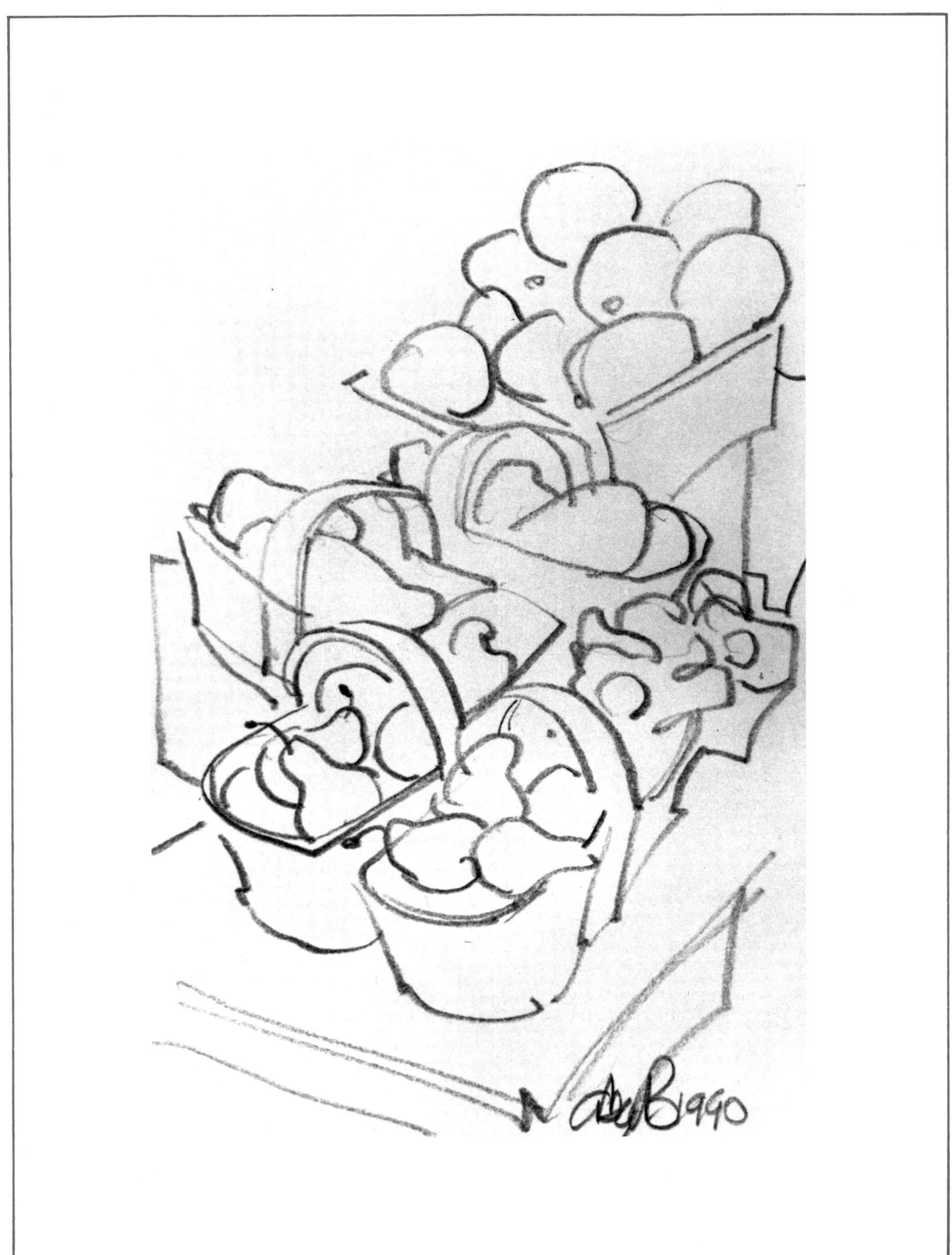

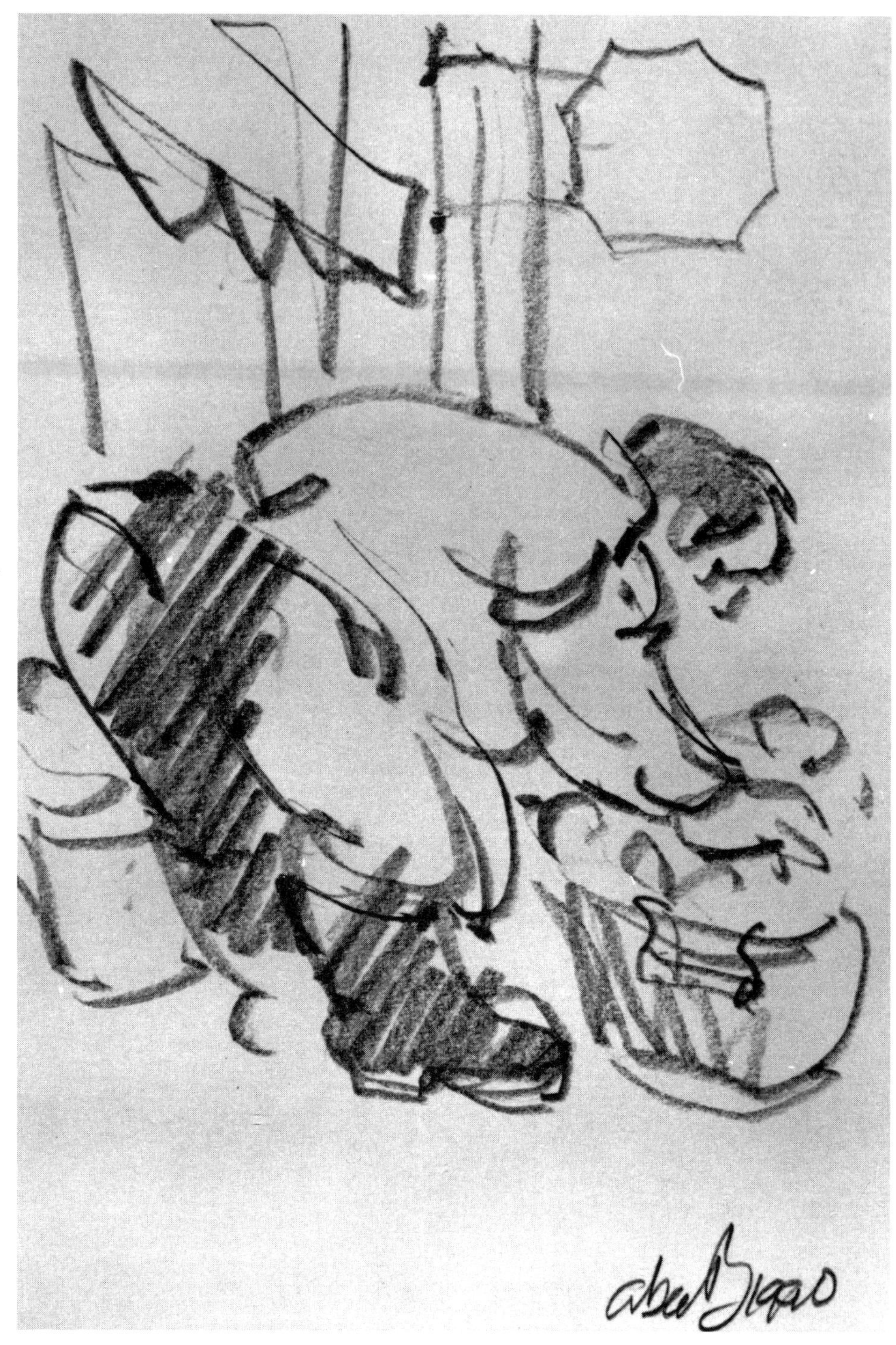

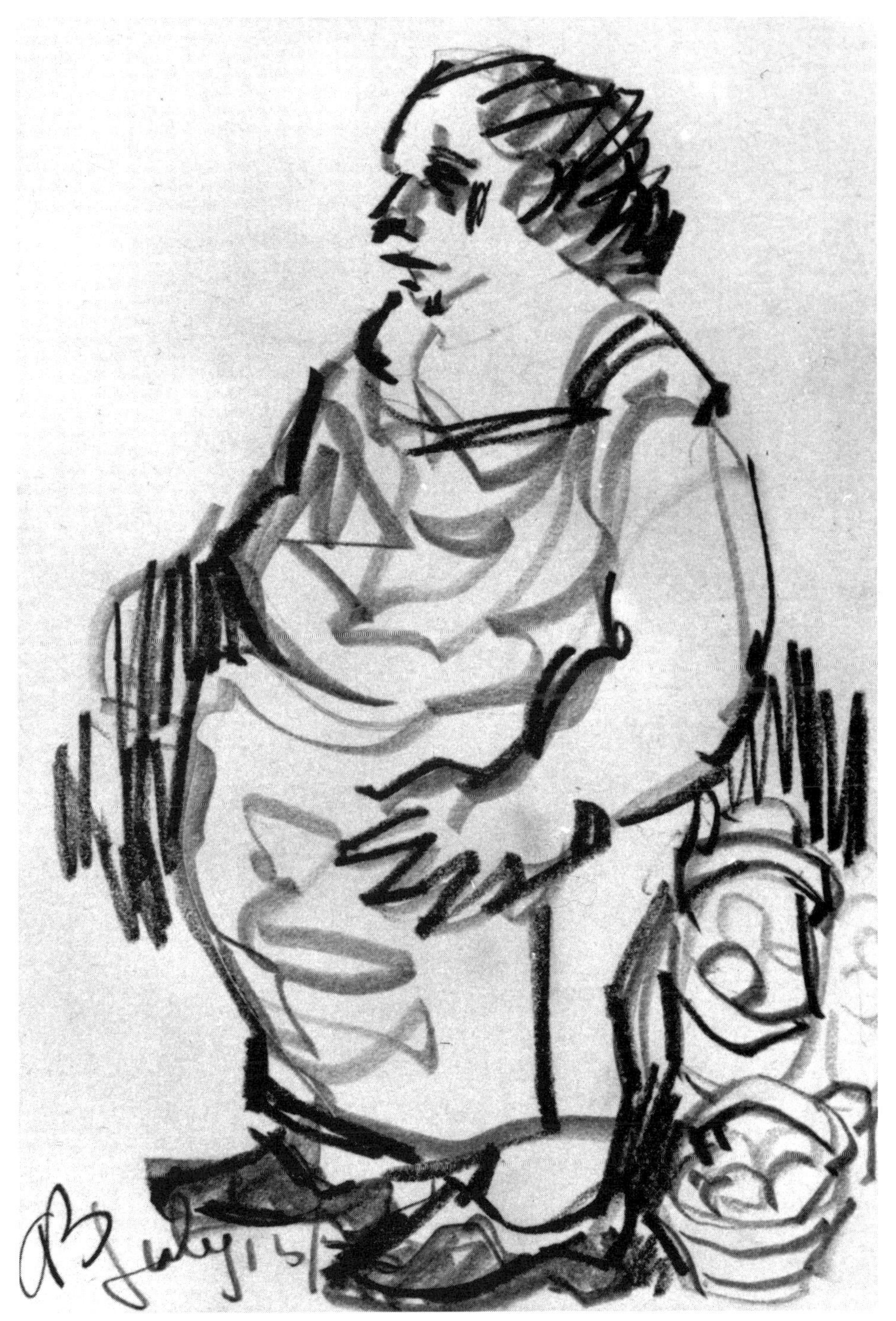

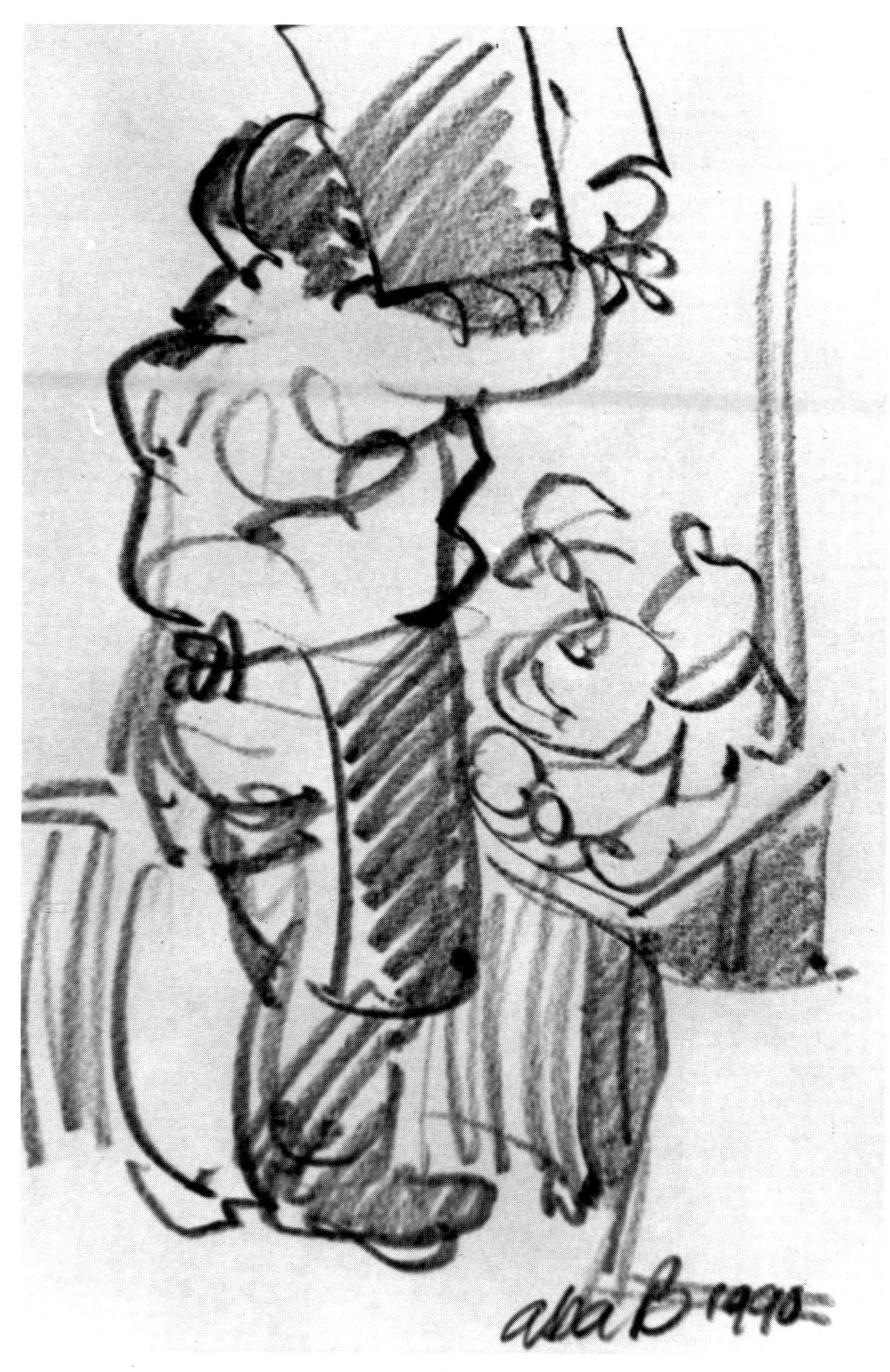

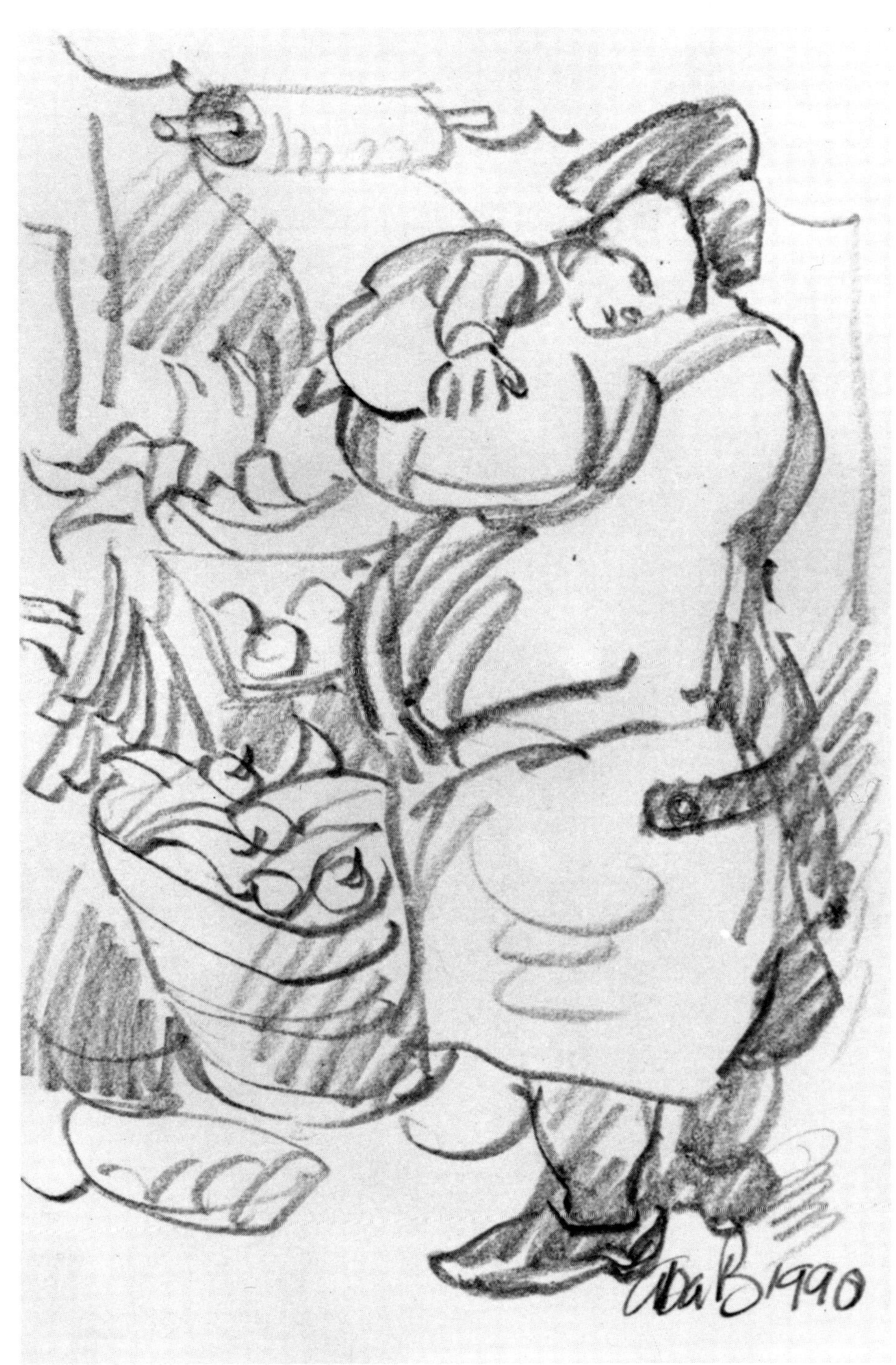

AdaB 1990

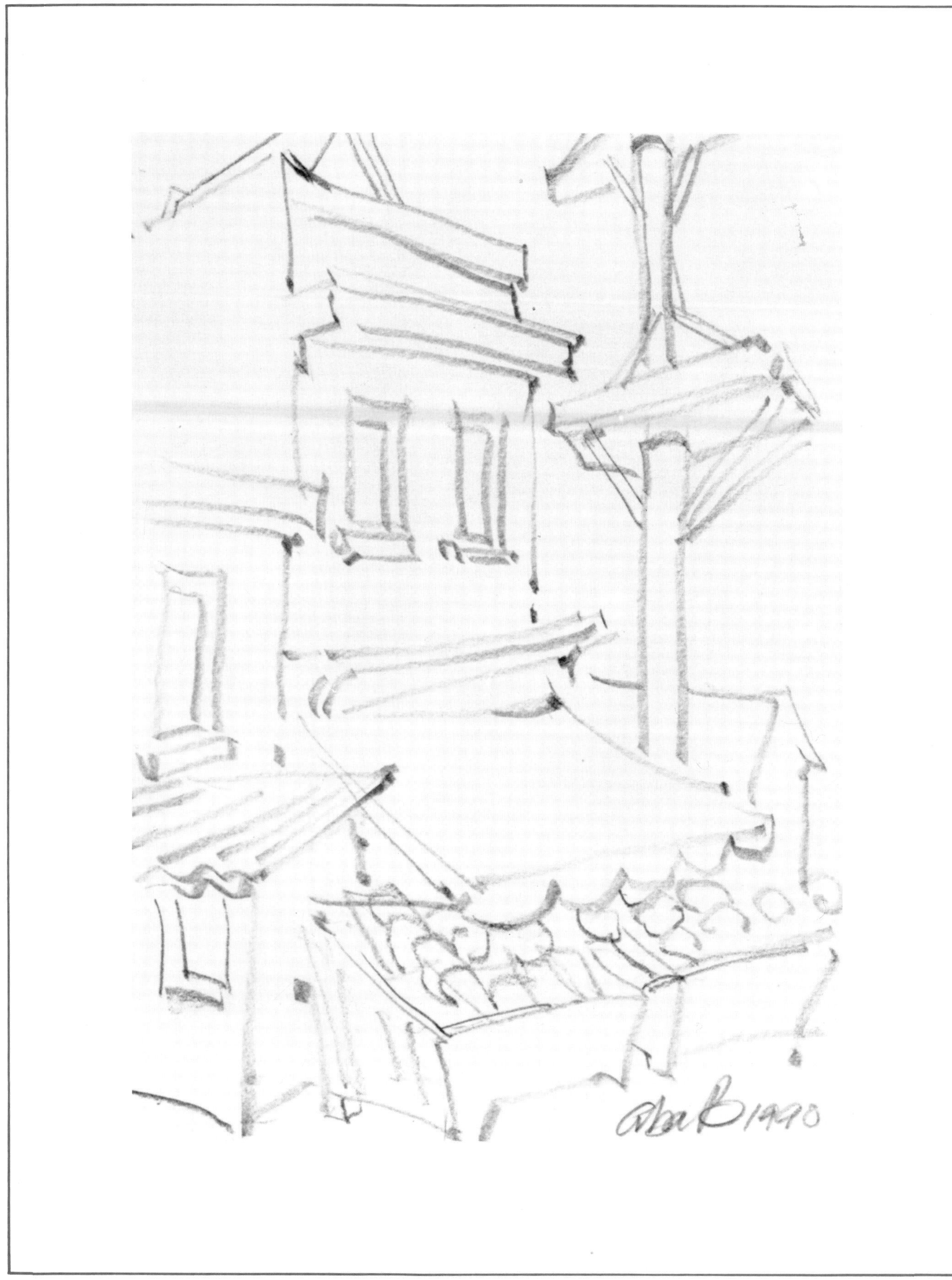

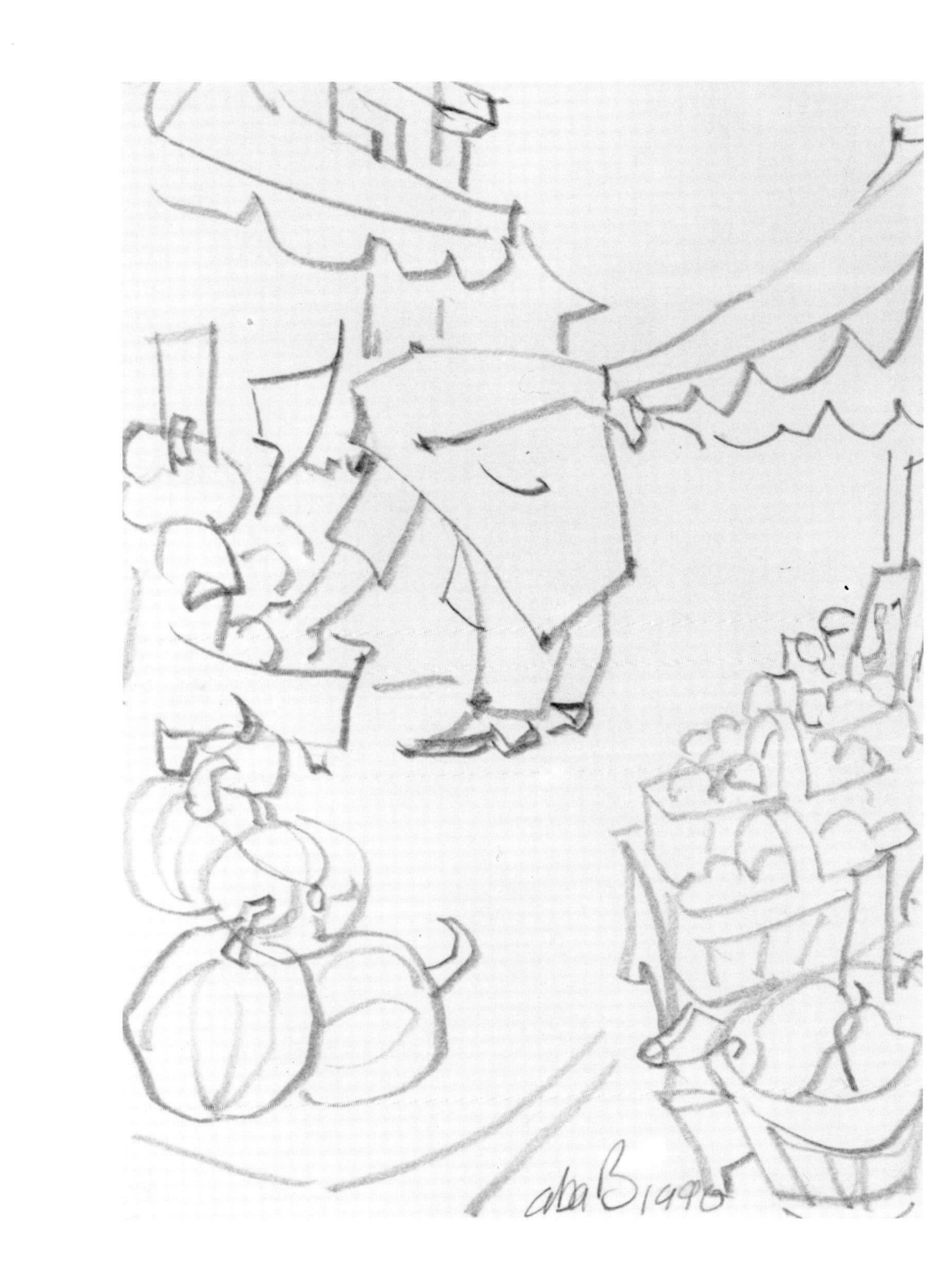

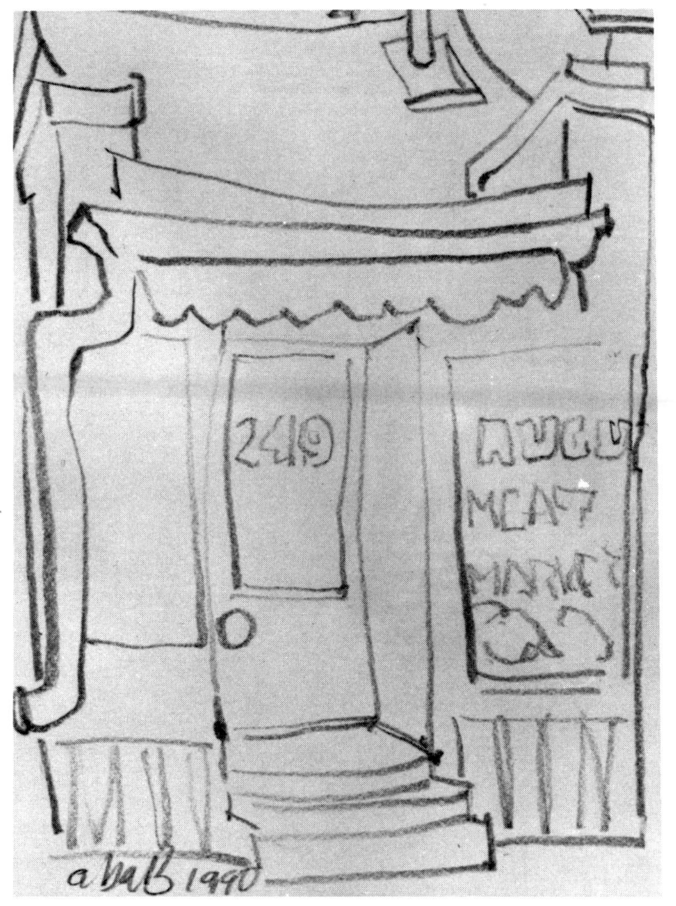
2419
MEAT
MARKET

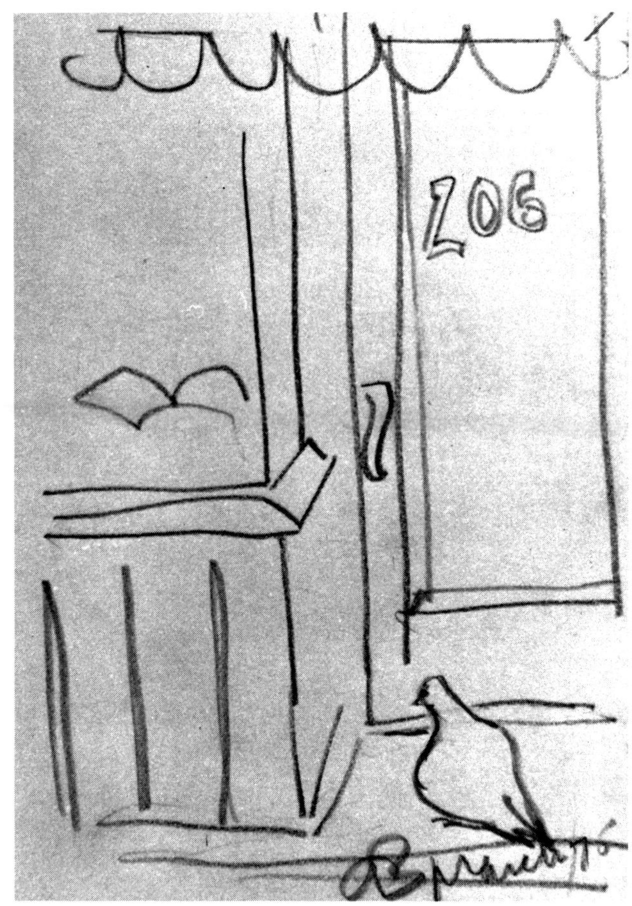
206

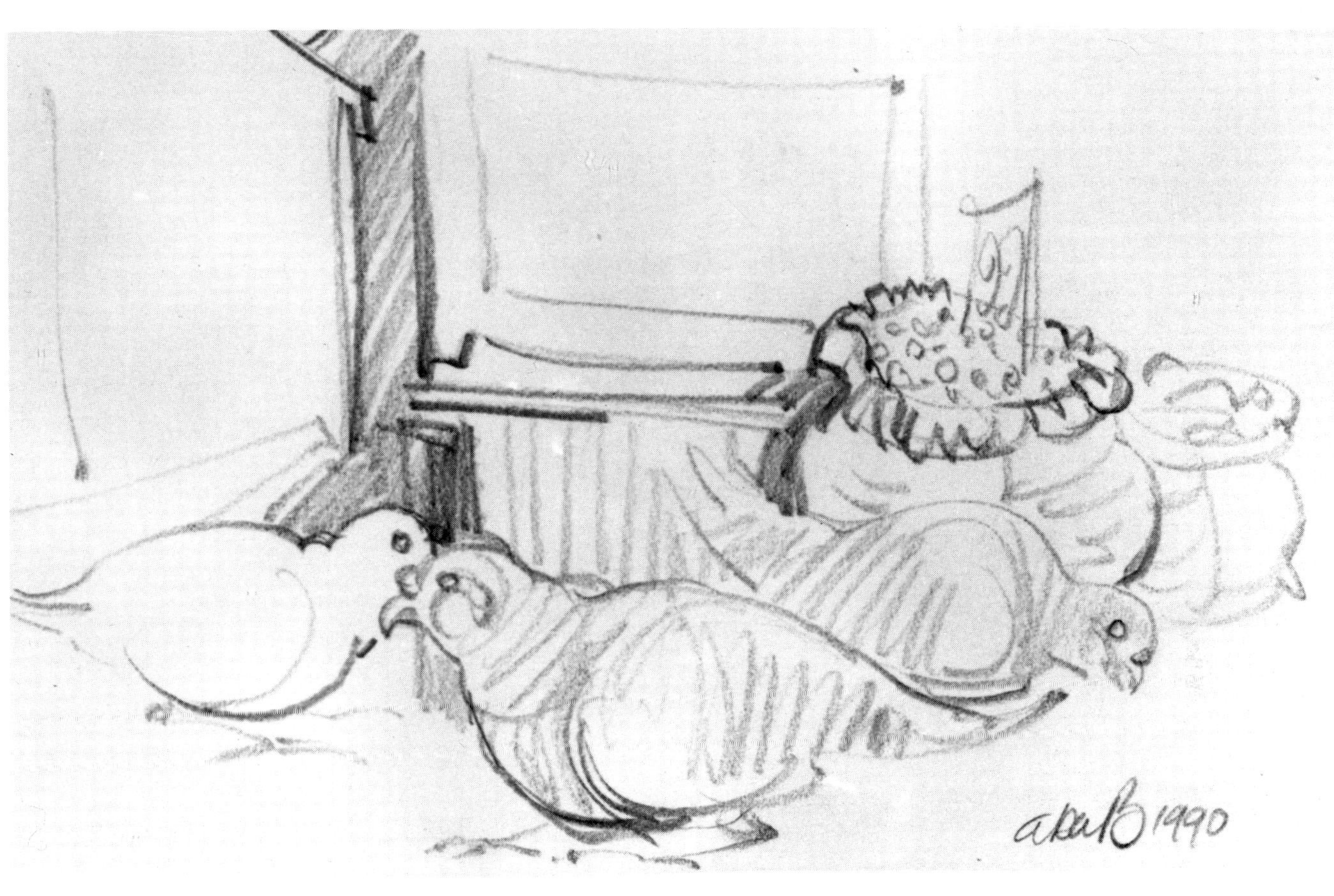

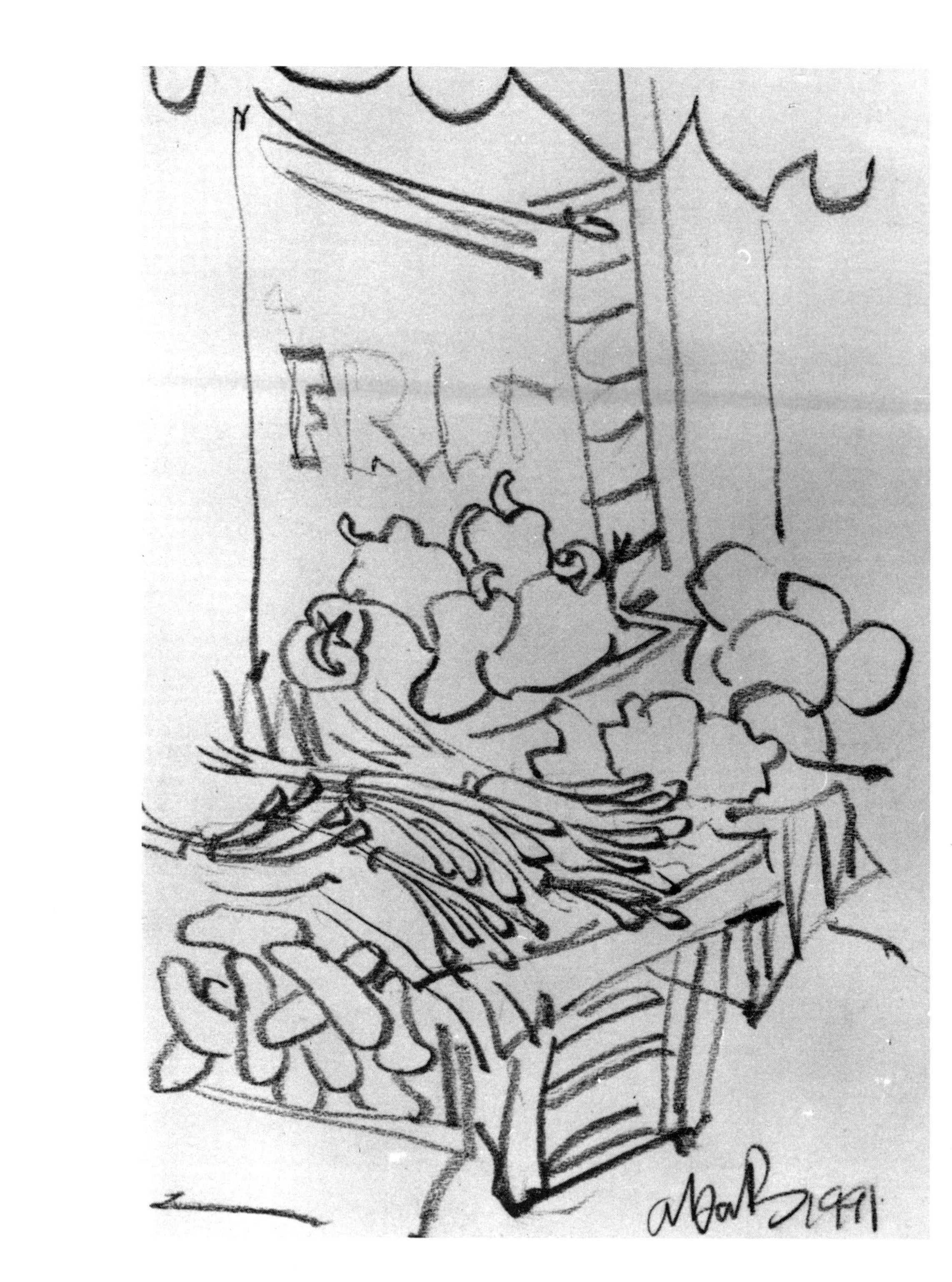

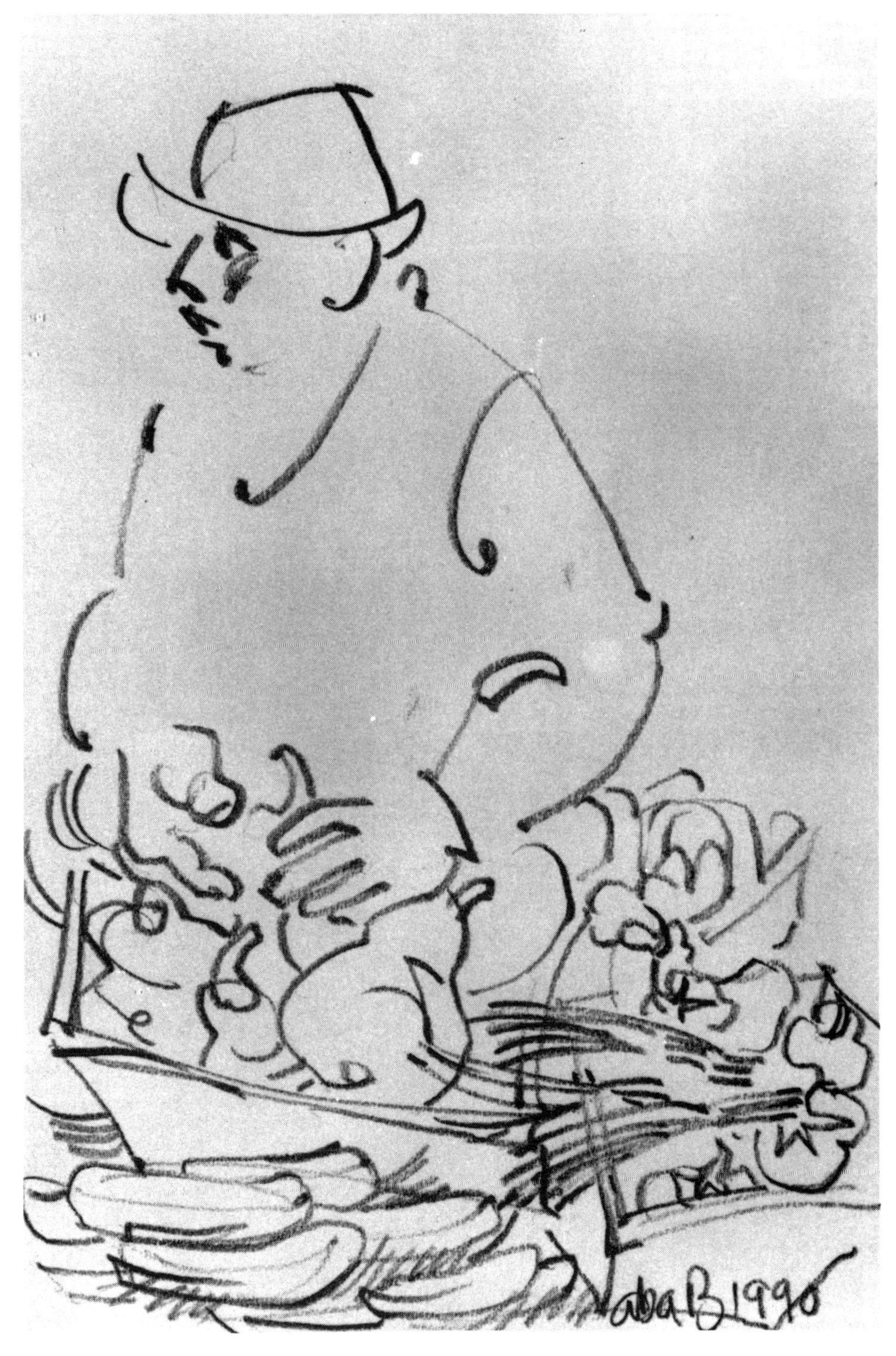

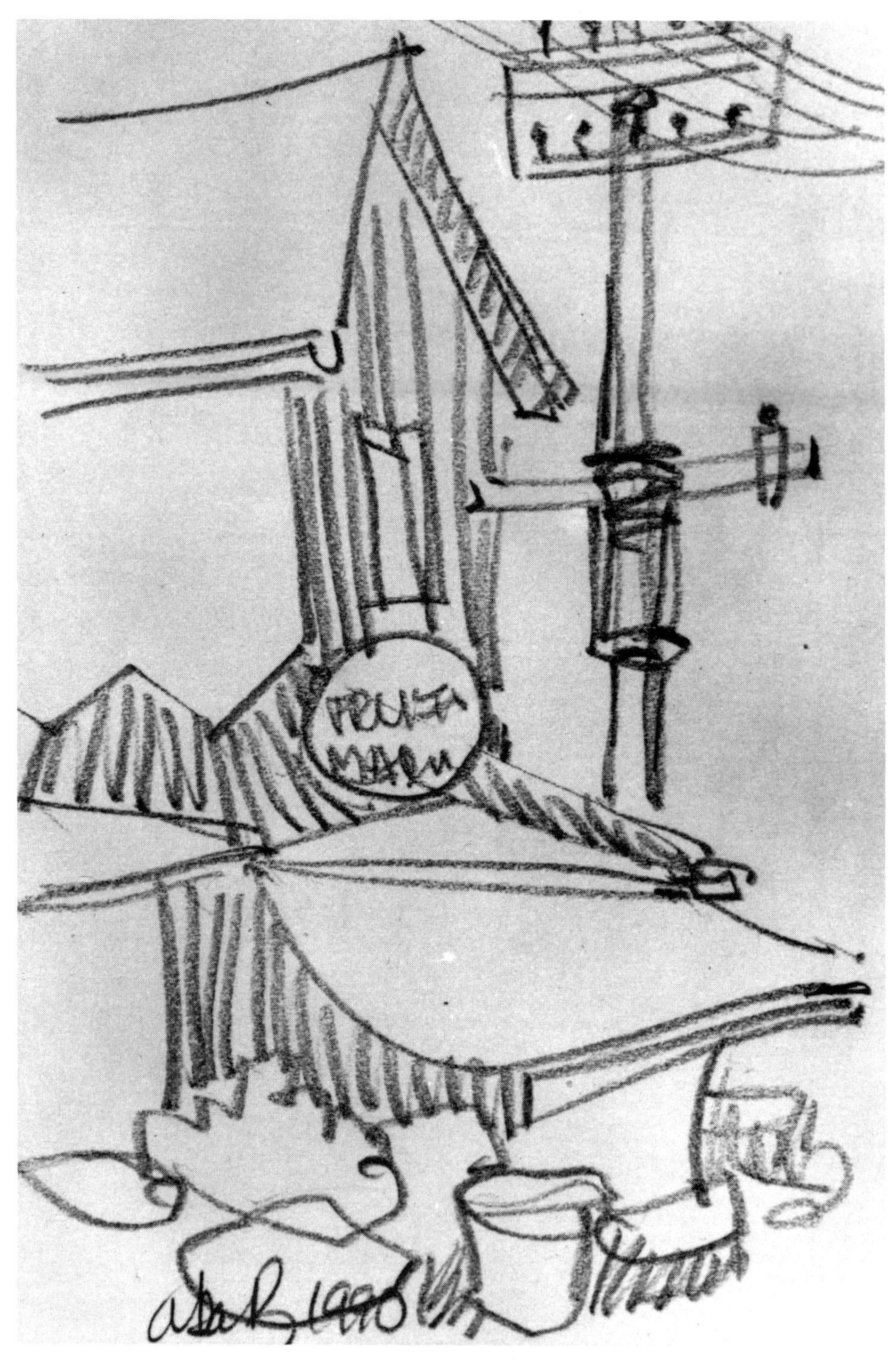

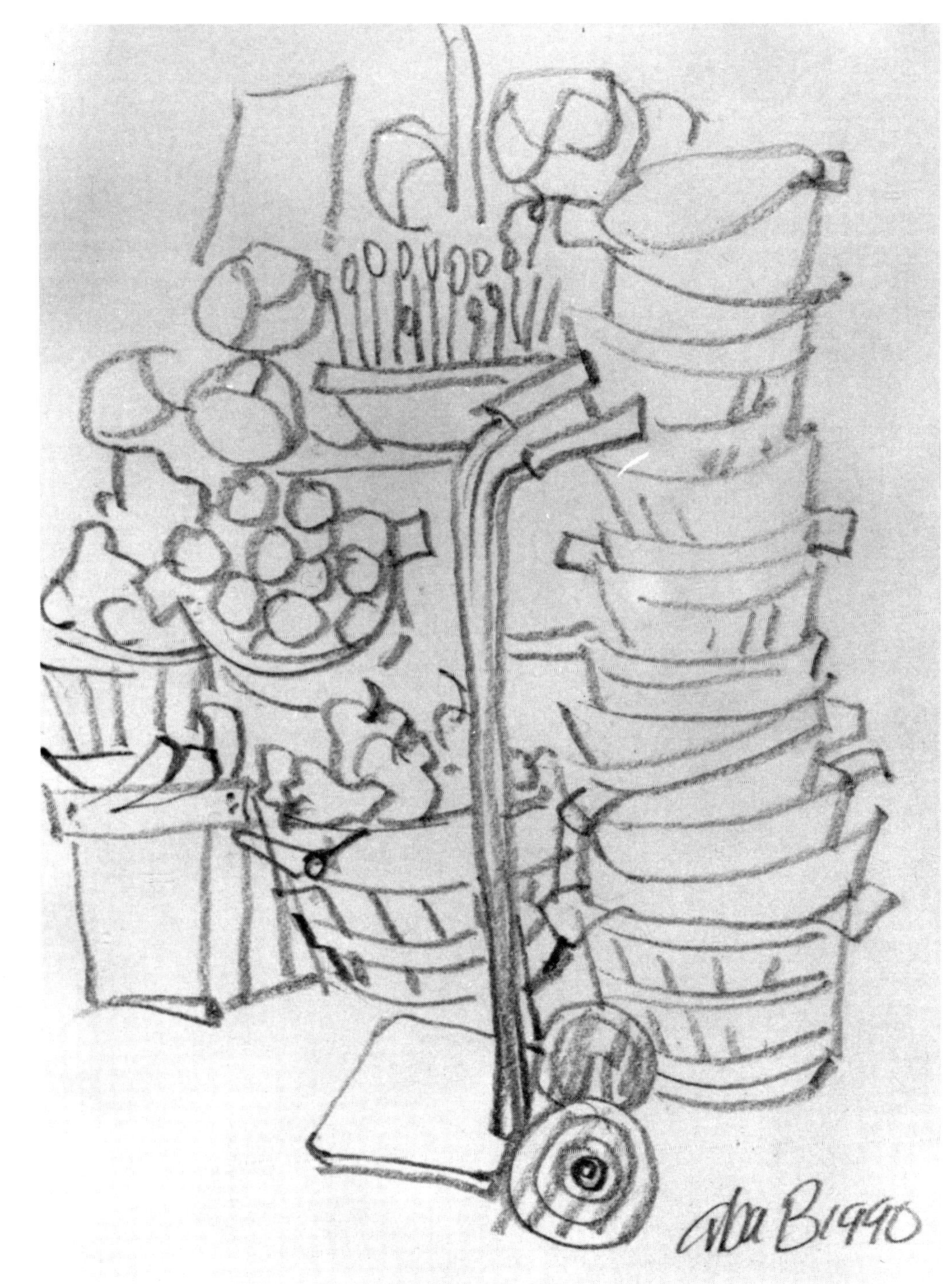

Alba B 1990

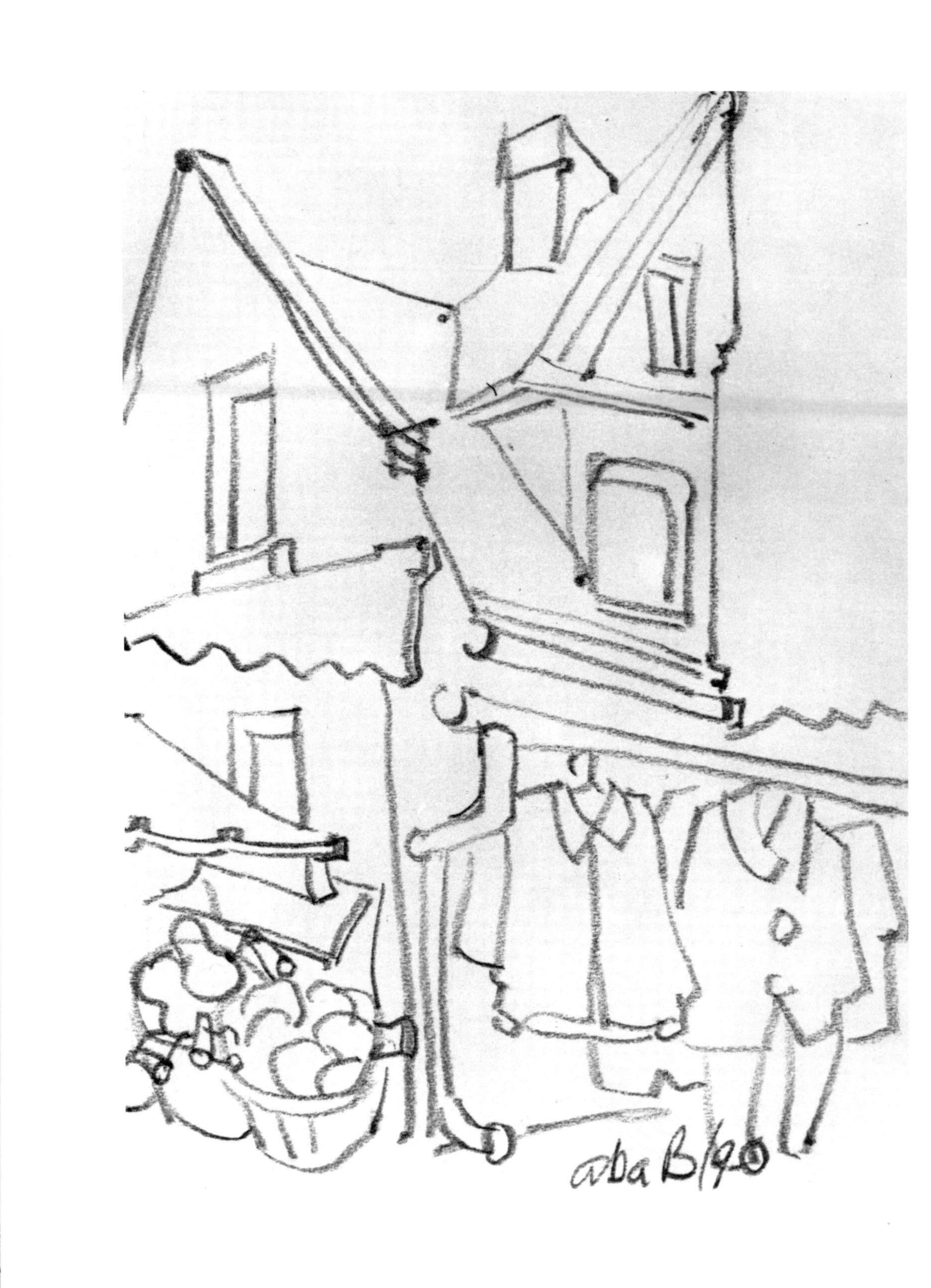

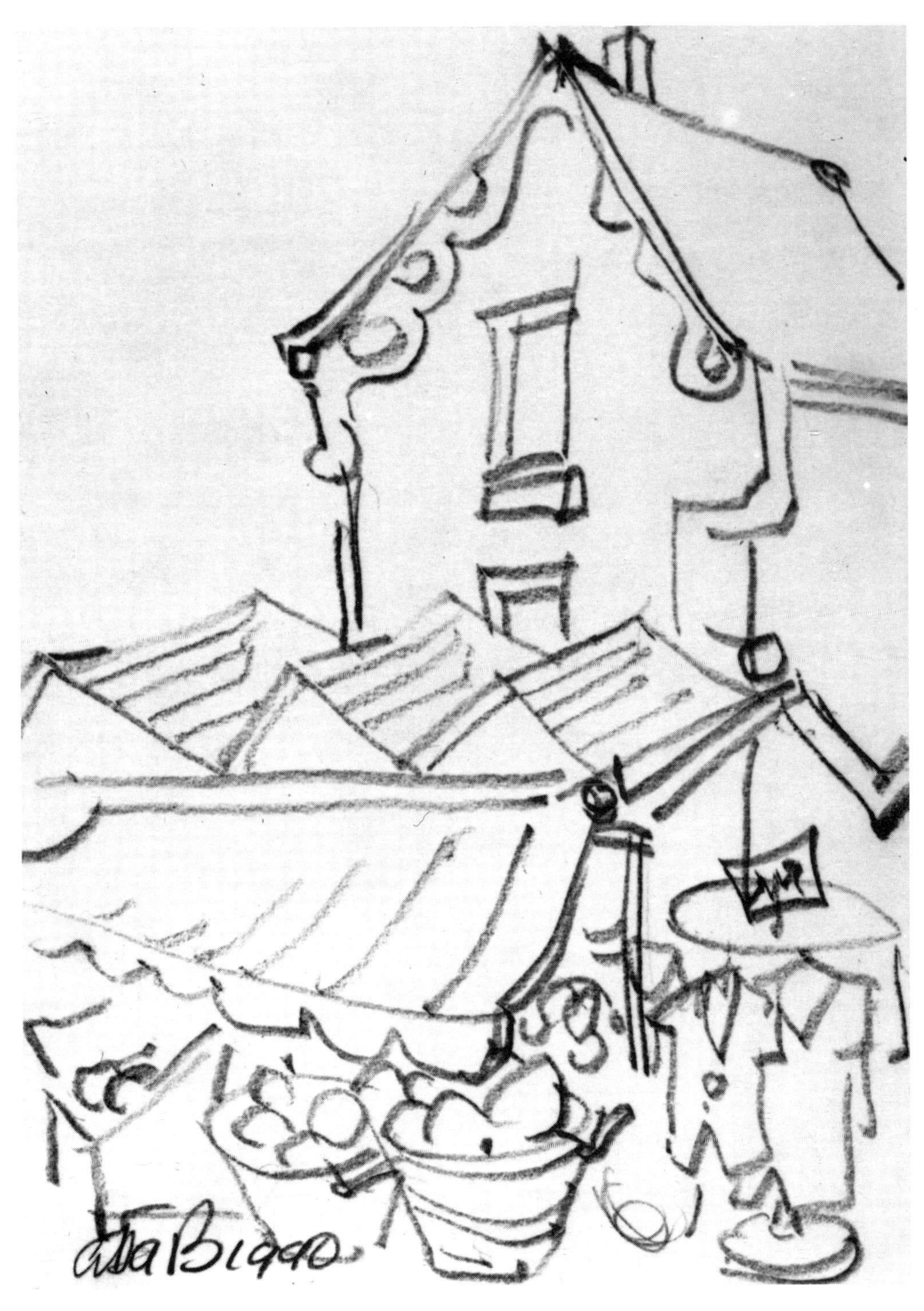

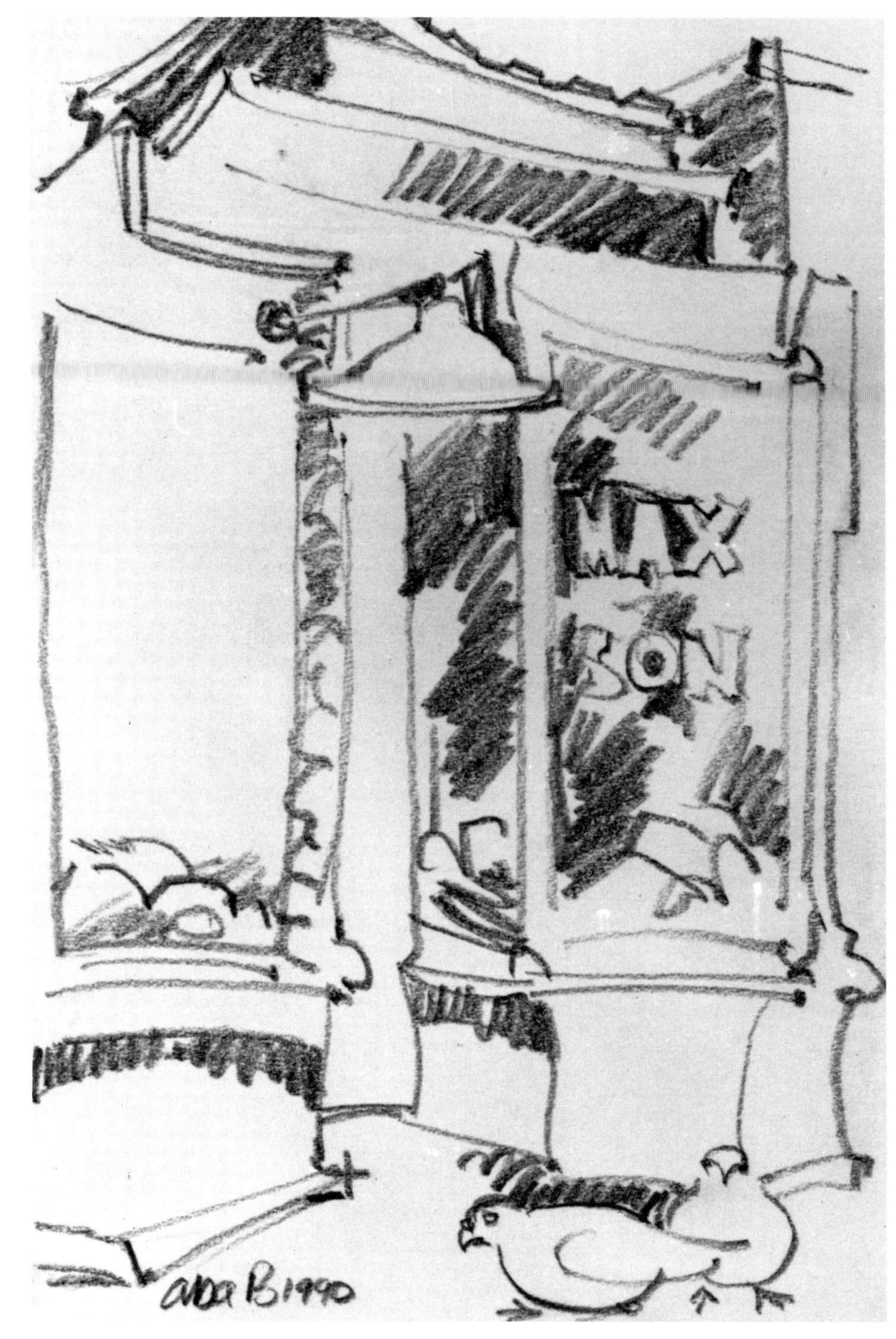

MAX
SON

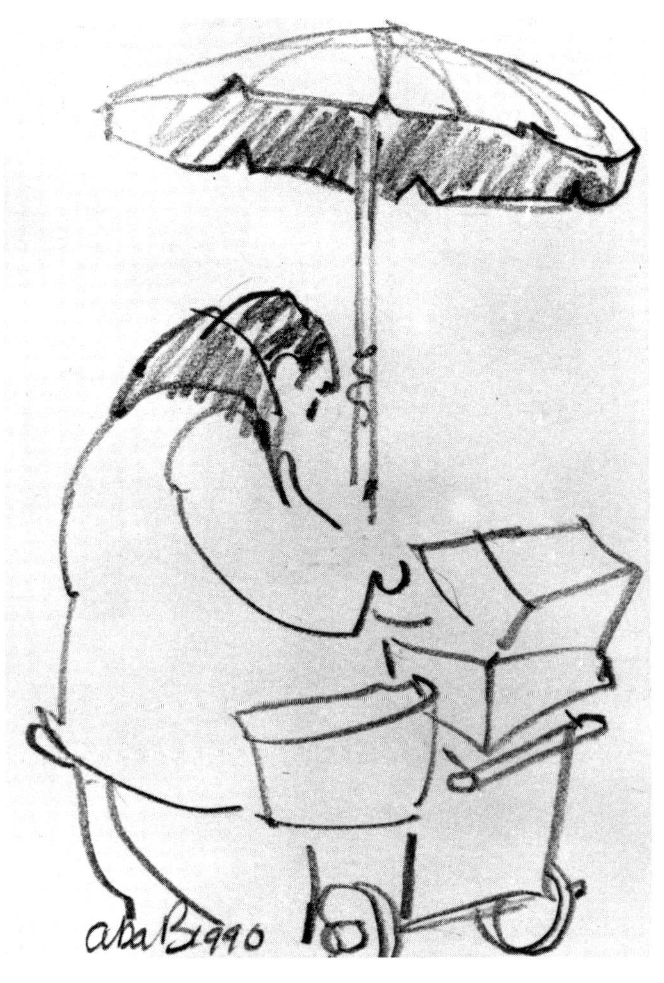
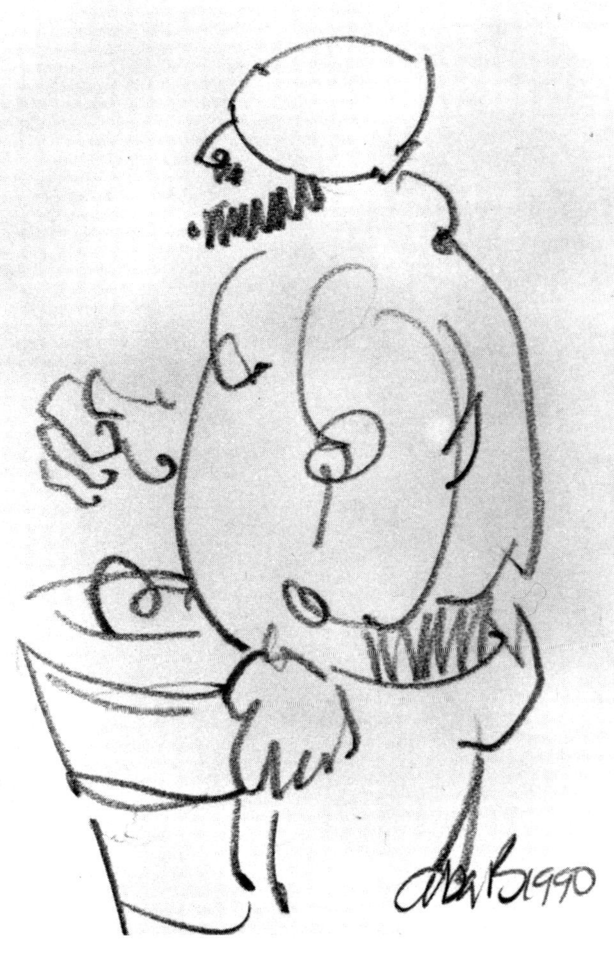

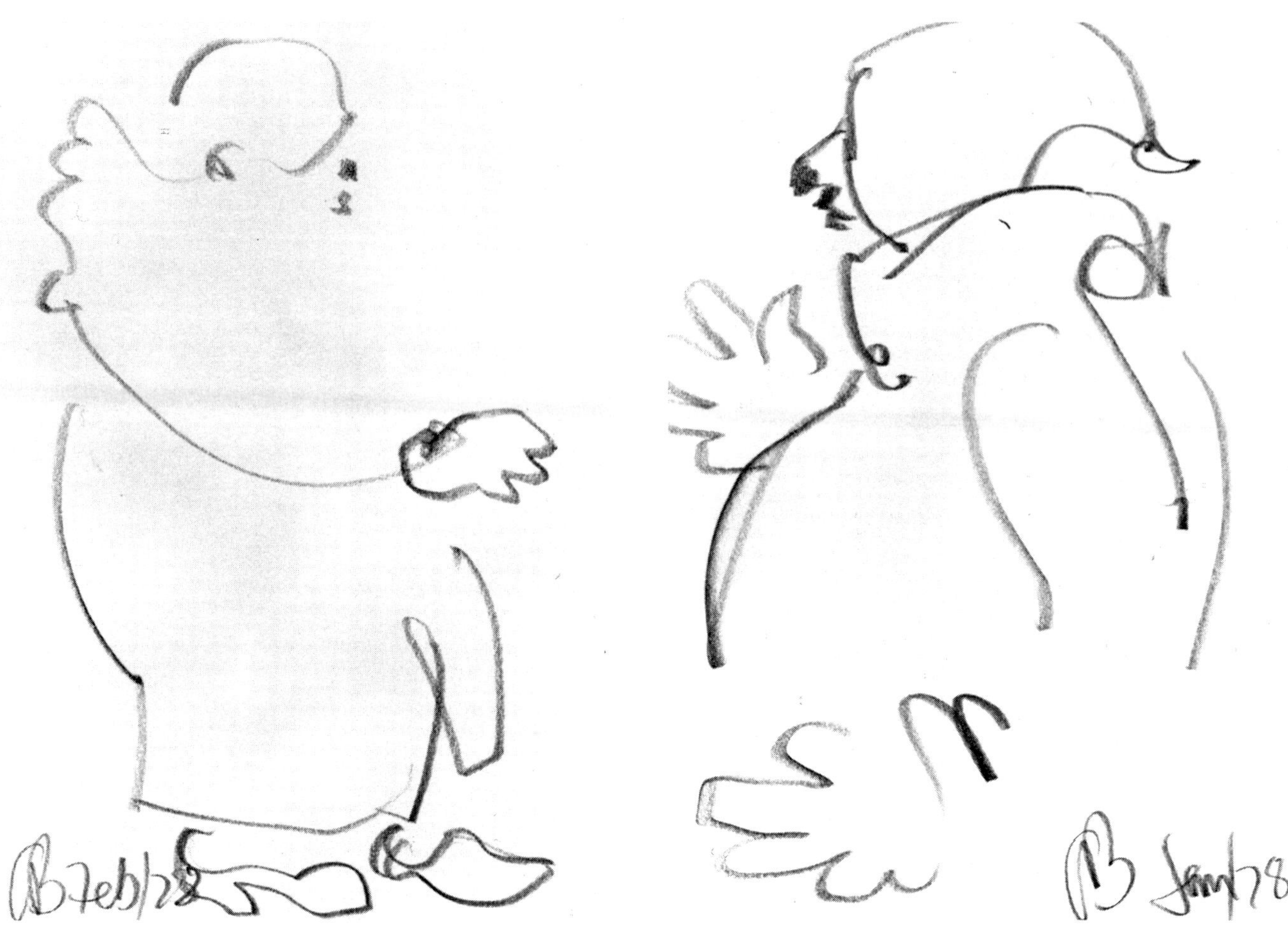

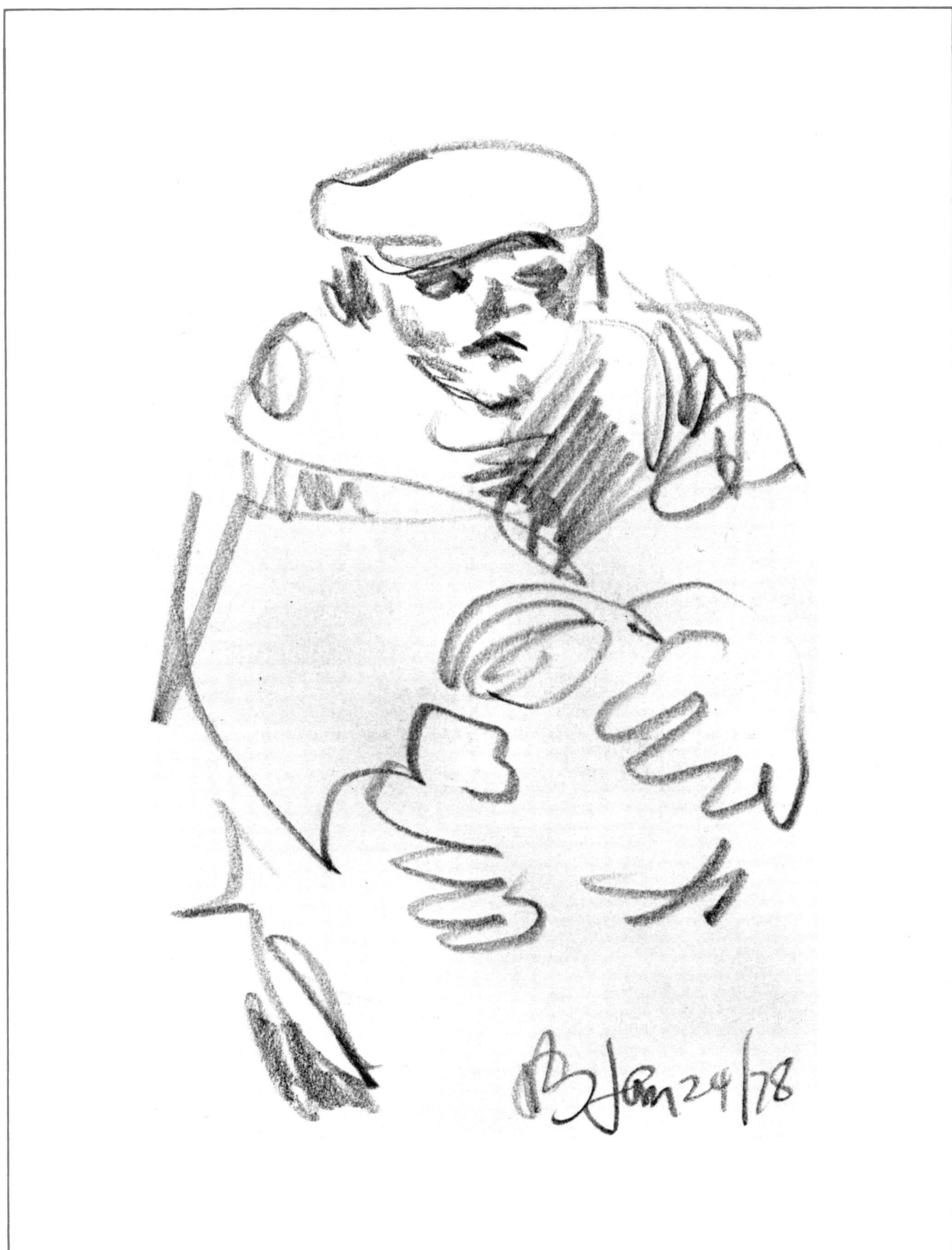

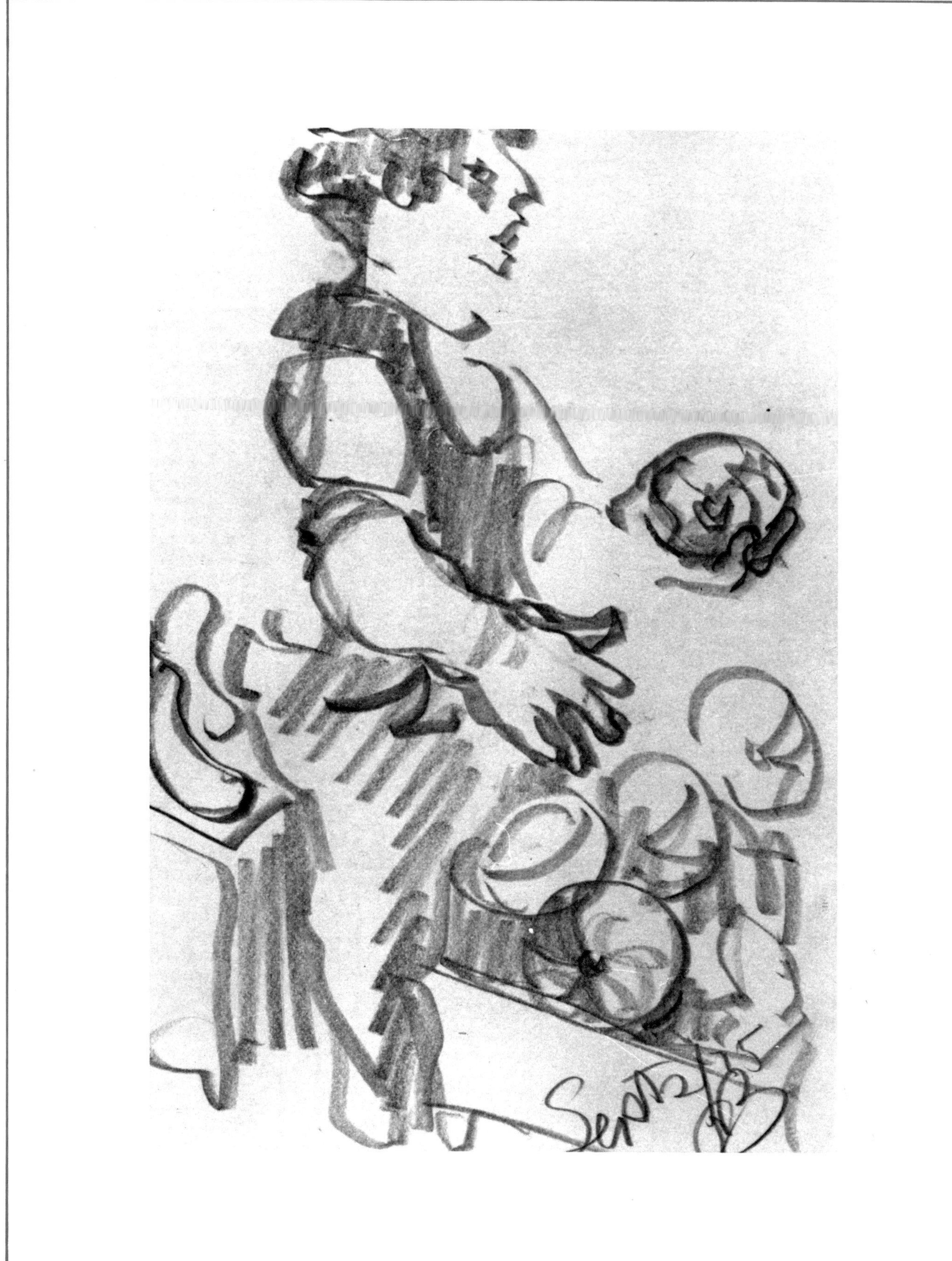

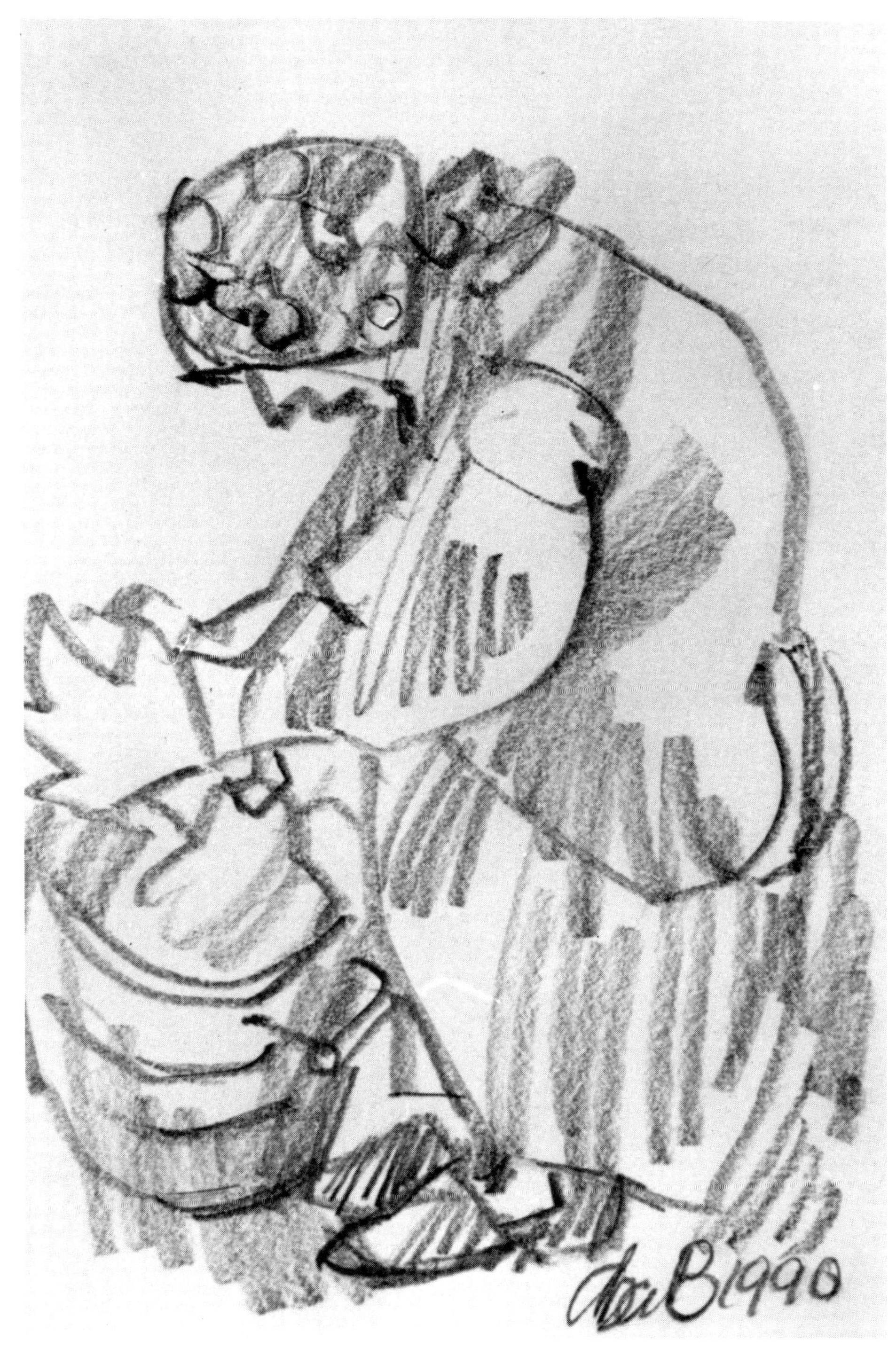

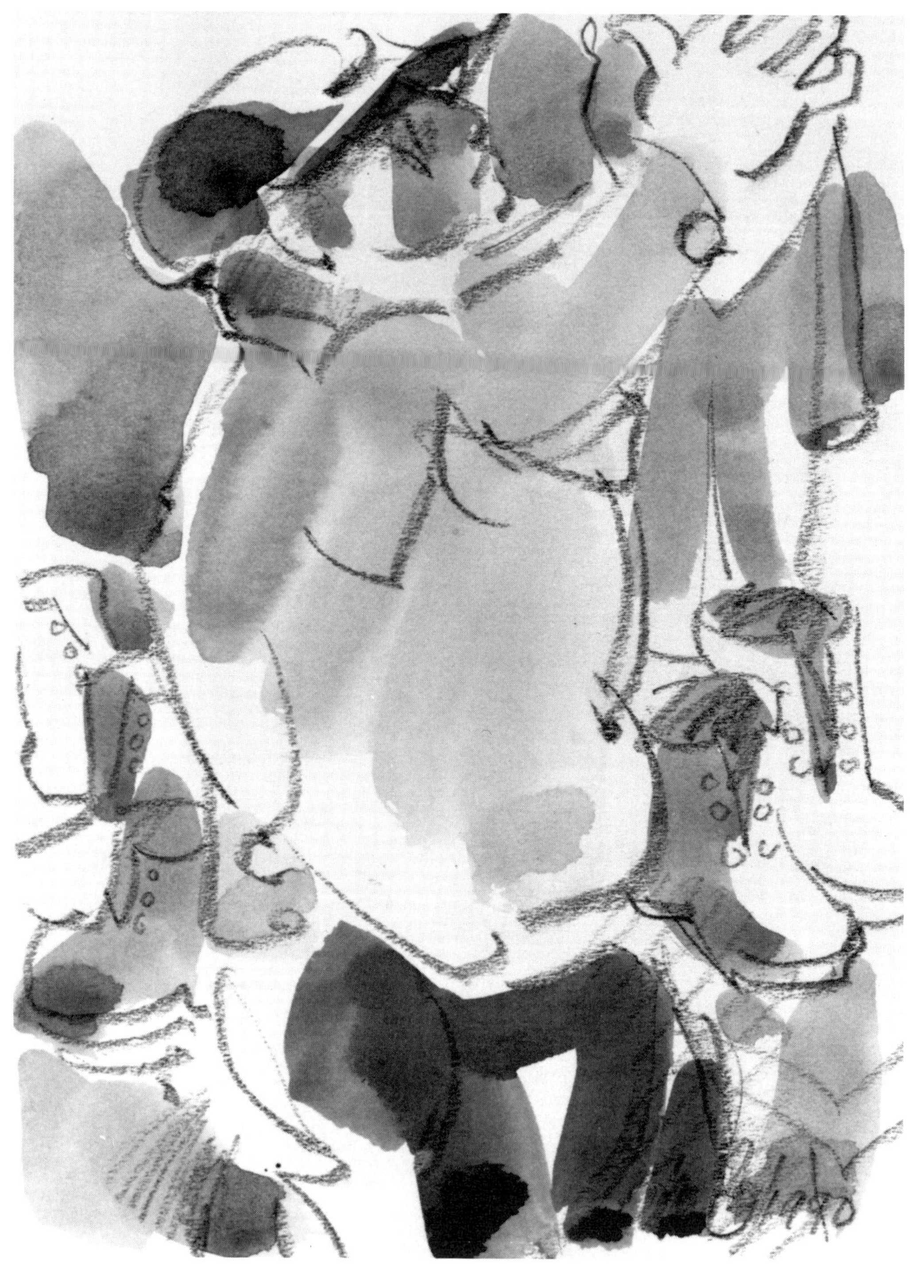

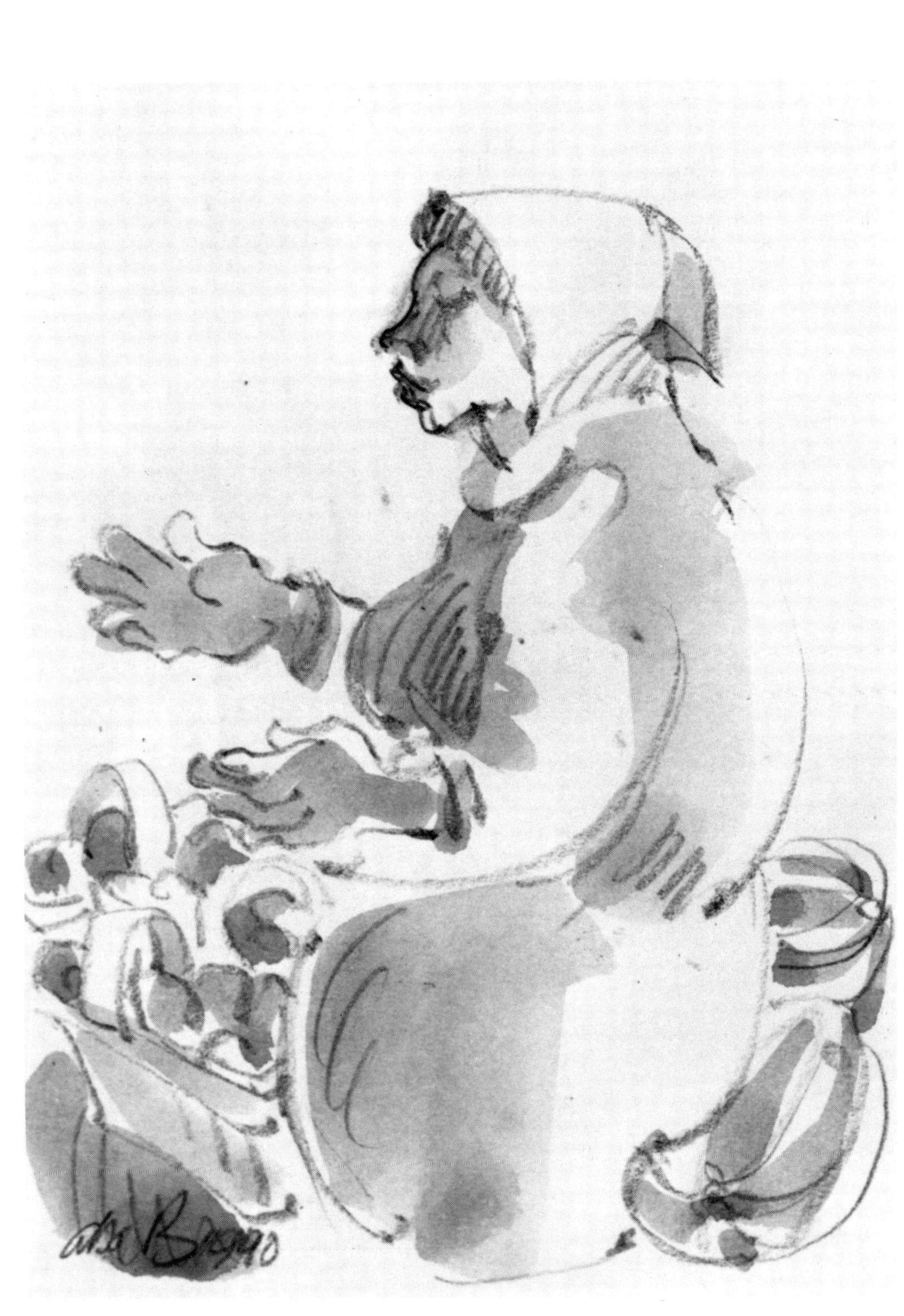

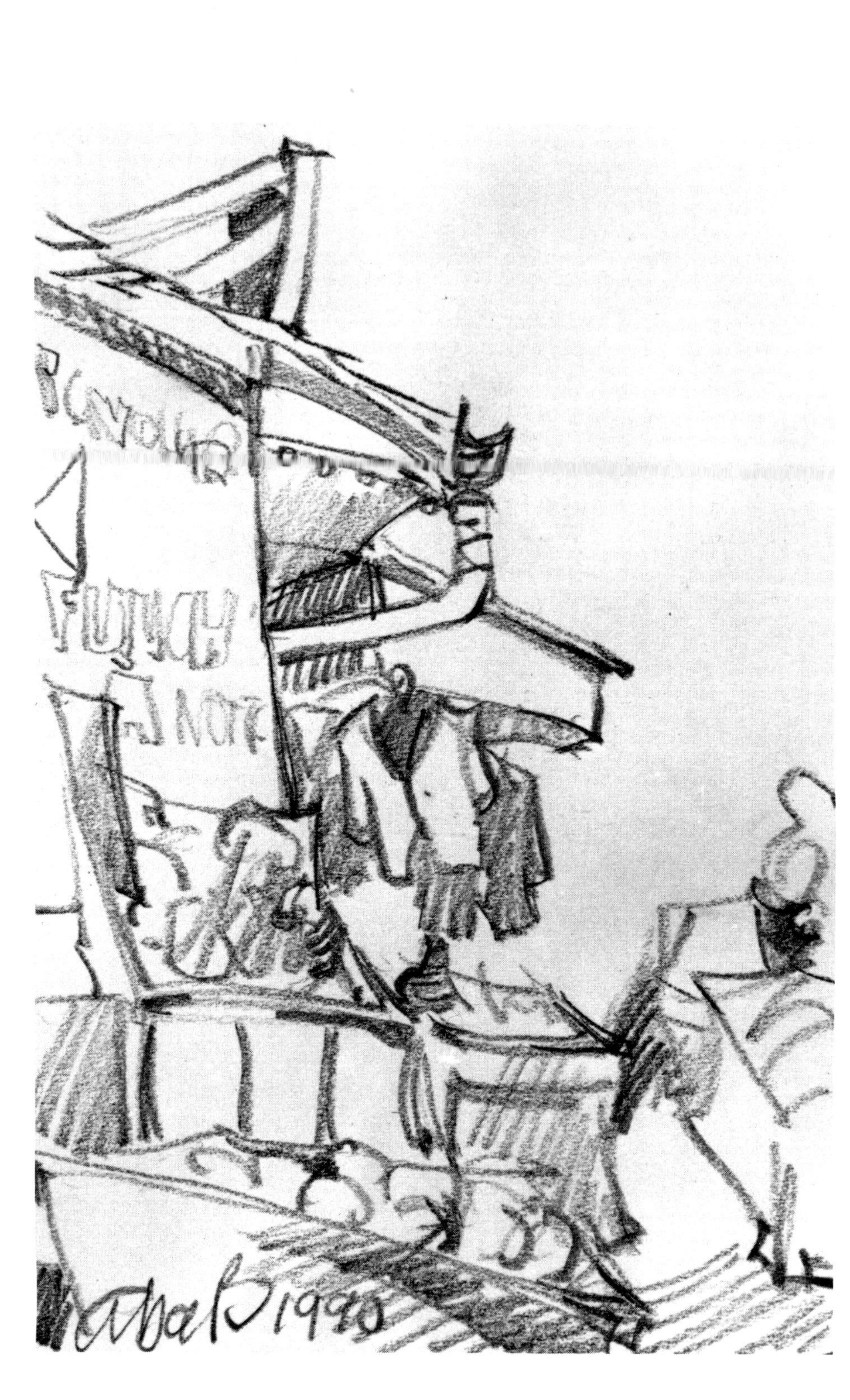

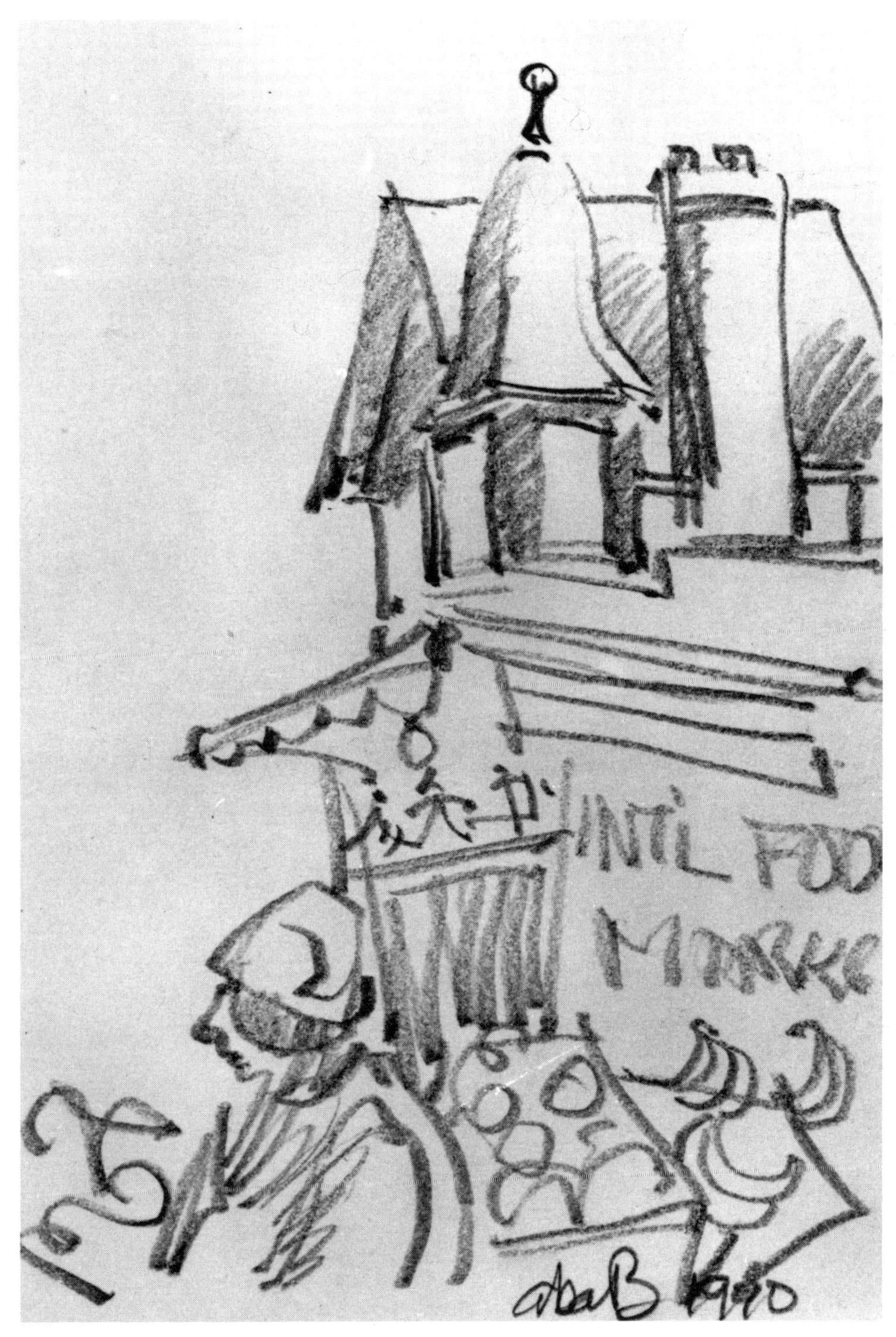
INT'L FOO
MARKE

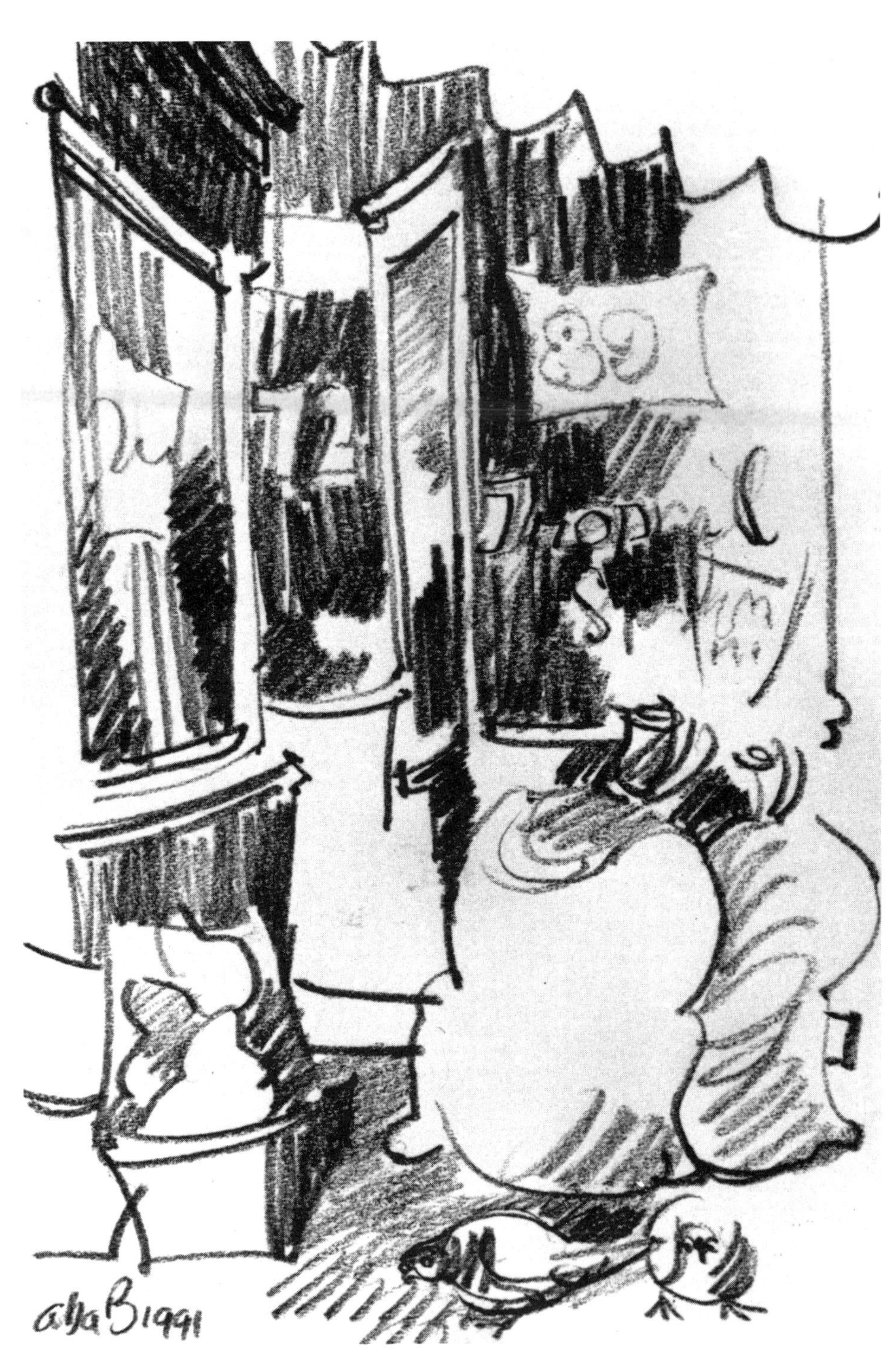

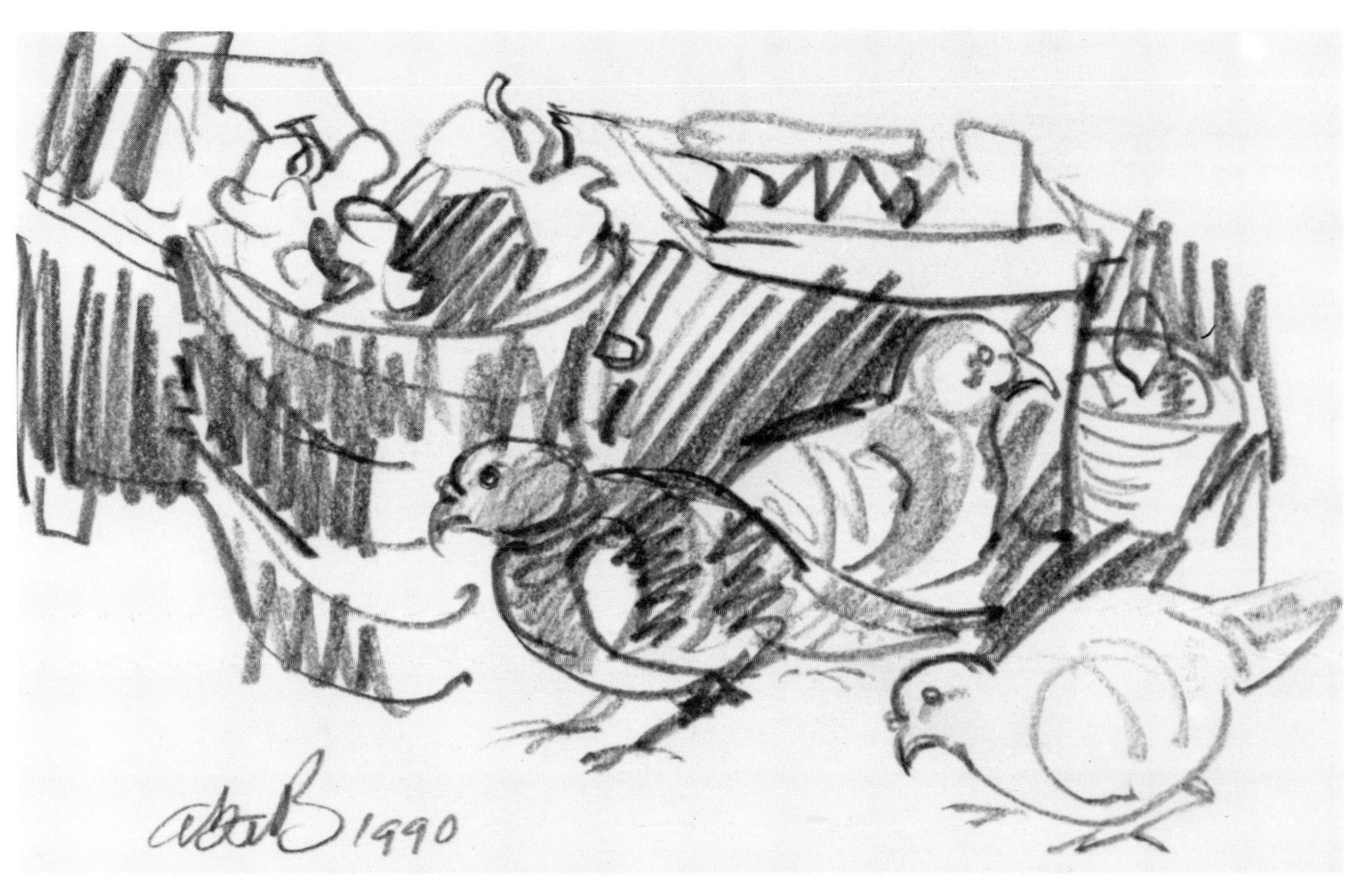
1990

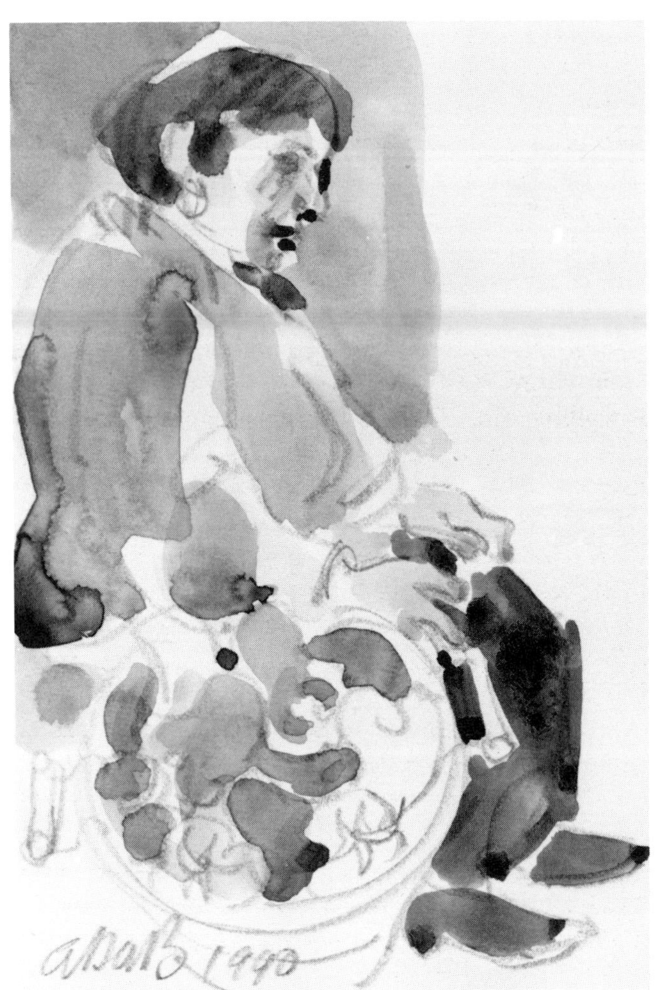 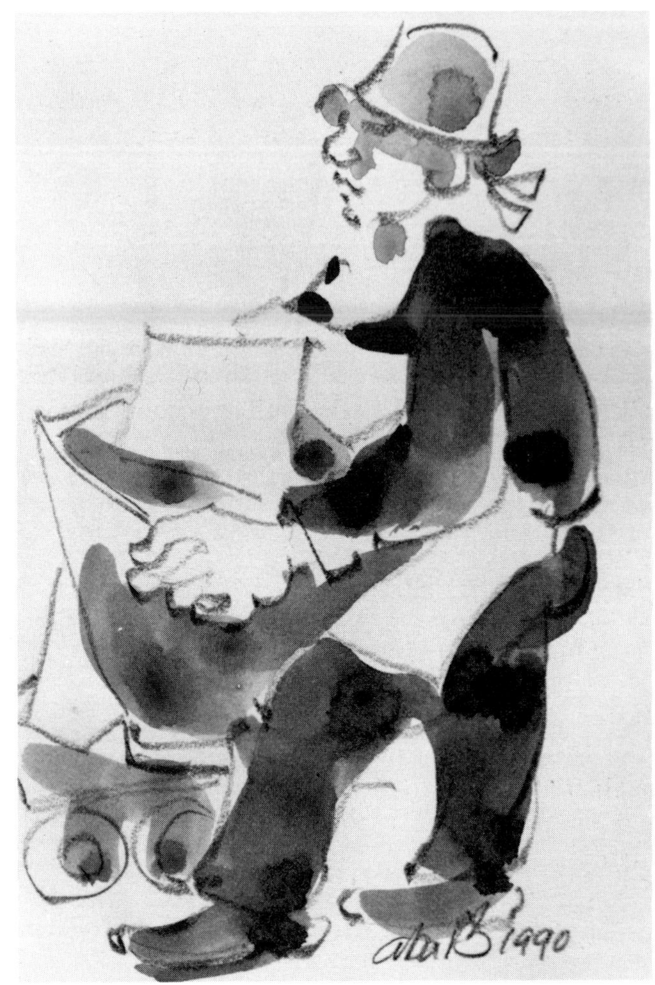

A MEMOIR by Ben Lappin

Localities, like individuals, rise from obscurity to become famous neighbourhoods such as The Village in New York, Soho in London, the Left Bank in Paris, and the like. Toronto, not to be outdone, has Kensington Market.

Little did the nineteenth century planners who laid out another copy of an English residential neighbourhood in yet another remote corner of the Empire, realize what changes it was destined to undergo. Only the names of the streets remain recognizable and even those vestiges are not enunciated as they once were. The first shift in pronunciation was from Kensington to Kenzigtn. Since then the time honoured name has been vocalized differently by each ethnic group that has been drawn to the area. Thus the variations on Kensington as it has been successively influenced by the intonations and cadences of Yiddish, Hungarian, Portuguese, Jamaican, Chinese, and others to follow, no doubt.

In his drawings Aba Bayefsky has captured the advent of the first non-Anglo-Saxon group. Whether it is the *shochet,* or ritual slaughterer about to dispatch a hen in the higher interests of chicken soup, or the butcher with his cleaver in hand chopping to order a section of meat for a customer, or the woman taking a retrospective look at her basketful of food items, each purchase accompanied, you can be sure, by a solid round of bargaining with the vendor — every sketch is vintage Kenzigtn.

Bayefsky takes us back to an era that preceded the constant changes Kensington Market has been going through since the end of the Second World War. It as a time of stability. In those days Kensington served the needs of the surrounding population exclusively. It was not the exotic bazaar it has since become for the entire city. In fact, it was virtually unknown outside of the ethnic enclave that coincided with the boundaries of Ward Four, extending from University Avenue on the east to Ossington Avenue on the west - the inner city locus of the

Jewish community back then.

That does not mean that Kensington was an out of the way market place where store owners bided their time anxiously waiting for customers, to show up. Far from it. A vendor wouldn't last a day in Kensington if he lacked the stamina to be at the beck and call of the buyers who came there in droves from early morning until late in the evening. Nor could he hold his own in the jaunty chaos that reigned in the market unless he came equipped with the lungs and vocal chords to holler out his bargains above the prevailing din. The stenortian haggling between buyers and sellers that accompanied paltry transactions...the thinly veiled threats that store owners and the street peddlers would exchange at the drop of a hat...the great rush to help anyone seen faltering in the heat or the winter cold...all of which lifted Kensington above the selling and the buying. Despite the clatter, despite the rumpus, Kensington was first and foremost a whimsy. Indeed, if a neighborhood can be described as eccentric, Kenzigtn was it. And so was the Avenue.

The Avenue? The full name was Spadina Avenue, though one called it either Spadina or The Avenue. Rarely both together. Kensington and Spadina were two centres that played essential roles in shaping the image of the Jewish community in Toronto. They had little in common other than that they addressed the same people many of whom earned their money as workers on Spadina and spent it as consumers in Kensington. It was Spadina that first clashed with the values of the community affecting Kensington specifically as we shall see.

In the early twenties Spadina emerged as Toronto's undisputed locale of the needle trades. The Avenue became a main source of employment for the newcomers who worked in its factories as dress makers, cloak makers, ladies' hat makers, men's cap makers, pocket book makers, button makers, and inevitably, button hole makers, etc. In short, the community had acquired something akin to an industrial base.

The bread and butter Spadina that provided livelihoods for the needle trade "makers" stopped at Dundas Street. From there the ideological Spadina took over. Between Dundas and College Streets the Avenue bristled with organizations social, cultural, and political. Along with these lofty resources there were, what one might call, the lesser diversions: a pool room or two, a bookie joint here and there operating in the rear of a barber shop. But the latter did not detract from the higher purpose Spadina fulfilled in the life of the community.

When the playhouse at Dundas and Teraulay, that hosted visiting repertory troupes from New York was destroyed by fire, the Yiddish theatre was reincarnated at Spadina and Dundas in a newly built, much more sumptuous hall that was named The Standard Theatre. The Toronto Daily Hebrew Journal was published on Dundas Street a few doors west of Spadina, while Dworkin's across the way was the local distribution centre for the mass circulation papers in Yiddish published out of New York. Further north the "makers" established their unions in the Labor Lyceum at the corner of St. Andrew, a minute's walk from Kensington. After the day's work, there were the organizations, and in the going hyperbole of the day, the mass movements with their forceful populists at the helm, their visiting lecturers, and local pundits who gave meaning, or better said, a variety of conflicting meanings to life. And after the lectures there was always Ladovsky's where waiters served steaming glasses of tea and lemon to the workers turned philosophers. At Ladovsky's passionate arguments raged into the late hours until the waiters threatened to put out the lights and lock the customers in for the night over that vision of redemption, this road to utopia, or yet another solution to the world's problems.

So numerous did these institutionalized amenities on the Avenue become in the twenties that the overflow of ideological groupings seeking accommodation had to be channelled into Cecil Street, a small tributary running off Spadina that connected the Avenue with Beverley Street where the professionalized social services and community organization agencies had taken root. But the Avenue remained the cultural hub as long as Ward Four was the major locale of the Jewish community. Though something of a challenge did come from College Street with its two movie houses, and the delicatessens (Becker's, Eppes Essen and others). But much more important, the YMHA was there functioning out of the basement in the building that housed the Associated Hebrew School on Brunswick Avenue at College.

The young seemed to prefer College Street over Spadina. No doubt the presence of the "Y" and the delicatessens made the difference. The banter over a corned beef sandwich and a coke (not sponge cake and tea) was in English. The conversations on College Street ran more to hockey and baseball than politics and the meaning of life that preoccupied the polemicists on Spadina in Yiddish.

Within this ecology of community functions, the cluster of streets collectively called Kenzigtn became the supply centre of foods and to a lesser extent, household goods, at bargain prices. The hawkers never tired of bellowing, "Bargains, bargains, bargains," *koyft* (buy) bargains," the one phrase that was dinned into the ears of the customers who flocked to Kensington all week, though Thursday was the big shopping day in preparation for the Sabbath. On Friday mornings the poorer shoppers came to pick over what was left unbought the previous day. The bargaining tone of the vendors with the Friday morning crowd was noticeably less deferential than with the Thursday ladies from Palmerston Boulevard and the other elegant streets.

Even when they were still a fair distance off the customers were invariably greeted by the yells and smells of Kensington. If the odours that came off the fruits and vegetables ripening in the sun assailed the nostrils, there was the redeeming fragrance of oven fresh bread and bagels wafting out over the streets from the bakeries, or the pungent aroma issuing from the creameries with their variety of cheeses, the trays of smoked fish, and gherkins pickling in barrels full of sour juices that made the mouth water.

Kensington was an in-group convenience meant strictly for the surrounding population. This was related, in some measure, to the nature of the community's economic ties with the larger world. This feeling of inwardness helped nurture a ready familiarity between seller and buyer of the same ethnic background. The haggling in stores and on streets gave off a visible informality; innocence would perhaps be a better way to describe it. Kensington was totally unaffected. It was years away from acquiring the savvy, the sense of style it now displays ''sitting'' for photographers and painters come to capture on paper or canvas Toronto's display of exotica. In those days the store keepers and the customers alike would have taken them as intruders, or worse, as *mishugoim*, crazies, who had descended upon them.

How then, you may wonder, did Bayefsky manage to catch so unwilling a subject in such a rich variety of attitudes? The truth is, he observed, studied and internalized these ''poses'' as a young child accompanying his mother on her regular shopping trips to Kensington. They became deeply etched in his mind. This process of absorption was reinforced a few years later by actual sketching sessions in the neighbourhood when he became a member of the Children's Art Centre sponsored by the Toronto Art Gallery and conducted by Arthur Lismer, who left his mark on Canadian painting as one of the Group of Seven. Children making like artists with drawing pads and charcoal sticks in hand, clustered around a nag with a low slung belly, or a push cart piled high with water melons were not likely to raise any eyebrows in Kensington. They also came through on Purim (the festival celebrating the downfall of Haman, the ancient tyrant who planned the destruction of Persian Jewry in biblical times) wearing fierce looking masks and behaving like knock about clowns. Children were entitled to their loony fantasies. After all, they were only kids. Their contribution to the general clamour on the streets of Kensington was not held against them.

And that's how those who came to shop remember the place — full of energy that rushed to the surface at the slightest provocation. However, those who lived in the area also have memories of Kensington in repose. On Friday afternoons, well before the Sabbath set in, a silence would descend on the entire market place. The vendors stopped hawking their goods and took brooms in hand. The cleaning was carried out as an imposition from without, a rendering unto the outside world what the health inspector demanded. Or else there was a fairly stiff fine to pay, and for the incorrigible *schlump,* the man who couldn't or wouldn't get around to cleaning his place up — a summons to appear in court. But inside the precincts of Kensington the physical act of cleaning up became a spiritual cleansing, for it marked a separation between the week long hurly-burly and the inner serenity needed for the approaching Sabbath.

Although this tended to reinforce an image of a self contained area it was not to be confused (which it so often is, unfortunately) with the infamous ghettos of Europe and the persecuting host societies that surrounded them. Ward Four, like the East Side in New York, or Whitechapel in London, was, as time was to bear out, a transitional enclave with a ramp leading to the larger non-Jewish world.

Socially, there already were the heroes who had made it in the great outer world. They shone like bright stars over the ramp luring and beckoning to the youngster in ethnic enclosures everywhere. Thus, the boy walking out of the house on a Sunday morning, carrying a violin case also carried his parents' prayers on the way to the music teacher that here was another Jascha Heifetz in the making. And the kid with the boxing gloves making his way to the

"Y" for a workout carried the same ardent parental hopes that another Benny Leonard was on the horizon.

While the immigrant parents prayed for their children's success, not a few were painfully aware that the role models for the young were no longer eminent Torah scholars, or charismatic rabbinical figures, as they had been for successive generation in the old country. This was not the only dilemma that people too fixed in their ways, or too old to dream new dreams had to ponder in their new land.

The open society is reputed to be a two way street with a ramp and all. Yes, but the ramp is deceptively one way, as any immigrant setting out to adjust to his new environment will tell you. Those who think they can escape the change that awaits them by keeping clear of the ramp will find change pursuing them on its own terms into the remotest clove of their ethnic retreat. This was the experience in Ward Four from the very beginning, for it became clear to the newcomer on arrival that economic demands of industrial Spadina below Dundas were arrayed against the religious sensibilities of the observant elements in the community. On Saturdays the fathers would attend services in the *shtibl,* a small type of congregation housed in a store, or a private home converted into a synagogue bearing the name of the town in Eastern Europe the congregants had left behind them. These *shtiblach* (the plural of *shtibl)* proliferated throughout the community. But the members congregating in them could not commune with the Almighty without feeling hypocritical, burdened as they were by the knowledge that while they were praying in the synagogues their sons and daughters were working at sewing machines on the day of rest. But alas, there was nothing they could do about it. The desecration of the Sabbath was a foregone conclusion. The forty-four hour work week of those days left no time for synagogue attendance.

The religious decline was not passive or gradual. It was immediate, dynamic, and moved with the force of a landslide, so that the wave of godlessness that flowed out of Spadina south and making its way northward soon began to engulf the Kensington cluster of streets. The volume of trade carried on in Spadina show rooms on Saturdays was not lost on push cart peddlers and store keepers in Kensington. The lure of an extra day's business became too much for them to withstand. At first, the bushels of fruit were brought out toward Saturday evening. Then they began to appear in the late afternoon. Then mid afternoon. The devout members of the community looked on in despair and with stifled fury at the tide of desecration rising from week to week.

Going into the Second World War, the use of Yiddish, indeed, the immigrant culture as a whole was in a state of decline. So was the Sabbath as a day of rest. It was not long before the streets were alive and thronging with Kensington going about its business on Saturday the same as on any other day of the week. And following the war, when the Jewish community made its third move en masse, this time from the inner core of Toronto to the northern rim of the city, Saturday became a favorite day for coming back on a shopping spree to good old Kensington. The second generation, whose use of English had displaced Yiddish, resurrected, of course, the correct pronunciation of the name. Although Ward Four was being replaced by other ethnic groups, Kensington still continued to serve, for some time, its traditional constituency, which was becoming increasingly remote.

Indeed the neighbourhood had become a place not only to shop, but to revisit. The parents used to enjoy taking their children to show them the inner city enclosure in which they grew up. Kensington became a past to reminisce about. Just as the grandparents told stories about the small *shtetl* localities in East Europe they hailed from; the parents had stories to tell their children about growing up in a *shtetl* of their own way down in the centre of

Toronto. Kensington became roots even more than the legendary Spadina.

....

What about Kensington now? What kind of yells and smells does the place exude these days? Well, there isn't much yelling to speak of. Yelling requires the informality that used to exist between the vendor and the customer, in the days of Kenzigtn. One gets the impression that the buying and selling nowadays is conducted with a certain restraint verging on formality. As for the Kensington smells, there is now a high industrial admixture to the food odours, whereas in bygone days the bouquet used to feature a high animal component. In other words, it is now stale gasoline and once upon a time it used to be stale horse droppings.

More important though, Kensington is being shaped by a consortium of ethnic groups rather than one element that once dominated the area. Those days it was Kenzigtn. Just that and no more. It now sports a surname: Kensington Market. It's part of the savoir faire the neighbourhood has acquired. It continues to be the product of ethnic genius but it is no longer an in-group convenience. It flaunts its universalized oddballness as a conceit of the entire metropolis and not of any particular grouping. This may in part be due to the fact that the ambience of Kensington Market has changed so drastically.

No more sleepy town surroundings. The back water exhibition hall that was once on Dundas Street across from Kensington has given way to the huge art gallery which extends for a full block. Starting at University Avenue the pale blue sky scrapers that look as if they were enveloped in Saran Wrap keep a big city watch over the Market from a distance. And coming out of Kensington towards Dundas Street on catches glimpses through the trees of Toronto's great hypodermic, the CN Tower, poking its needle up but not quite high enough to squirt an injection into the heavens. There is no getting away from it, Kensington is caught up in a sophisticated world the likes of which Kenzigtn never knew.

However, some things remain constant: as one strolls through the Market one hears the first generation struggling with the name. But the sons and daughters growing up in Toronto are having no trouble saying it. Kensington rises phoenix-like with every second generation from its fanciful pronunciations to regain the pristine sound of its name. Thus, allowing for predictable intervals of gestation, Kensington can be certain of its revived enunciation coming around regularly. But another Kenzigtn there will never be in name or in fact.
1991

CHRONOLOGY

1982-83 Three months of painting, drawing and travel in Japan and Korea; principally in the studio of Master Tattoo Artist, Mitsuaki Ohwada, in Yokohama, Japan.

1973 Two months of painting, drawing and travel in Israel.

1969-70 Four months of travel and painting in Japan; visiting major cities; lecturing at Chiba University, Tokyo; meeting with artists, notably the Japanese print-maker, Munikata.

1958 Three months of painting, drawing and travel in India.

1947-48 In Europe, completed a series of pen and ink drawings of people in camps for Displaced Persons in Paris and Milan.

1943 Went on active service with the Royal Canadian Air Force. Appointed Official War Artist 1944.

1941-43 Junior Instructor on the staff of the Children's Art Centre of the Art Gallery of Toronto, in classes begun by Arthur Lismer in 1927.

Painted with the "Studio" group, Toronto.

1937-42 Studied at Central Technical School, with Charles Goldhamer, Peter Haworth.

HONOURS

Bayefsky's Toronto: A Celebration of the City and Its People. The Market Gallery, City of Toronto Archives, Toronto. March 27 - May 30, 1982. Opened by the Mayor of Toronto, Arthur C. Eggleton.

Appointed Member of the ORDER OF CANADA July 1, 1979.

Special Exhibition of Drawings and Paintings by Aba Bayefsky. The Consulate General of Canada. Chicago, U.S.A., November 2 - December 15, 1978. Opened by the Canadian Consul General, Will Collett.

Prime Minister Pierre Trudeau presented Prime Minister Menachem Begin of Israel on his official visit to Canada the Portfolio *Tales From the Talmud,* "the perfect official gift". Fall 1978.

First faculty member of the Ontario College of Art honoured with a one-man show; to commemorate the 100th anniversary of the College. *Bayefsky at the Market.* November 1976.

Aba Bayefsky's (1964) oil portrait of the Scottish poet, Hugh MacDiarmid, reproduced and issued as a stamp to mark the poet's 80th birthday by the Scottish Philatelic Secretariat. 1972.

Canadian Embassy, Washington, D.C., Preview of Exhibition of Portfolio *Forces of Earth and Sky,* opened by the Canadian Ambassador to the United States, Mr. Marcel Cadieux. 1971.

President Tito, Yugoslavia, presented with *Portfolio of Earth and Sky* in Ottawa, "gift reflecting true spirit of Canada." November 4, 1971.

Canadian High Commission, New Delhi, India, Exhibition of Portfolio of *Legends* in one-man exhibition opened by Mr. James George, High Commissioner for Canada. 1970.

Aba Bayefsky honoured, along with Prof. John J. Weinzweig (music) and Rabbi Dr. Ernest Klein (literature) at Centen-

EXHIBITIONS

nial Citation Dinner, B'nai Israel Beth David Synagogue, Toronto, April 13, 1967.

Elected President of the Canadian Group of Painters. 1962.

Invited to be a member of the International Art Jury for the Second International Biennial Exhibition of Prints in Tokyo, Japan. November 1960.

Awarded a Canada Council Grant for travel in India. Travelled extensively, visiting Delhi, Madras, Bombay and Ahmadabad. 1958.

Elected an Associate Member of the Royal Canadian Academy of Arts. 1958.

Awarded the J.W.L. Forster Award, of the Ontario Society of Artists for *Market Place, November* oil. 40" x 50". February 28, 1958.

Elected Member of the Canadian Group of Painters. 1957.

Elected President, Canadian Society of Graphic Art. 1956.

Elected Member of Canadian Society of Painters in Water Colour. 1956.

First Purchase Award of the Canadian Society of painters in Water Colour for *The Doves (Yellow),* February, presented to the London Public Library and Art Museum, Ontario. 1952.

Awarded a French Government Scholarship for a year of study at Academie Julian, Paris, France and completed a series of pen and ink drawings of people in camps for Displaced Persons in Paris and Milan. 1947-48.

Appointed Official War Artist, Royal Canadian Air Force. 1944.

First prize "B" class, for watercolour *Going up for Gunnery Exercises* in world-wide competition open to air force personnel. 1944.

1989 John B. Aird Gallery. April.
Koffler Gallery Retrospective

1986 Retrospective Exhibition. *Carnival and Other Portraits.* Justina M. Barnicke Gallery, Hart House, University of Toronto. October 9 - November 6.

1983 *A Japanese Sketchbook.* One-man exhibition. Gustafsson Gallery, Toronto. November 22 - December 1.

1982 *Bayefsky's Toronto: A Celebration of the City and Its People.* The Market Gallery, City of Toronto Archives, Toronto. March 27 - May 30. Opened by the Mayor of Toronto, Arthur C. Eggleton.

1981 *Aba Bayefsky: Recent Drawings and Paintings on a Tattoo Theme.* The Kar Gallery of Fine Art, Toronto. October - November.

1979 Drawings and Paintings. One-man exhibition. Prince Arthur Galleries, Toronto. April 26 - May 12.

One-man exhibition. Drawings and paintings. Sarnia Art Gallery.

Drawing exhibition. Stratford, Ontario.

1978 Special Exhibition of Drawings and Paintings by Aba Bayefsky. The Consulate General of Canada. Chicago, U.S.A., November 2 - December 15. Opened by Canadian Consul General, Will Collett.

1976 *Bayefsky at the Market.* Exhibition of 60 paintings at the Ontario College of Art; to commemorate the 100th anniversary of the College. First major faculty exhibition at the College. November 23 - December 10. Recent watercolours and drawings of Kensington Market.

1975 Stong College, York University, Toronto. Aba Bayefsky, Fellow of Stong College, included in Stong Fellows Group Show, November 4-18.

1974 Images of the Land of the Bible. Galerie Heritage,

Toronto, February 12-28. Aba Bayefsky included in the group show.

1973 The Society of Wood Engravers and Relief Printers. 43rd Exhibition, August 29 - September 10. The Mall Galleries, London, England. Invited contributors.

Aba Bayefsky: A Retrospective, 1953-1973. Hamilton Art Gallery, April 5-22. This retrospective exhibition included works from *At the Market,* Portraits; Drawings; Prints; Paintings; and Legends.

Exhibition of two portfolios based on Canadian Indian legends: *Legends* and *Forces of Earth and Sky,* in the Canada Room of the Canadian Consulate General in New York City, February 6-23. Co-sponsored by the Canadian Consulate General, New York City and the Government of the Province of Ontario.

1971 *Forces of Earth and Sky* Portfolio, paintings and drawings in one-man exhibition at Agra Gallery, Washington, D.C.

Forces of Earth and Sky Portfolio, paintings and drawings, Preview of Exhibition, Canadian Embassy, Washington, D.C. opened by the Canadian Ambassador to the United States, Mr. Marcel Cadieux. 1971.

Forces of Earth and Sky Portfolio, paintings and drawings in one-man exhibition at Nancy Poole's Studio, Toronto.

"*Avinu Malkenu*", Series of paintings of Hebrew New Year prayers, exhibited at Holy Blossom Temple, Toronto, December 14.

1970 *A Japanese Sketchbook.* One-man exhibition. Albert White Gallery, Toronto.

"Fire Spirit" and "Spirit as Frog" (from Portfolio)

exhibited at Kathmandu, Nepal, at the international Art Exhibition, 1970, to honour King's 50th birthday.

Portfolio of *Legends* exhibited at Canadian Embassy, New Delhi, India. One-man exhibition. Opened by Mr. James George, High Commissioner for Canada.

1969 Hamilton Art Gallery. 20th Annual Exhibition of Contemporary Art, October. "Seated Woman" reproduced in Catalogue.

"*Legends*" - Portfolio of colour block prints first exhibited at Winters College, York University, Toronto.

"*Legends*" - Portfolio of colour block prints exhibited at Sir George Williams University, Montreal, Quebec.

1967 "*Legends*". One-man exhibition of paintings and drawings. Albert White Gallery, Toronto.

1966 A Retrospective Exhibition. Albert White Gallery, Toronto.

1965 The Penthouse Gallery, Montreal, Quebec. One-man exhibition.

1964 *Portrait Studies.* One-man exhibition. Victoria College, University of Toronto (including Northrop Frye, Claude Bissell, W.A.C.H. Dobson).

The Market Place. One-man exhibition. New Drawings. Gallery Pascal, Toronto.

1963 Drawings. One-man exhibition. Robertson Galleries, Ottawa.

Drawings. One-man exhibition. Gallery Pascal, Toronto.

1962 Drawings. One-man exhibition. Artlenders Gallery, Montreal, Quebec.

1961 Three Canadians. Art Gallery of Ontario. Bayefsky. (With Weisman, Filipovic) Exhibited portrait studies, including Barker Fairley, Northrop Frye, and "Paul Bunyan and Babe".

1960 Recent paintings. One-man exhibition. Park Gallery, Toronto.

1959 *An Indian Sketchbook.* One-man exhibition. Park Gallery, Toronto.

1958 *A Canadian Portfolio* - Exhibition of Canadian Art. Dallas Museum of Contemporary Arts, Dallas, Texas, September - November.

Pastels and watercolours (market and Paul Bunyan series). One-man exhibition. upstairs Gallery, Toronto.

Aba Bayefsky. Kitchener-Waterloo Gallery Association. (With Jack Bechtel)

1957 *The Market Place.* One-man exhibition. Toronto Central Library. March - April. Initiates new exhibiting policy at the Toronto Public Library.

Exhibited by invitation in the First Biennial Exhibition of Prints at the National Museum of Modern Art, Tokyo, Japan.

1956 Drawings and paintings. *Market studies.* One-man exhibition. Hart House, University of Toronto. March - April.

1953 Drawings. One-man exhibition. Picture Loan Society, Toronto. January - February.

1951 *Recruiting Posters.* One-man exhibition. Hart House, University of Toronto, November.

1950 Canadian Group of Painters. Annual Exhibition since 1950.

1949 First one-man exhibition of pen-and-ink drawings, pastels of displaced persons, done in Europe. Hart House, University of Toronto.

1946 Canadian War Art. Art Gallery of Ontario.

1945 War Art. National Gallery, London, England: Canadian War Art.

1944 Canadian Art, 1760-1943. Yale University Art Gallery, New Haven, Connecticut.

Royal Canadian Air Force, Exhibition of paintings and drawings. National Gallery of Canada, Ottawa.

1943 *Painters Under Twenty.* Art Gallery of Ontario March. "Park Bench", oil 28" x 23", purchased by the Art Gallery of Ontario.

1942 Canadian Society of Graphic Art Annual Exhibitions, since 1942.

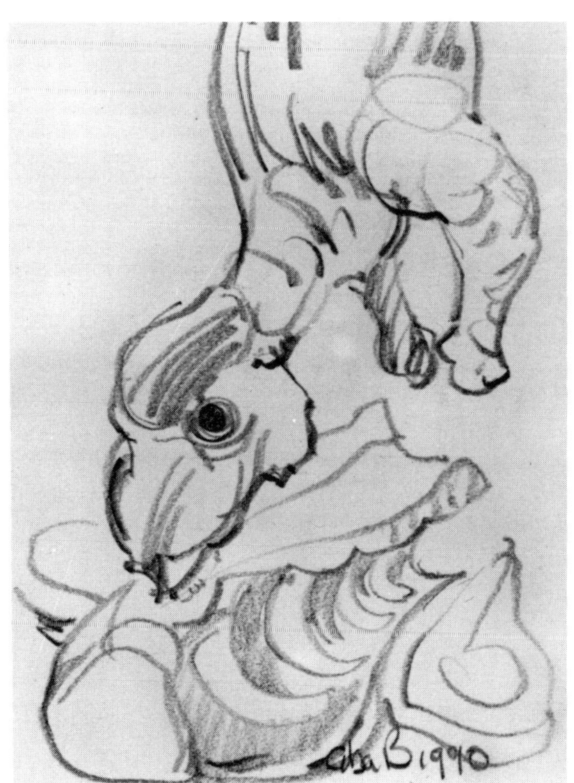

COLLECTIONS

Aba Bayefsky is represented in the permanent collections of:

The Art Gallery of Hamilton, Hamilton, Ontario
The Art Gallery of London, London, Ontario
The Art Gallery of Ontario, Toronto, Ontario
The Art Gallery of Sarnia, Sarnia, Ontario
The Beaverbrook Gallery, Fredericton, New Brunswick
The Corporation of the City of Toronto, Ontario
Ecoles des Beaux Arts, Quebec City, Quebec
Hart House, University of Toronto, Toronto, Ontario
Hebrew Union College, Library Collection, New York, U.S.A.
Hebrew University, Jerusalem, Library Collection, Israel
Library of Congress, Washington, D.C., U.S.A.
Loyola College, Montreal, Quebec (now Concordia University)
Massey College, University of Toronto, Library Collection, Toronto, Ontario
McMaster University, Library Collection, Hamilton, Ontario
Metropolitan Museum, New York, U.S.A.
The National Gallery of Victoria, Melbourne, Australia
The Public Library of North York, Toronto
The Public Library of Scarborough, Toronto
The Public Library of Toronto, Toronto
The Quebec Provincial Library, Quebec City
Sir George Williams University, Montreal, Quebec (Now Concordia University)
The Tom Thomson Memorial Gallery and Museum of Fine Art, Owen Sound, Ontario
York University Library Collection, Toronto
Prime Minister Menachem Begin, Israel, presented with *Tales from the Talmud* in Ottawa, "the perfect official gift", Fall 1978.
President Tito, Yugoslavia, presented with *Portfolio of Earth and Sky* in Ottawa, "gift reflecting true spirit of Canada". November 4, 1971.

Many other public and private collections in Canada, United States, Israel and India.

MURALS

A Song of Ascent. Mural in B'Nai Israel Beth David Synagogue, Toronto; based on a traditional form of Jewish Manuscript illumination. Completed December 1976.

A Mural commemorating 11 Israeli athletes who were slain at the Olympic Games in Munich, September 1972, was commissioned for the Northern Building of the Young Men's and Young Women's Hebrew Association, Toronto. 1973.

Mural, Temple Sinai, Toronto. 1970.

Decorative Wall Arrangement, Historic Museum at Saint-Marie-among-the Hurons, Midland, Ontario, 1968. Designs of flora and fauna were stamped in wet cement walls of the museum.

Commissioned to design and execute a mural for the Queen's Park Project, complex of Government Buildings Mowat Block, Toronto. 1967.

Out of Bondage, Mural, 11' x 15'; Polyvinyl Acetate, commissioned for the main entrance of Beth El Synagogue, Don Mills, Ontario. 1962.

Commissioned by Lipson and Dashkin, architects, to design a tapestry for the Shaarei Shomayim Synagogue in Fort William, Ontario. 1961.

Commissioned to design and execute three 9-foot panels for the Canadian Government. Canadian Exhibit at the Brussels' World's Fair, 1958. *Man; Woman and Child; Young Girl.* 1957.

Commissioned by architects Pentland and Baker, and Irving Boigon, to design a 26-foot mosaic tile mural for Northview Heights Collegiate Institute, Toronto. 1957

Mural, 3' x 10', for the Saracini Construction Co. Toronto. 1955.

PORTFOLIOS

Bayefsky, Aba. *Tattoo Drawings & Paintings*, c. Aba Bayefsky, 1983, printed in Japan. With an introduction by Julie Rickerd, Paul Duval, and Charles Goldhamer. 9 colour reproductions, 34 black and white reproductions.

Bayefsky, Aba. *Bayefsky's Spectacles*, c. Canadian Portfolio Editions and Edwards Books and Art, Toronto, 1980. Information and drawings; a visual history of the development of glasses from the 13th century. 50 original block prints and an original five-colour block print of Medieval London. Designed by Gus Reuter, Vancouver, B.C.

Bayefsky, Aba. *Drawings of The Market*, c. Aba Bayefsky, 1979, printed in Toronto, 49 black and white reproductions.

Bayefsky, Aba, Illustrator. *A Slight Trace of Ash: Poems of Recollection* by Walter Bauer, illustrated with 12 block prints. Tranlsated by Humphrey Milnes. 1976.

Bayefsky, Aba. *Forces of Earth and Sky*, second Portfolio of Indian Legends; with a foreword in English and French by Professor Humphrey Milnes, University of Toronto. Illustrated with 12 original Serigraph prints. Text in English, French and Cree. Text pages designed by Leslie Smart, using Cartier type. Hand printed by Canadian Portfolio Editions, Toronto, 1971.

Bayefsky, Aba. Production of 10 minute colour film: *Forces off Earth and Sky* based on the two portfolios of Indian Legends. (With Eli Kassner, Daryl Williams). Background track recordings of Cree people of Eastmain, Quebec, an Indian settlement near shores of Hudson Bay. 1971.

Bayefsky, Aba. *Legends,* a Portfolio based on Canadian Indian legends. Illustrated with 12 colour block prints, (4-5 colours each), with a foreword by Professor Humphrey Milnes, University of Toronto. Text in French and English in Cartier type designed in 1967 by Carl Dair. Also in Cree alphabet type developed in 1841 by Rev. James Evans. Text pages designed by Peter Dorn. Pouch and case handmade by William Poole. Handmade Hayle paper. Hand printed by Canadian Portfolio Editions, Toronto, 1968.

Bayefsky, Aba. *The Ballad of Thrym*, Icelandic poem, in an original translation by Prof. Humphrey Milnes, University of Toronto. Eleven illustrations in line-block. Hand printed by Gus Reuter, Village Press, Thornhill, Ontario. 1965.

Bayefsky, Aba. *Tales from the Talmud*. Trans. into English by David E. Newman. Illustrated with 18 lithographic prints. Text pages designed by Carl Dair. Letterpress hand printing by Gus Rueter. Foreword by Rabbi W. Gunther Plaut. Toronto, 79 pp., 55 cm. 1963.

Bayefsky, Aba, illustrator. *Rubaboo, Stories for Young Canada*, Toronto, W.J. Gage, 1962. 209 pp. Line drawing.

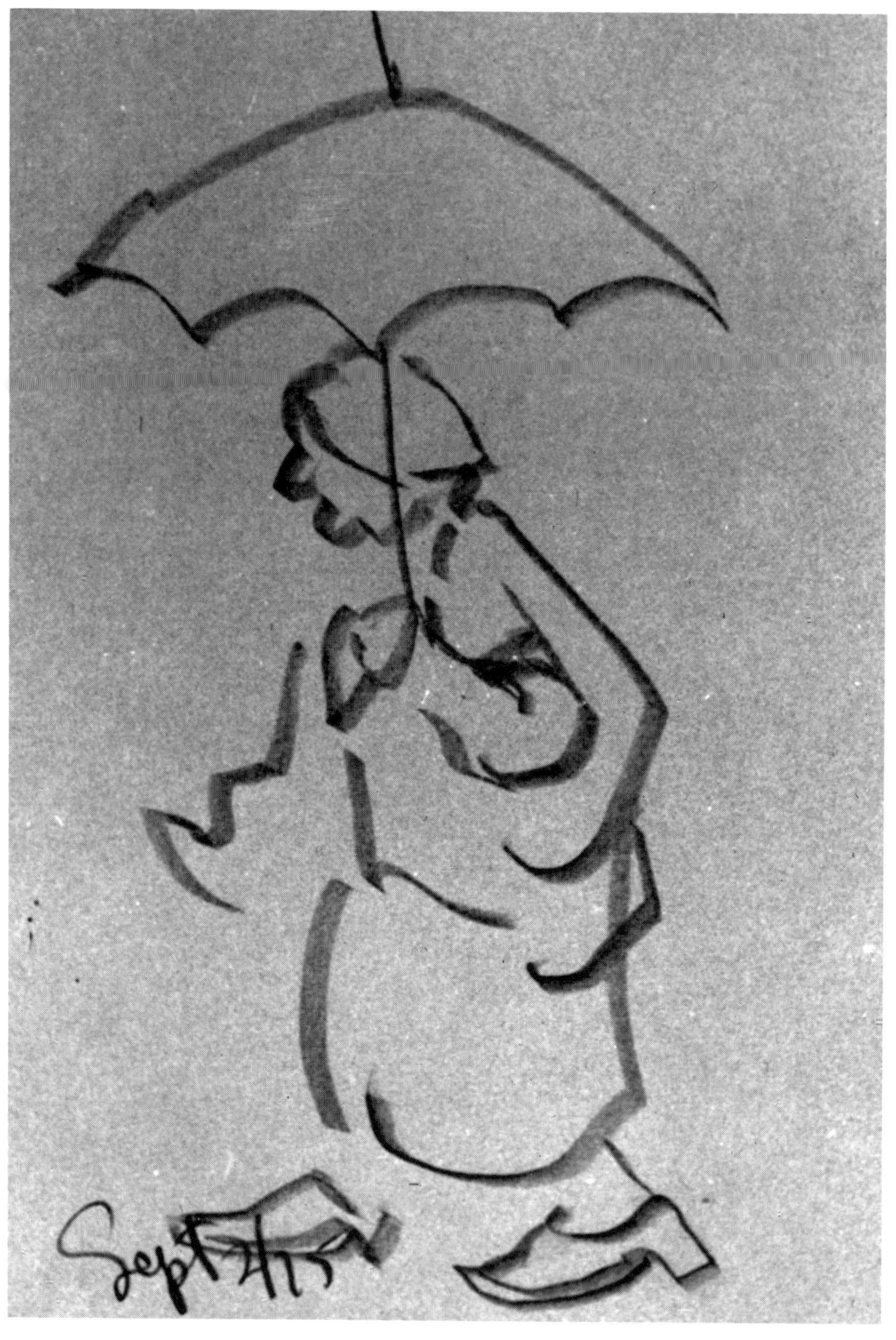
Sept